Praise for Ton

"Tony Irons' debut novel is a remarkable achievement. I was immediately grabbed by its vivid characters, its thrilling plot twists, and its profound insights into a generation of Americans split asunder by war."

—**Priscilla Long**, author of *The Writer's Portable Mentor: A Guide to Art, Craft, and the Writing Life* and *My Brain On My Mind*

"Tony Irons is equally gifted at creating characters and vividly rendering a troublesome history. He's a natural storyteller, with an original take on America in the 1960s, before today's battle lines were drawn or imagined."

—**Virginia Prescott**
New Hampshire Public Radio

"I was a soldier in the early 60's. A protester in the late 60's. I have never read a book that more accurately captures the struggle of those times. Both sides. This is a truly uplifting story."

—**Richard V. White,**
A1C, United States Air Force

"Who Am I" Words and music by Joe McDonald
© 1967 by Joe McDonald   Used by Permission
Joyful Wisdom Music Co, BMI

Published by RiverRun Select, an imprint of RiverRun Bookstore
142 Fleet St | Portsmouth, NH 03801 | 03801
603-431-2100 | www.riverrunbookstore.com

Cover photos © Charter Weeks
Author photo © Lee Irons

ISBN-13: 978-0-9885370-2-6
LCCN: 2012953919   ˎ

Printed in the United States of America

HOOVER'S CHILDREN

A Novel

TONY IRONS

For Peter

ank you.....

CONTENTS

PART ONE

THE SOLDIER

"Who am I, to stand and wonder, to wait,
while the wheels of fate slowly grind my life away?
Who am I?"

—Country Joe and the Fish

SOUTHIE

Before The Trail of Tears began, before Andrew Jackson ordered the Cherokee Nation to walk a thousand miles over lands they had never seen nor even knew existed to a place in Oklahoma where it was flat and dry and the winds blew brown dust from one horizon to the other, some years before the forced march began, high up in the Great Smoky Mountains of North Carolina a young Cherokee man; tall, bronze and straight black hair, lay in the moist morning grasses under a chestnut tree on a hillside below Thunderhead Mountain, making love to an Irish girl. Her family had fled starvation in Ireland. The potatoes had rotted. The Irish dirt was warm, damp and infected with fungus that turned the tubers to black mush. After two weeks of high seas and cold winds, the ship had docked in Norfolk, Virginia in November, 1846. Her father and mother, brothers and sisters were among thousands, many near death, who trekked west and south to seek work in the coal mines of West Virginia or the steel mills or railroads in southern cities like Savannah, Atlanta and Birmingham. They came from generations of hard physical labor and had become adept at existing on almost nothing. Their work was cheaper than slave labor. They didn't have to be fed or housed or nursed from sickness. They were Catholic, fair and freckled. They spoke in a strange way and stuck together like a tribe. On the hierarchy of the social structure, the Irish shared the bottom rung with blacks. Shunned, but like the slaves, economically useful.

Sometime around 1850, nine months after lying in the soft grasses of Thunderhead Mountain, Margaret Donnegad, sixteen years old, gave birth to a boy-child on the dirt floor of their shack on the outskirts of Ashville, North Carolina. The son of a Cherokee. He was brown-eyed and dark skinned. The Cherokee Indians had been stripped of the right to own land and banished from their ancestral mountains. The baby's father, with other braves, had ridden off towards the west behind Chief Going Snake, their tears falling from the thunderclouds in the sky. It was illegal for this baby to be alive in these mountains. To hide his identity, the family blamed the mutant eyes, skin and hair on an ancient aberrant European gene. They called him 'Black Irish'. The Cherokee gene was tough, tenacious and tribal, much like the lass who had coaxed it out on that warm Appalachian morning. Her father and the fathers of all the other children demanded from that day on, here in their new world, just like in their old world, Irish girls would have sex only with Irish boys. But the gene had melded and would be stuck in the helix of this family's core for generations.

Mary Donnegad O'Neal knew these things. She also knew that the gene she carried had something other than physical characteristics. Inside its husk was a wanderlust; a dark aloneness and an absolute fearlessness. Those who got it were rarely the same as others. They were either wildly successful or ended up as obituaries carefully worded to conceal the mayhem that had accompanied the young Irishman's death. She knew this because her father had told her.

"Papa, what really happened to Uncle Will? He didn't really die from pneumonia did he? I mean, he seemed fine when he was here for Christmas and then two days later he was dead. You can't die from pneumonia in two days can you?"

Mary, at fourteen, was a very serious and very factual young girl. Unlike her four brothers and two sisters she did not find humor in exaggerated stories that always made the teller seem smarter, stronger, more wily than they actually were. She was also her father's favorite. There was something about this girl that brought him comfort and solace. She, of all of them, was most likely to understand the things that he couldn't grasp. Things like how did money work in such a way that everything he had saved and invested had vaporized in one day in October of 1929. Mary, someday, would surely know the answer to that.

"No, you're right. He didn't die of pneumonia. He was stabbed to death outside a speakeasy in New York City. Stabbed by a pack of drifters who, I guess, just wanted his money. All the time he would just wander off into the bad parts of town looking for fun or looking for something. I don't know what." Her father said.

"Oh," she said, only partly satisfied that that was all there was to it. "Was he really my uncle? I mean, he didn't look like us. He didn't look like anybody in our family."

"Well Mary, I'll tell you a story. Come over here. Sit next to me. Back in about 1850, when everyone left Ireland because there was no food, Margret Donnegad, your great grandmother, had a child by a Cherokee Indian and ..."

Mary O'Neal remembered her father's story as she washed dishes in her chipped and stained porcelain sink, looking out the window into the backyard at her son Sean; only seventeen but tall, broad shouldered with black wavy hair, green eyes and a copper hue to his skin. He was

3

practicing throwing a knife into a board propped up among the brambles on the wire fence in their backyard. His best friend Cory McGivney was sitting on a trash can on the concrete pad outside the back door of the apartment. Cory was pretending to read an old LIFE magazine but he actually was just trying to get Sean's sister's attention. Gwyneth, two years younger than Sean and his constant companion, sat in the sun, not more than four feet from the board, reading her script for the school play. She was not happy with her role. In last year's play, her ad-libbing of the part of Elma Duckworth, the naive waitress in "Bus Stop", had brought the house down and brought ferocious frowns to the faces of the nuns. This year, the nuns had chosen "Journey to Jerusalem" and, in an effort to take a little of the prance, a little of the kick out of their headstrong filly, had cast her as the Virgin Mary. She was sitting on the ground wearing her high school uniform; plaid skirt, bobby socks, black shoes and a light blue oxford shirt with "Notre Dame Academy" embroidered just above her right breast. A cross on a gold chain hung around her neck. She had hiked her skirt up over her knees and thighs to let the April sun warm and tan her legs. Pale, freckled with long red hair, she burned quickly in the sun. When the knife would stick in the board, she would look up from her script and smile at her brother. When it would bounce off and fall her way, she would put her script down, throw it near his feet and go back to reading her lines. Cory threw a pebble at her. "Would you stop bothering me. Read your magazine or just go away." She pulled her skirt back down over her knees. "Hey, Cory, Don't bug her. You might get hurt." It was as if Sean and Gwyneth were two parts of the same thing. Mary O'Neal watched them and her stomach knotted.

Mary was the bright one in her family. Full of promise. The only one of six children who went to college. She had graduated first in her class from Notre Dame Academy,

Southie's Catholic high school, and got a full scholarship to Simmons College. She studied to become a librarian. Not an ordinary librarian. What she really wanted was to be a reference librarian. One who knew where to find all the answers. You didn't need to know everything; you needed to know where to find everything. Before the May Day festival she researched the pagan roots of the holiday and found innovative recipes for the traditional Strawberry Short Cake. She had adapted the Civil War fife and bugle tune, 'When Johnny Comes Marching Home Again' to a symphonic cacophony played with pots, pans, kettles, egg beaters and mixing spoons to lead the sophomores in their annual daybreak serenade of the seniors. She danced around the Maypole knowing why it all was happening.

Jimmy O'Neal, Mary's husband, was a barber. He didn't own his own shop but by 1963 he had worked in Paddy's Barber Shop on East Broadway for all of their eighteen years of marriage. Paddy had long since died and three owners had come and gone while Jimmy, every day, six days a week, at the same chair, with the same scissors, sharpened once a month by Old Man Kalowski, the same combs, cleaned every morning in hydrogen peroxide, and bottles of hair tonic, filled as needed, cut the curly hair of the Boston Irish. He heard everything. He knew everything but he never said anything to anybody about what somebody else had said. He sharpened his straight razors on a leather strop every morning before the "Open" sign went up and knew that if anybody heard that he had told somebody what somebody else had said and it caused them financial, legal or social pain, they would take his sharpened razor and slit his throat, wrap his neck in a white shoulder cloth meant to keep the hair off a man's clothing, stuff him in a trunk and throw him in the Dorchester Bay. They'd tell his wife and kids and the neighborhood that he ran off with an Italian whore and they'd produce the Italian whore's sister who would scream that it's all true and wail and flail her arms about. That would surely happen if he ever told one man what another man had said while sitting in his barber chair. Jimmy talked a lot because barbers, like bartenders, are expected to chatter. But always about nothing. Like a bartender, he bantered, keeping clients happy that they were having their hair cut in Paddy's Barber Shop where anything can be said and nothing can be heard. All the words are gathered up at the end of the day and thrown out in the trash with the hair. Swept clean.

The only person he could talk to was his wife, Mary. For years she would listen over dinner, after dinner and in the bedroom to the stories of Southie. She, pulling her blankets tight up around her, would hear about Vannie Druggan and the Spring Hollow Gang and how they ran the rackets; fixed the races, sold protection to the businesses, extorted the drug dealers by offering them a chance to keep their balls attached to their body for a cut of the money but, Jimmy told her, Vannie would always say no to heroin. Goddamned stuff will wreck a person, wreck a family, wreck the whole community he always said. 'Turns a good kid into an effin' zombie.' She heard about what teenaged girls would have to do to make a little bit of money and how most of the money men gave them went back to Vannie. She heard about how he liked his hair cut with just a slight trim and a shave front and back every week so it would stay curly and look full. She heard about the FBI guy who would tell Vannie what the Anguilo gang was up to and seemed to turn deaf when one of the Irish goons would slice up or shoot one of the Italians. She heard about the afternoon Sean was in the barber shop reading a comic book. About how Vannie, quiet, head tipped down while her husband shaved the nape of his neck, got tired of listening to a car salesman in the next barber chair babble on and on about how all the horse races were fixed and how the mobster softly reached behind his head, tapping Jimmy's arm. Jimmy stopped shaving, took the razor away from his neck, handed it to the mobster and the mobster exploded waving the razor in front of the guy's nose. "If you don't know what the fuck you're talking about, don't say nothin'. If you don't know nothin' about nothin', which you don't, just shut the fuck up!" Jimmy told her the car salesman pissed himself. When she heard that story and that her son was there she didn't want to hear her husband's voice anymore. She watched her children out of kitchen window and her stomach knotted. Her stomach knotted right in the middle just below the solar plexus every time she watched them being innocent and carefree. Mary wondered which way her son would turn as he grew old enough for that copper gene to start taking over. And her little girl Gwyneth was not a little girl anymore. She was sixteen and her body was fast becoming the type of young woman's body that every man wanted. And the knot got worse when she realized that whichever way her son's gene turned, Gwyneth would follow and there really wasn't anything to be done about it.

Sean was a junior in high school. A good student, an honor student. Ace pitcher on the school baseball team. He could read the poems of Jacques Prévert in French. He did his homework and didn't wise around with bad friends. Jimmy O'Neal didn't really care if his son did well in school. He knew he was smart and could get a good job and help support the family as soon as he graduated. Maybe Vannie could drop a word or two and his son could be a cop. Lord knows the family needs the help. Jimmy cut an average of twelve heads of hair a day. Out of the $1.50 a cut, fifty cents went to the owner and Jimmy got to keep a buck. He was bringing in about $300 a month. Good thing it was cash and he didn't have to tell Uncle Sam about it. He figured that saved some so whenever he talked to Mary about how much money he made, he would always add some to it because of the cash thing. Mary would nod and knew that money you don't get is money you don't have. They had just enough to pay the rent and buy the food and clothing. Jimmy always kept the buck from the last haircut of the day so he could stop at the pub on the way home and have a pint or two.

Jimmy had joined the Navy in 1943 and within a month had shipped out of Boston as a Seaman Apprentice on a destroyer headed for the Pacific Theater. He was a little man who looked a bit like a curly headed squirrel, spry and chipper, happy to do anything he was told to do. When he enlisted he had one talent: cleaning things. His father had been a drunk and his mother a washer woman. He dropped out of school at fifteen and worked in the fruit warehouses near Haymarket Square shoveling discarded bananas and apples and melons from the floor after the morning auctions. When he would get together for a pint with his buddies he would always tell them, every time he would tell them how hard it was to sweep grapes. Don't matter how stiff the bristle, don't matter how hard you push, the little crappers won't sweep. Won't shovel, neither, jus' roll around. It's a pisser. Jimmy never did tell them how he actually got the grapes off the floor. He never got that far. They'd tell him to shut his feckin' yap about the feckin' grapes before they smack his flapper shut. Jayeesus! He did become fairly accomplished at organizing cleaning equipment like brooms, mops, buckets, rags and various fluids and was quite proud of how shiny he could get the boss's toilet. "Effin' mankey jack shine like a babby's arse!" In the Navy, he became the ship's chief swabbie and the oiler of machinery. A perfect fit for his singular talent. From time to time he pulled night watch on the afterdeck looking back beyond the wake to see if there were bad things following. That detail ended when he was found passed out dead drunk in a life boat hugging an empty bottle of rum that had been smuggled aboard in a layover in the Canary Islands. He'd been out to sea two years when he came home to Boston to a hero's welcome. The Japs had surrendered. The War was over. We won.

As the destroyer pulled into the Coast Guard dock, the celebrations began. Wives and girlfriends, along with nurses, beauticians, secretaries and students from Radcliffe and Simmons, the women's colleges, had been commandeered to the docks, each given a handkerchief embroidered with the Victory "V". Bands with tubas and timpani played John Philip Sousa. The Mayor, the Port Commissioner and the Coast Guard Commandant all stood in salute as she nosed into harbor. Seamen stood at attention on her decks during the obligatory speeches given by the Important People and then streamed off board, down the gangplanks and, as planned, into the hugging arms of all the girls. Breasts and pelvic bones pressed into crisp white uniforms of sailors who had been at sea without female contact for two years. Sweet, sweet lips on proffered cheeks. Off they went in groups of ten or twenty, singing, laughing, arms around waists into the bars along the waterfront where drinks were half price and the night was young and happy. Jimmy ended up in the arms of Mary Donnegad and she ended up on his lap in the Shamrock Pub drinking rum and champagne. Jimmy's genes met the Cherokee gene at two in the morning in the backseat of a 1939 four door De Soto parked unlocked in an alley behind the bar. Jimmy became a barber. Mary, like thousands of other young girls across the country and every girl from Southie who got knocked up by a sailor, became a mother, a housewife and a part-time stitcher of pillowcases in a handkerchief factory. Not a librarian.

Southie is a place where people hang together on the street and there's a pub on nearly every corner. Some of the banks and public buildings are brick; new brick, flat and square with straight white mortar joints. No Palladian arches or curved cornices, just flat sand struck brick intended to retain the commercial real estate value with a minimum of maintenance, but most of the buildings are wood. In flush times, some of the clapboards and trim might have a coat of fresh paint but most of the time, and certainly all the time in the poorer parts of town, the two-family and four-family buildings are a damp gray and the wood rail porches list to one side or the other. Wood is cheaper and faster than masonry and there were trees in the forests of Ireland so a rudimentary craft of carpentry survived in the families through the New World migration. Not the fine craftsmanship of the English or the Scandinavians, but enough to get a duplex built.

In the Italian North End the buildings are all old brick. An irregular, hard, dark water struck brick set in thin mortar joints with a grapevine bead down the center. The window sills, door surrounds and eaves are a bas relief of elegant Old World craftsmanship. There are very few forests left in Italy. They were largely eviscerated during the Renaissance to satisfy the Visconti's, Sforza's and Medici's voracious appetite for warships, mansions and wine casks. The Italians became masons. Where they do use wood it is thick wood, wide wood, timber-like, stained dark or painted a Tuscan green. The Italian mob controls the money while the streets bustle with the business of food and wine. Chianti in the storefront windows. Big paper bags of two foot long loaves of hot bread and carts of dripping wet vegetables clatter along the brick sidewalks. The men who control the streets of the Old North End sit in cafes sipping wine, smoking fat cigars. The men who control the streets of Southie sit in pubs sipping thick, dark beer, smoking cigarillos. The words these men say among themselves are the same in both places, just spoken in different languages. The Southie streets bustle with trucks and vans painted like the old country delivering Guinness and

Bass. The streets are the common place where people, like-minded and like-blooded, hang together to keep traditions and religion from being siphoned off into the vast neutrality surrounding them. It is not that most of the people who live in Southie and the North End are Catholics. They are, but it is more fundamental. The communities as a whole are Catholic. The one word that could not be ignored was the word of Archbishop Richard Cushing. The weave that binds each town together is the fine fabric of the Pope's hassock. For Southie, the election of John Fitzgerald Kennedy as President of the United States brought ecstatic jubilation. Their own Irish Catholic in charge of the country. With the Pope, in charge of the world. Hot Damn! Effin' Right!

CHICKAPECKERS

Down past South Boston, the word of Archbishop didn't really mean much. They were Baptists and Methodists; poor and black. The sanitation trucks weren't regular down there like they were in Southie, Beacon Hill, the North End and most other places in the city. Even the streets around the docks and the fruit warehouses at Haymarket Square got fairly punctual attention. Not Roxbury. They might come, they might not. In City Hall, nothing about the place was on anyone's priority list. Nobody down there made enough money to amount to a hill of beans.

The great CITGO sign at Fenway Park could be seen from Dudley Street, flashing in the nightscape and even though a black face couldn't be found in the bleachers at a Red Sox game, baseball was in the blood of almost every boy from the Roxbury streets and vacant lots. As long as they stayed out of jail and stayed off smack, they could swing the bat.

Elroy Jenkins was serving twenty five years for assault on a federal officer during the commission of a crime. Out in ten if he kept his nose clean. Armed robbery was the crime. An off-duty Treasury cop named Bill Whitcomb was the officer. Elroy had neither robbed anyone nor had he assaulted Mr.

Whitcomb. That didn't matter. The country was beginning to boil from one coast to the other and the big cities where white people lived near black people were becoming cauldrons of anxiety. For those folks who lived and worked in the inner cities, the days were stressful, the nights dangerous and often when a boiling bubble burst, people died. Usually shot or stabbed.

From Dudley Street to Cedar Street was just like that. The Nation of Islam had brought into its fold young black men in their twenties to re-organize the social structure of the Roxbury community. Malcolm X had grown up on these streets and his voice rang loud, angry with the white man. They set up after school programs, soup kitchens and drop-in centers. But Elroy knew it wasn't just the police and judges that kept them all behind the eight ball; it was also and maybe even more so, the insidious, ubiquitous smack. The heroin that was pushed through the pinhole eyes of dirty needles into the veins of the prostitutes, into the veins of the young men who could now never hold a job or be a father and into the veins of the young men's children. This dope was corroding their communal soul.

Elroy's troubles began on a summer evening. He sat with two men and a woman in the back room of a makeshift recreation center they had built out of a small abandoned warehouse. They had gotten the money for it from a few successful bank robberies in Chicago. There was a short basketball court, not regulation size, the ceiling too low to arc a three pointer, but good enough, a room with a pool table and a ping pong table, an area with comfortable chairs, mismatched and ripped with stuffing spilling out, but comfortable. Shelves on the wall beside the chairs had thirty or forty books on the history of Africa and the black man in America. A phonograph and records of Ella Fitzgerald and the

Supremes sat off to the side. It was quiet inside. Dead quiet. There were no children there, just Elroy and the two men and the woman sitting in fold-out metal chairs around a card table in the back room office. Elroy was agitated. He shouted about how all the kids were out on the streets shooting dope, not basketballs. That they are hustling money, not pool games and how they are reading. Oh Yeah, you bet your ass they're reading; they're reading their own names on a goddamned arrest warrant.

Shauna, Skinny and Big Pete listened. Worried. Saying nothing. They had seen Elroy get like this a few times before. For all his strength, his determination and clear vision of their path, he was like a bomb. A big one. Megaton. When his detonator got set it ticked and ticked and ticked until it blew. BOOM!!! Then he put the pieces of whatever got destroyed back together and kept on working, kept on talking, kept on building.

Elroy lived alone. He had left his mother's house after a homemade bomb he was building for the purpose of blowing up the local police station had instead blown up in the face of his kid brother, Jimmy. Now the kids called Jimmy, Popcorn. It didn't blind him or make him deaf, nor did it take an ounce of power out of his swing on the ball field. It just wrecked his face, turning it into a pock-marked moonscape. His momma had screamed, "Elroy, you gonna kill us all with your hatred! Elroy, why don't you g'won back down to Birmingham. You can live with Uncle Jim. He'll get you work in the rail yards. You stay here, Elroy, you gonna kill us all!" He hated Alabama, he hated Uncle Jim and the tin shack he lived in. Elroy had never been happier than the day his momma took him and Jimmy north, away from his papa and his papa's brother, Jim. They were mean people. Elroy was starting to think that they never going to succeed in the mission of building a strong black nation without the help of hundreds, maybe thousands of white people who shared a vision of a new order. White people who can get money without robbing banks. White people who can talk to a judge without their sentence getting doubled. White people who can get the cops to stop the dope dealers. And Elroy became angry. Depressed, rejected and angry. He told Skinny and Big Pete to go out on the street and get some boys down here to play some ball. Grab'em by the neck and drag 'em down here if you have to. Shauna was ordered to go find the mothers and have them get their damn kids off the street and into some place safe and doing something good for themselves. Go on! Go do it! Elroy told them he was going to go straighten out a score. He said he was going to scare the everlovin' shit out of that prick on Tremont Street who's selling junk to our babies.

The night was never dark or quiet in the Combat Zone. Neon flashed outside the bars, the liquor stores, the pool halls, and the pimps and prostitutes shouted out, advertising their wares and tires screeched and sirens screamed and trash cans and doors banged all night and into the hard dirty mornings. The hawkers and shills barked, cajoled, and music, music up and down the street; rock and roll and blues and jazz spilled out the doors, horns blew in the bars and horns honked on the street and once in a while a siren screamed and no one paid any attention. All the pavement was festooned with sandals, with patent leather shoes, with boots and high heels that clicked, clicked, clicked and the curbs were awash in the cuffs of suits, of bare ankles lifted high up by heels and the black jack boots of children and police and every door and window was decorated with bare bellies and bare belly buttons so particularly beautiful that all the men forgot everything they had been taught by their mothers, by their wives or even what they should have learned from one of their God given children about what God said was right or what God said was wrong.

Elroy weaved his way along the sidewalk trying not to rub up against the breasts of whores as he walks through their clutches. 10:55 PM. Simon Weintaub's pawn shop was still open. Simon was taking the money out of the register, counting it and putting it into a metal briefcase which he would lock in the $15,000 safe bolted to a concrete pad under the counter. He paid a lot for a hefty insurance policy. Simon had never carried his money out the door at night. His son would come in daylight, with two armed friends and take it to the bank. Simon was getting ready to put up the "Closed" sign, slide and padlock the steel grates shut. Elroy waited, leaning against a street light pole until the sign was up and Simon had turned his back towards the street. He bounded into the store, wrapped his thick arm in a headlock around Simon's neck and jammed his snub-nosed .38 caliber into his temple just behind his eye socket. "Listen, you motherfucker," he growled, "You sell one more gram of that shit to any kids in my neighborhood and I'm gonna put a bullet hole right between your ugly little beady eyes. If you even..."

"Police!!!. Drop the gun! Drop the gun! Back off, hands in the air!"

Elroy dropped his gun on the floor, stretched his arms out to the sides and turned around. As he turned his hand grazed Bill Whitcomb's 9MM service revolver and Whitcomb pulled the trigger ripping a hole the size of a quarter in Elroy's shoulder.

Elroy's attorney, Charles Moussa-Faki, tried to ask Whitcomb what a Treasury Department Inspector was doing on those streets at 11 0'clock at night and what was the name of the whore he had been upstairs with a few minutes before he shot an unarmed man but the Federal District Court judge shut him off mid-sentence, declaring those circumstances irrelevant to the charges brought against Mr. Jenkins and instructed the jury to disregard the question. The jury, three white woman and nine white men, found that Elroy's version of the events and his reason for threatening Mr. Wintaub to be lies and all he really wanted was the briefcase full of money. Whenever Mr. Moussa-Faki would stand to speak, most of the jury would stare at him, mouths hanging open, eyebrows up. He was a short man with a very large clean shaven head, a goatee and skin so black and shiny it was purple, like a very ripe eggplant. He spoke in a lilting French African accent. Whether Elroy Jenkins intended to steal the man's money or whether he intended to slap the cop's gun really didn't matter. A duly sworn officer of the law found him in the act of strangling and pushing a stolen loaded gun into the head of a shopkeeper with a box full of money not more than two feet away. One way or the other, he was penitentiary bound. Twenty-Five to Life in the Big House.

Seanie, pitch 'em tight. Don't hang it out over the plate. These are big boys. Long arms. Don't let 'em get a full swing on it. Keep backin' 'em up off the plate. When you got 'em backed off, throw some heat to the outside. Keep 'em off balance. Cory, whenever there's a guy on first, set up behind the plate ready to make that throw to second. Get your left leg set so you can jump and throw without takin' a step. These are fast boys. I've seen them run. They'll steal on anything. Be ready to throw 'em out on every pitch. Listen up everybody. Everybody! You, Weeks, get over here. Pay attention. Listen up! This is a game we can't lose. You hear me! All of you kids hear me? This one's for your mother and father, for your sisters and little brothers. This one's for us, for our town." He rolled up his sleeve to the elbow and pointed to the tattoo on his thick forearm. It was a shamrock with a cross through the middle and the word "SOUTHIE" in green Gaelic script emblazoned around it. "This is about honor, m'boys; honor and family. Play hard, play rough if you need to. Just win."

The City Council had been unable to gerrymander the seedings for the All-City baseball championship tournament in such a way as to prevent an all-white team meeting an all-black team in a Boston neighborhood. When it became clear that Southie would face Roxbury in the finals, they considered canceling the entire tournament. They couldn't come up with a legitimate reason other than there might be a lot of people hurt no matter who won. That was such a damning statement about race relations in the city of Boston some members began looking into more creative, less obvious, downright obscure reasons that might come from somebody in the city other than them. They talked to the Mayor who wanted nothing to do with it. They talked to the Superintendent of Schools who wanted nothing to do with it. Then they hit on it. The Director of Public Works was instructed to find serious maintenance related traffic problems and issue an order to dig up, remove and repave the entrances to both ball fields, effective immediately. Reluctantly, they said, there must be a change of venue. Quietly they looked for someplace neutral where the demographics were not all one way or the other. Someplace hard to get to. Someplace nobody lived. They found a baseball diamond abandoned by Boston University three years before. It worked. Almost no one was there. The nearest bus stop was a mile away, the subway didn't go near there and very few people in either Southie or Roxbury had cars. Jimmy the Barber, Mary and Gwyneth O'Neal got a ride with Eddie McKenna in his brand new Buick. Maybe a hundred other people made the trip. Five Boston plainclothes cops were in the stands. Even the home plate umpire was an off-duty patrolman name Charlie McGloughlin.

19

Three batters up, three batters down, three innings in a row. No runs, no hits, no errors. A pitchers' duel. Fourth inning, top of the order. "Strike One!" Sean had put it right where Coach Dan had told him to but it wasn't a strike. It was inside. The leadoff batter jumped backwards a bit but didn't look back at the umpire. Didn't complain. He held his bat straight up in front of him and looked at it from the bottom nub up to the crown on the top and all the way back down, slowly, as though he was trying to figure out how the thing worked, what the trick was, where did it want the ball to hit it. It was talking to him. He tapped the dirt off his spikes and set himself up away from the plate. "Strike Two!" It caught the inside corner. The batter looked at his bat again, impassively, quizzically, the same slow search. He looked at his coach, took the sign and set himself up close to the plate. Hit me and the leadoff runner is on. Go ahead, pitcher, thread the needle. Coach Dan had a furious frown, slapping signs all over his ears and neck. Hit him, it said. Sean shook his head. A short, quick shake, almost imperceptible, like a tic. No. The next pitch was outside but not quite far enough. Given where the batter had set up, the sweet spot of the bat met the ball straight on. A solid single into right field and Coach Dan was out of the dugout jogging his way across the infield to have some words with his star pitcher.

"When I tell you to hit 'em, you hit 'em, you understand? You better teach these black boys some respect right now 'cause if you don't they're gonna slap you around. You want to win, m'boy, you better make them afraid of you. That's how you win. Fear breeds respect. Don't let 'em look you in the eye. Hit em!"

"Sorry, sir, no disrespect to you, but these are ballplayers, just like us. You want somebody to hit them on purpose, get somebody else. Not me." Coach Dan put his hands on his hips and turned around, surveying his dugout.

Any other pitcher and his Southie team was sure to lose. "Coach, I'll pitch them tight, I'll pitch them hard but I'm not breaking some guy's ribs just because his skin is black. That could turn out bad." The softened glare in Coach Dan's eyes belied a perfect misunderstanding of his pitcher's mind. "Don't be scared of 'em, Sean, you can do it. I know you can." He patted him on the butt and jogged off the field. Everyone behind the plate, in the dugouts, in the field and in the stands knew exactly what the Coach's conversation had been about. Many shifted forward in their seats, a little more tense. Players smacked their fists into the ball pocket of their gloves, getting ready. Umpire McGloughlin held his long arms out, palms up in a stop signal as though he was holding up traffic at an intersection, one outstretched towards the Southie dugout, the other towards the Roxbury dugout. He held that stance for a full ten seconds looking back and forth between the coaches then, with a slow nod to Sean on the mound he shouted, "Play ball!"

A very light rain had begun to fall as the next batter came to the plate. He was big, football big. If he caught up with the ball it would likely be out of the park but his swing had seemed slow. He had an awful lot of neck, shoulders, arms and chest to pull around in time to catch up with the ball. Cory put his leg half out ready to throw to second. The runner had a big lead and would surely go. Cory held one finger down, stationary. No wiggle. He was calling for a fastball right down the middle of the plate. The big guy might have seen Sean's two fingers split wide on the seams as he began his wind up. He might have heard Cory's fist smack his mitt directly in the center of the plate behind him. His bat came around in perfect sync with the ball coming in. They met dead center in the middle of the plate but he got nothing underneath it, nothing to lift it over the outfield. It was a line-drive smacked straight back to the mound, belt high. Sean, bent down towards the plate at the end of his delivery caught the ball just below the right side of his neck, snapping his collar bone and slamming shut his windpipe before it ricocheted off his jaw. He was down on the mound, out cold as the benches cleared. McGoughlin called an ambulance on his police radio. Five cops all blowing their whistles dashed onto the field. The shriek so stunned the players they stopped moving; stood stock still. Only two sets of punches were thrown. The first was a single hard right to the chin by Jimmy Byrne, Southie's assistant coach. Coach Dan had grabbed a bat in the dugout and Jimmy knocked him ass over water bucket before he got to the stairs. The other was a set of ten or so flailings that went wholly unnoticed by the recipient. Gwyneth had managed to climb the chain link fence that separated the fans from the field and run through the police and the clot of players around the mound and flung her fists onto the back of the big black batter who was kneeling over Sean, begging him to wake up. The umpire called the game due to inclement weather. Zero to zero.

Sean came to and looked up into a portrait of his sister's face tight against a black man's face, her long red hair spilling half over the black man's head. Both of them eyebrows up. Both of them mouths open. "Who are you?" Sean asked.

"I'm the guy who hit the ball into your head." He said.

"Seannie, Seannie, are you OK?" Gwyneth's hand was on his forehead.

"Nice hit."

"Seannie, are you OK?" She was struggling to elbow the big guy out of her way.

"Yeah. Wish I got more under it."

"Yeah, that would have been good. What's your name?"

"Popcorn."

"Popcorn?" Gwyneth stood up putting her hands on her hips, looking straight into his badly scarred and pockmarked face. "Popcorn? Jeepers, that's a weird name. Where'd you get that name?" The medics pushed them aside and put a cot down on the grass next to Sean, humped him onto it and carried him off.

That was the day Sean, Gwyneth and Popcorn Jenkins, Elroy's little brother, became friends. That was the day when the mutant gene from a hundred years ago found a soul mate. The three of them developed the deep sort of friendship that is born out of a shared rejection. Neither their families nor communities would tolerate their kinship. This made the bond as special as the bond among outlaws or orphans in an orphanage. Their time together was always spent in a neutral zone. Somewhere other than Southie and other than Roxbury. The three of them could not be seen together in either of those places, nor could they go to a Red Sox game. This was understood without words. They met by the banks of the Charles where they would sit for hours watching the crewmen and the small sailboats or in Harvard Square where the beatniks and eclectic mix of students took no note of their inter-racial camaraderie. Once in a while they would venture to the North End where bars were so packed and loud no one cared if they were too young to drink. It was risky to be together there, but not, like Southie and Roxbury, suicidal. Sean's friends came to know about Popcorn and their knowledge made them necessarily, by virtue of their own social mandate, drift away. The last time he saw Cory was months ago when he walked by a group of classmates and someone muttered, "nigger lover" and Cory didn't say a thing. Just looked away. That was the way it was on those streets.

"So," Sean said one evening when he and Popcorn were smoking dope in an alley behind Puguli's Pub, near the Old

North Church, "how about we walk around the streets and pick up a couple of girls."

"Oh, my man, how young and foolish you are. You don't know nothing about the ways of the world. These Italian girls are birds. They won't have nothing to do with us."

"Birds?" Sean said. "What are you talking about?"

"It's like this. Black people mate with white people and have little brown babies. Not black not white. A mixture. A half-breed. White people mate with Orientals and have little light yellow babies. Tall, curly haired but with slanty eyes. A mixture. Dogs are the same. A German Shepard and a Pekinese can get it on and have a weird looking little mutt. Same with a Cocker Spaniel and a Doberman. Cats are the same way. Lots of mutt cats. And horses do it like that too. A fancy racehorse and one of them ponies can have something that folks just call a horse. Cows too. People and all the animals that live with people, you know, domestic animals, they do it with whatever breed they want as long as they're the same type of animal. Then they have little mutt babies. But not wild animals. Not bears. You don't see a black bear getting' on a grizzly. They don't do it. Not fish. You never heard of a great white flounder, have you? Or a humpback dolphin. Nosiree. That don't happen out there." He took a long deep toke on the joint and handed it to Sean. "Birds are the same. Chicadees only get it on with other chickadees. They don't do it with woodpeckers. Then you'd have a chickapecker. You ever heard of one of those? Nosiree. Italian girls are like that. The only men they get it on with is Italian men. They're birds. That's what I'm saying. Birds. Your Irish girls are like that too case you never noticed."

"Chickapecker. Oh my God that's funny." Sean was laughing so hard he had to hold onto a 'No Parking' sign. "What about a, a, a, a, titmouse and sapsucker? What do you have then? A titsucker! And then, and then, Oh my God, and then you get a chickapecker and a titsucker and then what do you have?" They held onto each other laughing until Popcorn saw a cop cross the street a block up and they ran down the alley, off into the maze of Little Italy looking for some candy or cookies or anything to eat.

In the light of the next afternoon, sitting on a bench in Harvard Square, reading a Boston Globe article about how President Kennedy had ordered all Special Forces troops to be truly special by being the only ones who wore a different hat, a green beret, Sean and Popcorn made a pact: join the Army and go off for adventure to a place where it didn't matter who you were, it only mattered what you could do. Within a month they were both gone. Sean's room was empty. A mausoleum. To his sister, the air was dead. Silent and still. There was no Popcorn laugh, no big arm around her shoulder, no brother tousling her hair.

Every week on Thursday after school, Gwyneth began a ritual of walking from their tenement on Silver St. through Perkins Square, the center of Southie, down Broadway to Saint Peter and Paul Cathedral to give confession. Through the persistent efforts of the nuns at Notre Dame Academy, she had come to believe that she had a great deal to confess. A great deal more, she thought, than other girls who couldn't possibly share her affliction. Her loneliness had given way to unbridled thoughts. When she watched the hard muscles of a handsome man knot as he worked in the winter sun, a warmth would come between her legs. A warmth that drove her to dutiful confession. Weekly, she would trek to the other end of Southie to sit in the dark booth on the hard wooden seat to hint to the priest of these dreadful yearnings hoping his words would assure her that she was not evil or demented, not sin incarnate but just a young girl who needed to give penitence and stop sequestering herself in doorways and alleys, watching men, afraid that if she gave in to these yearnings a floodgate would open that couldn't be closed. For a number of weeks he did just that. Twenty Hail Marys and admonitions to contain her inner emotions, to date young men of her age, albeit in a proper manner, and apply herself to her school work and family household chores. Had Father Bigg cared, he probably would have divined that it was her loneliness that led to those nascent desires. But he didn't divine any such thing. What he did divine was that she was exquisitely beautiful, full of unrequited, painful passion that had welled up deep inside her and that he could, and, as time went by, became convinced that he should, make every effort to relieve the pressure in her soul. To uncork the dam. Father Bigg was unusual in the congregation of priests. He loved women and girls. Not a pious celibate nor a fondler of young boys like some of his bretheren. He was a fornicator of the first order.

On a cold but bright March afternoon, a Thursday, Gwyneth went far beyond her normal, somewhat abbreviated, edited, descriptions of her inner desires and told the priest a lyric story, almost as D.H. Lawrence or Henry Miller would have told this story, about exactly how her body felt as she sat on a bench with her legs crossed, but moving, as she watched a crew of shirtless young men fill potholes in the street by Perkins Square. She was weeping softly by the end of her tale. Father Bigg's hand was inside his cloak as he listened, rubbing himself. He suggested that it was time for him, as her priest, to put an end to her suffering. She said, please, and he led her by the hand to basement of the rectory where he took her virginity.

NOT OLD

On Sean's eighteenth birthday, July 15, 1964, eight months after John Kennedy was assassinated, Sean and Popcorn both enlisted in the Army with a request for the expedited Special Forces testing and training. The military had set up recruiting centers for the Army, Navy and Air Force throughout Boston as well as every other major and many minor cities around the country. President Kennedy had ordered the Army to provide for more soldiers wearing the Green Beret. There would soon be a massive effort to enlist young men for the burgeoning guerilla war in Viet Nam. What had started under Kennedy as a few thousand highly trained Special Forces soldiers advising the South Vietnamese Army commanders would, within a year, escalate under Lyndon Johnson to more than one hundred thousand soldiers of any kind, any type. Bodies were needed to fill the uniforms, uniforms needed to fill the bunkers and mud hut forts from the North Vietnamese border all the way through the country to the southern tip of the Mekong Delta.

The South Vietnamese Army, the ARVN, Army of the Republic of Vietnam, had proven to be incapable of matching the stealth, endurance and discipline of the Viet Cong guerrilla forces. They slept late, wouldn't fight at night, didn't dare wade across rivers because there might be crocodiles in the water and whole battalions would stop marching so a few soldiers could go take a shit in the woods. The ARVN officers spent their time devising ways to milk more money, more piasters out of the Americans and concocting elaborate war plans designed to ensure they would not end up confronting platoons of VC guerrillas. They were afraid of them. The Special Forces men knew that war, stripped of its raw reality, stripped of good luck or bad luck or no luck, is no different than sports. Those who are afraid of their competitor are those who are going to lose. Always. It wasn't a matter of having a healthy respect for the opposing team, it was a matter of actual fear when they thought about stepping into a nest of Viet Cong. So they listened to the Advisors' advice and ignored it.

By early 1964, months before the American Congress passed the Gulf of Tonkin Resolution, it was clear to all the Special Forces advisors that the war would be disastrously lost unless American soldiers, under American officer's command, flooded the country to beat back Ho Chi Minh's Communist forces from the North. The Colonels told the Generals and the Generals told the President, "If you want to win this thing; if you don't want a humiliating defeat of your finest fighting forces, then give us the means of going out in the mountains, out in the jungles, out in the rice paddies and getting the job done. If we don't kill them they will kill us and thousands of innocent civilians. If you want us to teach these South Vietnamese chickenshits to fight, we need to show them how, not tell them how. Words are cheap, Mr. President, lives aren't." President Johnson heard them and at that juncture he was still brave about it. Every young man who was not a priest, student, war worker, homosexual or medical or mental catastrophe was drafted. The Pentagon, with the approval of the President ordered a five-fold increase in recruitment. They knew that children who volunteer to fight by and large make better soldiers than children who are ordered to fight.

Jimmy the Barber, the proud father, borrowed Mr. McKenna's Buick LaSabre and drove his son to Fort Dix, New Jersey. Just the two of them. Popcorn took the Greyhound. Eddie McKenna had made Jimmy go around the block first to make sure his neighbor knew how to drive. He showed him where the lights were: high beam, low beam, the windshield wipers. Jimmy talked and talked while he drove, one hand easy on the wheel, elbow out the window. He talked about the War in the Pacific. He talked about the Nazis and the Fascists and Admiral Nimitz. He talked about the big guns on the destroyer and how important it had been to keep them nice and clean and oiled. He told his son how winning was hard, it wasn't easy son, but we stuck to it and beat the Krauts, the Wops and the Nips. There was this time when he had drawn midnight watch and it was about three o'clock in the morning. Black as pitch. No stars. You couldn't even see the whitecaps on the water. Somewhere off the west coast of Africa, maybe near the Canary Islands, headed for Cape Horn and the Indian Ocean. The Captain, Jeremiah Bogart, we called him old Blowfart but he really was an OK Captain, he got us home safely didn't he? Well, he came out on deck and there I was just leaning on the forward gunwale sipping a bottle of cheap rum that Dougie Higgins had given me and there's old Blowfart up at three in the morning. What's he doing up at three in the morning I don't know. That's when I got transferred to the galley as chief dishwasher and also the ship's barber. Oh sure, the first round of haircuts the sailors got made them look like mental cases but I got the hang of it. After a while the boys stopped complaining and threatening to keel-haul me. It was a stroke o'luck for me because now I make good money cutting hair and that's where I learned it. Thanks to Captain Blowfart.

But Seannie, you don't want to do what I did when you're in. Don't mix fighting and drinking. The brass don't like it. And he told him about the glorious day his ship had pulled back into harbor at Boston with all the fireboats spewing their water in huge arcs and blasting their horns and marching bands and how pretty his mother had been standing on the dock with a hundred other girls, waving her handkerchief. How she was the prettiest one of them all and that's what you get when you win the war. You get the prettiest girl on the dock. So go out there and give 'em all you got. You're a good boy Seannie, you'll make this country proud. Give 'em all the devil in ya m'boy and come home safe.

He was waved through the front gates of the Army Base by an unsmiling soldier who pointed towards the civilian parking lot. Sean got his bag. They looked at each other for a moment then shook hands. Jimmy the Barber watched his son walk away, duffel slung over his shoulder, long strides. He headed back to Boston, both hands gripping tight on the steering wheel, scared to death that something might happen to Eddie McKenna's Buick.

For Sean, boot camp at Fort Dix was not much different than baseball practice. Sergeant Jeffries barked the same way Coach Dan barked. Nothing was ever good enough for them. Nobody was ever listening up close enough. Nobody was ever good enough but in their eyes Sean could tell he was doing fine. One hundred sit-ups in two minutes, one hundred push-ups in two minutes. He could run two miles in eleven minutes flat and almost always came back first or second after jogging for hours in the sun carrying a forty pound backpack. And the rope. He loved the rope. Fifty feet in fifty seconds straight up without using his feet. Hand over hand. Sliding back down perfectly balanced so the rope stayed straight with no whip to it landing on both feet with knees bent. Only ten guys in a thousand could do that. An intelligence test, a psychological test, a French language test. All good.

"O'Neal, Major wants to see you. Now. On the double." Major Gould was tall, lean, rugged looking with a flat top buzz cut and hard cold blue eyes. Popcorn was already in the office doing his best to hold down a big grin. "You're both in for Special Forces training, soldiers. Good work. Tomorrow 0800 you ship out to Fort Benning for airborne school. If you get jump qualified, and that's a big if soldiers, you'll spend three months in a guerrilla warfare course jumping out of choppers at night into the middle of snake infested swamps and learning how to kill people with nothing but your hands. You walk out of there in one piece with a big smile on your face you'll be sent to the Special Warfare Center at Fort Bragg. Welcome aboard, sons. You'll do fine." He shook their hands and handed them their papers.

Nine months after enlisting in the Army, Sean O'Neal was nearly fluent in French, could kill a man with a single punch or break his neck or garrote him without a struggle. The trick was to take the guy out in the first thirty seconds. After thirty seconds your chances of staying alive diminish rapidly. He could put ten .30 caliber rounds through a half dollar sized circle at fifty yards and slice the head off a water moccasin with one swift stroke. He could fieldstrip, blindfolded, both American and Russian submachine guns and pack and detonate plastic explosives to take out a bridge with one blast. He could dig a well and thatch a roof. When he could do all these things, when the alignment of his senses, his body and his mind were balanced, when his actions and reactions were automatic and he knew it, he knew he was willing to take enormous risks to accomplish a goal. It is that characteristic that made the Special Forces the perfect fighting force in Vietnam. President Kennedy recognized the conflict as a true guerilla war and wanted men to be able to bring that kind of fight to that enemy. Unfortunately, the fighting force that shared this characteristic was the Viet Cong. Also unfortunately, the Americans could neither fight nor give orders. They had been 'advisors' to the South Vietnamese whose commanders had the final say in all military decisions. That was changing slowly. Not before they shipped out.

In June, 1965, the US Air Force Military Transport plane carrying Sergeants First Class Sean O'Neal and James "Popcorn" Jenkins with fifty other freshly trained men all wearing the Green Beret with the flash of the 5th Special Forces above the left eye, touched down at Nha Trang airfield one hundred and forty miles north of Saigon. When the cargo door opened, the plane sucked in the dense, humid 100 degree air of Southeast Asia. In the morning at 0600 ten men, an A team component, were flown by a Huey UH-1B chopper to B509, a Special Forces encampment in the western mountains, two miles from the Cambodian border. Everybody on the helicopter wore a headset of padded earphones and a mouthpiece to talk into. Ten minutes into the flight 'BB' said, "Good Gracious this thing is loud!" The pilot responded. "That's the sound of freedom, soldier." 'BB', who was raised in the Pentecostal persuasion in rural Arkansas fully understood the curative power of deafening persistent noise, barked back, "Roger that Captain." They touched down at a square fort looking north and west into the thick green mountains and gorges, southeast across wide, flat scrub lands. The perimeter was lined with sandbagged walls, machine gun ports and concertina wire. Two years earlier the Special Forces had set this encampment high up on a ridge on the edge of the central highlands between Kon Tum and Dac To, deep in the mountain forest overlooking the green hillsides descending gently into the vast flatlands, the wet lands, the rice lands of northern Cambodia where it abuts the southern tip of Laos. It was a small camp of twelve or so Green Berets and dozens of

Montegnards, Vietnamese highlanders, just two miles above the Ho Chi Minh Trail. The camp could not be seen from down below through the thick canopy of oak, thitka and calamander trees nor did the soldiers have to worry about being heard. By day, the endless screaming chatter of black monkeys, gibbons and squirrels masked all noise they made. The maddening cacophony also made it certain they would never hear the Viet Cong climbing, creeping up towards their camp. The bamboo huts with roofs of stretched camouflage tarps were bounded around the perimeter with sand bags and barbed wire coils. On the front facing west, facing down the mountains where the North Vietnamese moved supplies along the Trail, the men had dug a trench wide enough to sit in, just deep enough so that, when standing, the sandbags were belt high, rifle high to the average kneeling soldier. Every twenty feet or so a bunker had been dug at the bottom of the trench, a place where hand grenades and ammunition for the rifles and machine guns could be stored so that the soldiers didn't have to get up out of the safety of the trench until all the bullets and grenades were spent and each man was left with only his fists and his knife. The new huts and bunkers were low and white with thatched roofs. By that November, one hundred fifty men were there, fifty of them South Vietnamese Rangers, the elite force of the regular army, twenty Americans and the rest were the hill tribesman who harbored a special hatred of the Viet Cong. The French called them the Montagnards. They were Degar, people indigenous to these mountains of central Viet Nam, many of whom have been converted to Christianity by the French. They had not always been indigenous to this place. They were an amalgam of tribes that had been pushed out of the rich farmlands up into the hills by a population that considered them stupid, backwards, savages. "Moi" they called them. But it was over these mountains that the Viet Cong could most effectively infiltrate to the populous centers of

South Viet Nam. It was here that the American military command sent the first Special Forces personnel into the mountains to befriend and train the Montagnards. The mountain people had in large part fought with the French and were fiercely independent and antagonistic towards the bulk of the Vietnamese population. The relationship between the Green Berets and the Montagnards became close and effective. As a fighting force they were far superior to the South Vietnamese Regular Army and as a people, much more similar in temperament to the Special Forces soldiers.

Night is still hot. Even in the highlands the heat hangs in a fog shroud. A breeze might blow it away for a moment, might cool the sweat on a man's face and neck but then it's back. Sound doesn't travel well in hot, moist air. The wavelengths become longer, slower. Noise is dull. There is no echo. In the Artic night, the sharp crack of a rifle can be heard for miles and then heard and heard again as it ricochets off sharp ice. Here, it's a dull Blat! Blat! Blat! If you hear it, you're lucky you're not dead. It didn't come from far away. Whoever is pulling the trigger can probably see you. It is not likely in this place, in this war, that you can see them. Soldiers who fight in the Artic wear white, the color of ice and snow. Soldiers who fight in the desert wear khaki, the color of sand. Those who fight in the jungle wear tiger suits that look like tree bark and green leaves. Men who fight at night wear black pajamas. Their shoes are soft-soled sandals and they lift their feet when they walk putting each step down with measured weight rocking their toe or heel back so the twig underfoot won't snap. If you try real hard to see through the dark and listen through the dull to see a man or an undulating platoon of men before your head is level with the bead at the end of their gun, your senses are drawn so tight exhaustion sets in soon. The random shriek of a gibbon can shred a man's nerves. Patient soldiers in black pajamas waiting, crouched in the damp dark could imitate the primate screech. A few seconds after the man-monkey screamed, when the grunt in the trench was jerking and blinking, they'd storm the sandbagged walls, grenades lobed into the gun turret trenches, submachine guns on full automatic.

The VC main western headquarters was thirty miles inside the Cambodian border, due west of camp B509. Far enough in so that the 1954 Geneva Accords prevented any incursion into the "neutral" country by the Americans or the South Vietnamese without precipitating an international diplomatic disaster. Smaller encampments were scattered along the border. Thousands of Viet Cong and North Vietnamese regulars were fed from the main camp to the smaller outposts to conduct platoon sized raids and ambushes inside the South. Neither the Cambodian nor Laotian governments said anything to anyone about the presence of these camps nor the movement of armaments along the Ho Chi Minh trail inside their borders. B509, like five or six other bases along the Laos and Cambodian borders, was there to disrupt traffic on the Trail and try to staunch the flow of the VC over the highlands and down into the sweet underbelly of South Vietnam.

When Sean and Popcorn arrived at camp B509, it was a new base, construction not yet completed. The only part that had been there for long was the mud hut barracks of the Green Berets inside its own concertina wire gate and fence. Ten men, and, from time to time, a CIA operative constituted an A team that rotated in and out of this camp in three month stints. Up until the time Sean's contingent arrived, only Special Forces advisors were there. In the expanded war, non-com regulars were flooding into the WZ, the war zone. The new soldiers spent their first days working with the Vietnamese building concrete grenade-proof walls and roofs on the ammo dump, finishing the control room where the officers met to plan strategy and building latrines that could handle twenty men at a time.

There was no running water at these camps. Water was gathered in buckets from a nearby stream and hoisted by pulley into large elevated plastic containers. The larger one was for bathing and washing. The smaller, for drinking and cooking, got iodine tablets for purification. The first week was spent working on the camp and sitting through training, briefing and strategy sessions with the Base Commanders. It was a certainty that the VC would strike this base soon. It was a mystery as to why they hadn't yet. The base was incomplete, the arms and munitions exposed and the number of men grew as every week went by.

Captain Hank Bryson, the Special Forces Commanding Officer (CO) thought that a VC strike at a small base would not carry near the strategic impact of a major victory at a significant American base. They were waiting, he thought, until the base was staffed with lots of new men but not yet organized or constructed. The new soldiers were clumsy in action, slow in response. Bunch of Howdie-Doodies. Gumby-footed Howdie-Doodies, the Captain called them. Attack time was any time now.

The Regulars, both American and ARVN stayed clear of the Green Berets. "Greenies" they called them in most camps but after Private Jimmy Littleworth of Hoboken, New Jersey looked out the mess hall window and saw one of them shirtless, face smeared with black grease carrying, in one hand, a live squealing monkey by the throat and in the other hand the creature's severed arms and legs, he shouted out, "Them fuckers give me the heebie-jeebies. Black heads like killer-man hoods and them white eye-balls. They give me the heebie-jeebies!" After that everyone at B-509 base called the Green Berets, "G-Bs." A black soldier sitting next to him said, "Gimme one of them guys any day compared to the opposite; white

36

pointy hoods with little black eye-holes. Talk about getting' the heebie-jeebies. Lord, Lord, Lord them fuckers are scary."

The Green Berets stuck to themselves and nobody went into their fenced area without being invited, which was almost never. The G-Bs came and went as they pleased. Mostly they slept during the day and would slide out at night in groups of three with a score of Rangers and Montagnards. Slide out black-faced into the dark with a knife, a garrote wire, grenades and a light weight, sliding stock 5.56 MM Colt Commando CAR-15 assault rifle. Sean's first foray out was on a night the moon never rose. Thick clouds stretched from the South China Sea to the Bay of Bengal. Captain Bryson paired him up with Popcorn and Master (Weapons) Sergeant Howlin' Henry, a three month veteran of the high jungle. Howlin' Henry LeCroix, son a French hunting expedition guide and a Mormon schoolteacher lady, was from the mountains of northern Idaho. After a kill, when the coast was clear, he would crawl around and howl like a wolf. "I howl 'cause the dinks don't know what it is. Never heard a wolf. Freaks 'em out. Makes them think we're animals. Crazy animals." Henry didn't know it, but he was spot-on right. Even the hardest core of the Viet Cong were afraid of these guys.

Folks in this part of Indochina live in hamlets. Little villages of mud huts with a common well. The vast majority, more than 90%, are Buddhist. Most of the people in these hamlets sympathized with the North because the rulers of the South, Jean Baptist Ngo Diem and his family were Catholic and all the perks and appointments went to Catholic family and friends, especially military appointments. Mr. Diem and his brother spent much of their political capital persecuting the Buddhists and appropriating land to the coffers of the Church. His father had been a counselor to the Son of Heaven Emperor Thanh Thai during the French occupation and later rose, if you will, to become Keeper of the Eunuchs. After the French deposed the Emperor because they believed him to be raving lunatic, a condition which he likely feigned to be able to escape death at their hands, Diem's father became a poor farmer but Diem and his brother cozied up to the French. They became major players in the Catholic Church of Vietnam and in 1955 Diem, with the help of American diplomats, became President. He dedicated the country to the Virgin Mary and at all state gatherings, he flew the Vatican flag. None of this sat well with the Buddhist farmers in the paddies and hamlets. Ho Chi Minh knew how the peasants felt and knew that "armed propaganda" was highly effective. He had said, "Do not take a peasant's land. It's too easy to kill innocent bystanders with guns and bombs and accidental killing of the innocent will alienate peasants from the revolution. If assassination is necessary, use a knife, not a rifle or grenade." The Green Berets were of the same opinion. They also knew, because their CIA operative guy, Heindrick Moller, a Danish commando from the Korean War, had told them that it was from these hamlets the Viet Cong originated. They were Viet Minh, the fathers and sons of these hamlets, southern communists fighting under the command structure of the North. These fighters found food, shelter and support throughout the villages of Vietnam, Laos and Cambodia. It was in the night into these hamlets that the three men teams would creep, knives drawn.

This moonless night Sean, Popcorn, Howlin' Henry and six Rangers walked ten miles down the gorges, over the ridges, along the river banks to the village of Duc Tom. Captain Bryson had said a woman from the village, a sympathizer with the South, had told of a shipment of food and arms being dropped there for the Viet Cong. It was to arrive at daybreak, but the soldiers would be there tonight. As they walked they used their hands to talk but inside their minds their thoughts were as loud as cannons. James Jenkins, 'Popcorn', went over and over what he was going to tell his older brother Elroy about how fighting for his country was not a bad thing. About how there was honor in serving and how black men like him fighting right alongside all the white men would make black people's place in society better by being a part of defending our nation from enemies. The Viet Cong might be brothers in your eyes, Elroy, but they are ruthless killers to the poor people of Vietnam. Butchers, murderers. What you're doing with those Black Panthers, Elroy, is wrong; killing innocent folks because you don't like the government. You're no different than the Cong. And he would tell him that with his hands down at his sides, peaceful, but strong and sure. In his thoughts he couldn't get Elroy to answer. Elroy just stared at him and so he would start all over again. And again. And then again.

Henry James LeCroix, named after his mother's favorite author, had long conversations with his dog. A spaniel-like mutt afraid of his own shadow. Henry had always wanted a malamute or a huskie, something ferocious, but when, at sixteen, he had passed out dead drunk behind the bowling alley in Coeur d'Alene and woke up to this abandoned pup licking the snow off his cheek, he fell in love. Strike, he called him. When Strike saw another dog coming, he would put his tail down between his legs and hide behind Henry. It didn't matter what kind or how big the other dog was, they terrified him. Henry figured he'd been a runt thrown in a kennel of sled dogs and he'd somehow made it out alive. Then somebody just chucked him out on the city street in the middle of the night. Henry thought that if he could get Strike over here to Nam then maybe the constant danger, the persistent fear would raise his dander and he would be OK. He would be tough like him and his buddies. Sean, who they now called Geronimo, thought about...Blat!...Blat! Blat!...Blat!.. Blat. The Viet Cong's AK 47s spit bullets into the soft dirt ahead of them and they all dove face down and rolled until they found a tree or rock hide behind. They unshouldered their rifles, fingered the triggers, waving the barrels slightly back and forth, waited for more. They couldn't tell where it came from. Somewhere ahead and up above but there wasn't anything to see. Nothing moved. It was night quiet again. More than quiet. Deadly quiet and deadly dark. They waited; listening, looking, straining to find something that didn't fit. A crackle or a whisper or a rustle or a click or a darker darkness that moved. Nothing. After four or five minutes Popcorn caught Henry's eye. Henry jerked his head up the hill, behind them, back from where they had come. They crouched up the hill slowly from tree to tree and then eight miles back to camp. "Yeah, it might've been just one guy and we could've gotten him, but more likely there was a bunch of them further on and they wanted us to think there was only one of them. But, also, they didn't know for sure how many of us there was. Best how that came out." They got back to camp and told about it, just how it was and everybody agreed it was best how it came out. Everybody but Dick, who didn't need a nickname, who called them all pussies and went back to smoking his dope.

They went out most every night. Often they found VC, or VC sympathizers or people who might have been comforting the enemy and sometimes they killed them. Not every night, but sometimes. They usually shot them if they figured a fire fight wouldn't bring more, or, if they thought it would, they killed them with their knife. Sometimes, as when silence was mandatory, when they were inside the hut of a sleeping hamlet, they used the wire garrote. They didn't kill many. It was the presence, the pressure, the constant nightly pressure that was most important. We're here you fuckers and you better not sleep. We're better at your game than you are. We don't wear medals or march in columns or shout orders but we sure as hell aren't going to let you seep into this country without a fight. The VC knew they were there, all along the border, and who they were and what they could do and that knowledge alone was instrumental in keeping them in check while the Marines built up their strength at all the inland bases. It was a good plan. A plan that eventually wouldn't work for reasons much more political, religious and historical than military but, on the face of it, given what there was to work with, a good plan nonetheless. At the Marine bases in the States, Colonels and Majors and Generals were beginning to figure out that helicopters might be like horses. In the Officers' Mess Halls and the bars they were talking about how the cavalry, small bands of mounted men could ride over rough terrain and down into the camps of the enemy, strike and ride out. Like they had done in the Sierra Madres of Mexico in 1848. Like Teddy Roosevelt had done with the Rough Riders on San Juan Hill in 1898. Why couldn't we do the same thing with an agile helicopter packed with a ten man, jump trained strike force?

The time most difficult for Sean was down time. No work, no thinking, no training; just hours of time the military thought important to give each man once in a while so they could relax, rejuvenate, write letters that never got past the sensors in Saigon. When you knew you were going to attack or get attacked, when you knew that any minute you would be killing people, shooting them or stabbing them, wrapped in slippery tight to their foreign sweat breathing in their mouth odor before breaking their necks, the last thing that came easy was doing nothing. Sean had developed a repetitive monotonous ritual that heightened his sense of preparedness, of awareness. His knife, issued by the Special Forces, was a masterpiece of both design and craftsmanship. American made combat tactical knife with an eight inch high carbon 420 stainless steel blade an inch and a quarter wide with a very shallow "blood gutter" running down the center of each side.

The black handle was glass filled nylon, cross-hatched, with a finger slip at the hilt. Sean sharpened this knife after every time he used it; whether for whittling, cutting meat, rope, bamboo, slicing bread or opening sacks of rice. With a thin carborundum stone he started sharpening with the edge of the blade that faced away from him. This side was harder because it sharpened through the pushing stroke and the pressure was from the elbow. The other side was more natural; the pulling stroke was from the wrist. As the forearm tired and began to ache, the easy side was last so he knew he could finish all the strokes. Holding the blade just slightly angled off the stone, maybe five degrees, with the point in the middle of the stone, he pushed its full eight inch length until the wide heel slid off the end, then pulled it back and off the stone in a long sweep towards his body. That's one stroke. He pushed it and then pulled again through the second stroke, the third, the fourth; fifty times on each edge. One hundred strokes. Inside the soft grinding noise of each swipe, the steel sang. The pitch was high where the blade was skinny and dropped lower where the blade was fat.

Done, he put the stone down, dropped his right arm and shook the soreness out. He wiped the blade clean on his fatigues and took out his wide leather belt, hooking it through its buckle on the end of his bed frame. With sweeping theatrical slaps of steel on leather, he would hold the belt taut and use it as a strop to burnish off the invisible burrs; twenty strokes, each alternating side with a flip of the wrist at the top. When he stropped his knife this way, he remembered his father. He remembered a little boy sitting in a big barber's chair watching his father sharpen his straight razors on a wide leather strop. When the knife was once again wiped clean on this pant leg, he shaved a small patch of hair off his forearm, making sure the knife is sharp enough to slice fast through human veins, arteries, organs, and taut, thick muscle with a minimum of effort.

"Why you do that all the time when it ain't even dull? You're gonna grind that thing down to nothin'." Popcorn said sitting on the cot across from Sean, leafing through an old Captain America comic book. Sean looked up at him and shrugged. "I don't like that noise, that grindin' noise. Give me the willies, like scratchin' a blackboard." Sean looked up at him again, shrugged again. "Listen Geronimo, don't you do that to me." Popcorn stood up, all six feet two inches of him, all two hundred ten pounds. "Talk to me." Sean put his knife in its sheath and said, "Humanitarian reasons. Dull knife hurts, sharp knife kills clean. No pain, just dead." Popcorn smiled. "Ain't you the soft touch." He was quiet for a while. "We going to win this thing?" "No." Sean said. "No? How come?"

"Do you care if this place is two countries or one?"

"No."

"I don't either. That's why we aren't going to win." Down time was hard.

Sean, Popcorn, Howlin' Henry, and six of the other seven G-Bs returned for a second three month stint in the camp after two weeks of R&R in Saigon. Dick didn't come back. He didn't get to go to Saigon. Dick wasn't going to go anywhere or come back from anywhere. Wherever he was, was where he was going to be forever. A few nights before they left for the city, Dick, who had always been basically a callous, kind of get it while you can loner, had been becoming increasingly unhinged from the fear, fatigue and massive quantities of dope. At a bend in the trail a hundred feet away there was a clutch of young girls washing clothes in a stream outside a VC mountain hamlet. It was early first morning light. Pinkish. The oldest of the girls bent far forward over the scrubbing rock so her blouse fell away from her plumb breasts and with upbent face gathered her sillion black hair and threw it with a flick back over her shoulder. She smiled at Dick. He walked straight towards her in a lustful stoned stupor, grinning back, arms hanging at his sides, ape-like. The girls, in what he thought was about the most seductive move he'd ever seen, lay flat down in the stream, only their pretty wet asses up out of the water just as his left boot hooked snugly under the brown #16 detonator wire loop of a Bouncing Betty landmine and BOOM! there were two Dicks. One from the rib cage up at the edge of the stream looking dead-eyed down at the prostrate girls and the other, parts and pieces strewn back on the trail. Nobody came out shooting. There were no VC there. Women and children only. Captain Bryson wanted to know how in the name of the Good God Almighty they were ever going to win this war as he and Sergeant Bob Johnson, gathered the parts, put them in a poncho with a pole and humped it back to camp. "Getting our asses kicked by a bunch of goddamned Buddhists." he mumbled.

The VC attacked B509 two weeks into Sean's second tour. Only three of the G-Bs were there; Heindrick Moller, Howlin' Henry and a Cajun boy named Robby Billidoux. He'd grown up in the swamp outside Houma, Louisiana. He was the son of a roughneck who worked the oil rigs in the Gulf of Mexico. His daddy had wanted him to join the Navy because he had grown up on boats and always lived in a house on stilts in Bayou Cane but Robby wanted to find out what it was like to spend a couple of years walking on solid ground and listening to regular Rock 'n Roll music. No fiddles. No accordions. The rest of the G-Bs were out in the night somewhere. Too much time had passed for the attack to be a guerilla action alone. The camp was too big, too many men, too many munitions. About fifty VC and a 100 man battalion of the North Vietnamese Army's 325 Division's 101B Regiment under the command of Lt. Colonel Nguyen Trong Cao struck in a two phase, three pronged assault. VC first at the north wall followed by the NVA hidden in the ravine about a quarter mile, or 10 minutes away over the south and west embankments. Five of the six Montagnard Ranger scouts patrolling the lower ravines and grasslands to the south were dead before they got the button pushed on their radios. One got through to the radio shack. Two minutes later, while one of the communications men was pounding on the Base Commander's door, the man-monkey screamed about five feet from the face of an 18 year old Private First-Class Allan Pritchard who was lost far deep in thoughts about his woodworking shop at Lincoln High. He jumped so hard he dropped his gun, and a bayonet thrust clean through his chest. A more seasoned soldier about twenty feet away recognized it all for what it was. Before they could cut through and fully breech the fence, he spun and squeezed the trigger of the .50 caliber machine gun spraying rounds along the sandbags, into two or three scrambling VC, all up the chest and head of an already dead Private Prichard and then off into the night sky as he took a round in the neck. The CO had hit the alarm. Men were running fully dressed, half dressed, hardly dressed at all, firing M-16s, lobbing grenades as mayhem broke loose. Howlin' Henry fought the whole battle with a load of shit in his pants. He'd been in the latrine in the early seconds of taking care of an explosive case of diarrhea when he heard the .50 caliber pop. He missed a step or two at the outset but, all in all, it didn't slow him down a bit. Just another thing.

Three miles away over two ridges and two streams out past the Ho Chi Minh Trail in a in a dense thicket of oak and calamander..."What's that?"... Sean, Popcorn and the ten Rangers stopped. Don't talk, stay still..."What's that?"...They could just make out the faint distant dull thud of grenades. The almost soft "Puuu"..."Puuu" and the muted staccato of the perimeter guns, "Bop,Bop,Bop,Bop,Bop." The men stood silent looking back up into the hills of Vietnam and then took off at the fastest lope, the most nimble scramble they could manage. Explosions of mortar rounds began. A half an hour later they were at the bottom of the west ravine watching retreating VC and North Vietnamese Regulars pulling south towards Cambodia. No matter how well trained, no matter how disciplined, how experienced a soldier is, certain human actions can trigger immediate, equal and opposite human reactions. Sean didn't know if it was a beaten battalion running home or a victorious battalion retreating to re-group; what he saw at the tail end, headed north directly towards them was a fistful of soldiers who were hundreds of yards away from the retreating battalion. They were not NVA or VC. They wore khaki shirts and pants with a Mao-type cap. They seemed to be laughing, jogging down the hill. As if they were alone. As if they were happy. Popcorn rose out his crouch behind a thicket of shrubs and unloaded his clip. Three went down, two didn't. Sean pulled the pin on his grenade and lobbed it towards them. A poor pitch. Way out of the strike zone. It bounced off a tree and fell to the thicket in front of Popcorn just as Popcorn took rounds across both kneecaps and he buckled down, flat down spread out wide with the grenade nestled under his great belly like a little unborn baby. The ground was soft and wormish. The grenade rolled down a hollow hole into the forest floor. There is no such thing as a specific time or a specific place. They are both relative to the observer. Albert Einstein made that clear in his Special Theory of Relativity and all important scientists eventually agreed that he was right. Most important psychiatrists also agreed that, to a certain extent the theory applies to the inside of the human mind. What a person sees happening and when they see it happen is entirely dependent on where their conscious and subconscious minds are in time and space and where in that mind space they might link together to make a cohesive image. Sean's immediate consciousness was, in the instant second, trying to will his body to jump and dive, to roll the body of his buddy off the unblown grenade but his subconscious was lying on the baseball mound looking up into the faces of his sister and a black man, her red curls falling over a pockmarked face. "Hit 'em!" Coach Dan had said. "Hit 'em!" If I had done what my coach had said, Popcorn would have walked to first and we never would have met. If I had just done what I had been told to do Popcorn would be in college somewhere, not be lying on my hand grenade in a sweaty fucking jungle full of weird little laughing people with puffy little hats and I wouldn't be here glued to the ground with a pin ring hanging from my forefinger, waiting, waiting to see him die.

Road builders, when they run into ledge, drill holes in the rock, put sticks of dynamite in the holes and put a mat on top. The mat is woven steel wire. When the sticks blow the heavy mat humps up a bit but because it is wide and pliant, essentially in a "plastic" state, it forces the explosion downward, fracturing the rock. Nothing can be faster than the speed of light but the speed Sean's thoughts traveled from the crack of the bat all the way through his friendship had to be faster. It seemed a month but it was a micro-second. When the blast came, Popcorn's big body humped and jumped bit but the thick calamander roots nestled in bed of wet leaves and rotting undergrowth made a plastic mat.

Even the finest soldier is nothing more than a man. All the training possible cannot change that. Sean rose out of the bushes, pointed at the Rangers and pointed at the body of his friend, now entirely limp. He jerked his thumb towards the top of the hill. He pointed at himself. He pointed at the puffy-hatted soldiers running down the hill, crossed himself and took off after them, weeping as he ran. He followed at a far enough distance so he wouldn't be seen or heard. At 0530 he finally caught up with two of the men four miles to the north-north west. At the far side of a field the two men turned and looked behind them directly at the gulch where Sean lay crouching. They looked off to their right and off to their left and back again across the whole expanse, then laughed and joked with a very old man who seemed to be hoeing dirt behind a hut of a small encampment. They hadn't seen Sean. One of them stayed out with the old man occasionally looking in a long slow arc from side of the field to the other. The gulch was a drainage ditch for the wet season. It was dry now, two feet deep, three feet wide. Sean couldn't be seen as he crawled on his belly around the perimeter of the field to the south head of the town. There was an arched gate, more ceremonial than secure, old and cracked with faded, peeling paintings from better times long past. Inside the gate was what might have once been a small village common. A metal bucket on a rope and pulley hung over the well. The place seemed deserted except for three people; one of the soldiers with his rifle, a man with a very long beard and a young girl with the khaki clothes and Mao hat, sitting on the edge of the well, talking. Sean eased back to the edge of the building, fifteen feet away from the farmer and soldier in the field. Their backs were turned and within seconds he had slit their throats. Not a sound. Sean checked the safety on his Colt Commando, spun around the post...'don't hit the girl...don't hit the girl' and emptied half of the thirty round clip in three seconds. Fourteen of the fifteen rounds were right on target. One had slipped a bit to the left. She went down. Sean headed off at a full run into the woods, south by southeast. There was no one there who could chase him. The only other person in the little hamlet was the grandmother, folding clothes in a mud hut.

He was back at camp at 0845. What Sean didn't know then was that the man with the long goatee was Bounsouan Kahmphoukeo, provincial chief of the southern Pathet-Lao, the girl was his granddaughter and that the killing had taken place four miles inside "neutral" Laos. Nor did he know that official outrage about this assassination would reach the American Department of State within a day.

No one of course could ever be sure who had done the killing so the State Department responded that they believed it likely to have been carried out by one or more Hmong commandos working under contract for the Royal Lao Army. No one was sure except Base Commander Major Dryden. He had been told by Captain Bryson that Sergeant Sean O'Neal had been heard talking about it with another Green Beret in his group. Talking about that and talking about Popcorn. How the medics just took his body on a stretcher, put a sheet over it and shoved it into an idling helicopter. "Get O'Neal out. Get him out now!" That was the order. The last image Sean had of combat in Vietnam was, just at the tail end of taking fire at the edge of grasslands one mile to the south of camp, the unmistakable retort of a Colt SAA forty-five caliber pistol coming from behind him and a searing pain in his right calf. Only the CIA guy, Heindrick Moller, like his hero, Gen. George S. Patton, carried that weapon. He was a good shot. It missed the bone. Before Sean was airlifted out to Nha Trang that afternoon, Major Dryden came to his bedside in the clinic and personally awarded him the Purple Heart. Right there. On the spot. The major said, "Good work, son. Your country thanks you."

"I killed Popcorn."

"No, soldier, you didn't. Popcorn didn't die. Hurt pretty bad, but he didn't die."

"I killed Popcorn." The Major didn't reply.

"How old was the girl?" Dryden said nothing.

"How old was the girl?" Nothing.

"Major, Goddamn it, how old was the girl?"

"Not old."

*   *   *

In June, 1966, twenty three months after enlisting at the Army recruitment office next to the Post Office at L and 14th Street in Southie, Sean was shipped home.

MURDER IN THE NORTH END

It was late 1966. Cool and brisk in Southie. The summer leaves had browned and mostly fallen from the trees. Occasionally, on a quite cold morning, breath could be seen. People wore jackets and hats. No snow yet, but each day as the earth tilted ever so slightly away from the direct rays of the sun, precious daylight was lost to longer nights and the sky chilled more quickly. Soon, the moisture in the clouds would freeze and rain would fall as snow, dampening sound and slowing down the daily bustle. Sean O'Neil was back from Viet Nam. In the weeks and months after he was flown from Nha Trang to the Army Air Force base in Stuttgart, Germany, perfunctorily debriefed, flown to Fort Dix, New Jersey, released from service with an honorable discharge and put on a bus home to Boston, his mind could not latch on to a single, whole thought. That was it; home again, no hero's welcome. Gwyneth, his mother Mary and his father Jimmy met him at South Station. Nothing more. No girls waving handkerchiefs, no Important People saying thank you. For five months he'd walked the streets at night, his limp worsening each day as the earth and sky cooled. The wounded calf muscle ached. He didn't look for work. He slept at home in his old bedroom.

During the day when his mother and father were off at work and his sister was off at school, he read mystery novels and listened to the records Gwyneth had left him. Ramblin' Jack Elliot, Bob Dylan, Country Joe and the Fish, The Rolling Stones, Joan Baez. Most of the songs they sang were about what a bad idea the war was or how a new day was coming. Sean sensed that however virgin these young singers were, however untouched by bullets, unbeaten by dark fear and mayhem, they were likely right but right only because they weren't wrong. Not because they knew anything. To know it's not right to kill a man you have to have..."Goddam it!" he shouted as he became confused. His hair was getting long. He left it that way. But he shaved every morning; cleanly, closely. A little of this, a little of that. Baby steps. Go either way.

Sean stuck to Southie. For him, the rest of the city was changed. A place he didn't know. There were anti-war posters and protesters and marchers and peace symbols hanging in the windows of coffee shops, book stores and clothing stores where they sold bell bottoms, tie-dyed t-shirts, sandals, incense. dope pipes. Brass peace pendants hung around almost every neck.

He stuck to Southie. It was like an old place that would stay old forever. A house got painted once in a while, a new restaurant opened here or there, a crosswalk was added where old Mr. Weeks, then ninety-two, was finally run over after having teetered on his cane twice a day for forty years, jay-walking from his apartment on the corner to the Olde Dublin Pub diagonally across the intersection.

Surprisingly, it was on his way to the bar, stone cold sober at 10 AM when he was creamed by a mail truck that swerved to avoid a Cocker Spaniel and a Doberman copulating in the street. The Irish brogue that once was on every corner, in every shop had lost a little of its lilt, but not a lot. Once in a while someone would say, "Hey man, dig it, it's cool!" but not a lot. It was an old place.

Sean avoided his classmates, the kids he had known before he went in. If they hadn't gone to Nam, he had nothing to say to them. They would ask him this and that and want him to talk about himself. He wasn't going to do that. If they had gone to Nam, and had come home, he had nothing he wanted to say to them. They would surely ask him this and that and he would have to talk about himself. He didn't want to talk about himself because he didn't know anything about himself.

Everything he had known for sure about Sean O'Neal had been sucked out in some stinking jungle 10,000 miles away. What was left was not much more than an amalgam of anatomical parts. Feet, knees, hips, shoulders, arms, head. He wandered the streets at night, drinking beer here and there, chasing it with shots of cheap whiskey, thinking. Thinking the same thoughts over and over and over. As though the record in his mind was scratched. Just as the second verse of Country Joe McDonald's lamentation on the nature of being was about to begin, it skipped. *"Who am I, to stand and wonder, to wait, while the wheels of fate, slowly grind my life away?"* Skip. *"Who am I...Skip...Who am I...Skip...Who am I?"*

Some nights when the shops were closed and the clutches of youth had thinned from the sidewalks, he would walk past the Army Base along the waterfront, by the docks where the stevedores in their black watch caps, high laced leather boots and pea coats worked all night under lights, across the bridge into the maw of the inner city all the way to Tremont Street. To the Combat Zone. He would pay ten bucks, lie with his pants around his knees on filthy mattress ticking staring up at a peeled yellow ceiling, motionless, mute, while someone's daughter, likewise mute, quickly fucked him.

The only person he wanted to talk to was his sister. He was sure that she could, and would, gently reach into him, lift the needle, rub out the scratch and let a whole song fill him up. Talk to him. But the want was in his heart and the talk was in his brain. The strap between the two had come unbuckled.

Each day when she got home from school, she ran upstairs to his room and sat on the end of his bed, cross legged, talking rapid fire about what this Sister said and what that Sister did and the trouble her friend Beth or Missy got into. How did you like the book I left you? Did you listen to that Rolling Stones album? Slowing down, she asked her brother for his advice, about the merits of having boyfriends, which she neither had nor really wanted, about going to college, which she really did want. She asked him these things partly because she wanted to know what he thought but mostly to pry him open, to hear him speak. Last week, Sister Mary Margaret had told the class to dissect the poem "'The Windhover, To Christ Our Lord" by the troubled Jesuit priest Gerard Manly Hopkins. To take it apart and find out why the poet used the words he used. What were all the different references to Jesus Christ and God? What each word meant by itself, alone, separated from the whole thing. Gwyneth loved that poem. She kept a copy of it folded up in her purse. She thought it the most beautiful thing she had ever read. Gwyneth, the "A" student, handed Sean her homework paper, graded. Across the top was written "*F*". *"You seem to have chosen to ignore my assignment"*. Across the bottom, another "*F*". Sean read her handwriting; perfect penmanship on an unlined page.

THE WINDHOVER

I am doing something here I have never done before and don't want to do. That is to reach inside my favorite poem, and, as though it was the dead body of some rare bird, take out the organs, dissect them and try to figure out what made this creature what it was; to find the bird's soul, or maybe the poet's soul. I don't know. I am told his bird was a kestrel; the only falcon that can truly hover in one spot without a headwind, like a hummingbird or a pied kingfisher. But as I slice the wings off looking for some special reason he could do this, I realize that it, now wingless, is no longer a magnificent 'dapple dawn drawn falcon', but now just a heap of dead parts. I become sad. I didn't need to know how the wings worked. I didn't even need to know that it was a kestrel. I only needed to know that whatever it was, it could 'ride the rolling level underneath him steady air' and then sail off like a 'skates heel sweeps smooth on a bow bend'. I already knew that so why look any farther. I look because I have been told to.

So I reach inside the poem again and pull out parts; individual words like Buckle! with an exclamation point. I inspect it and see it could be a hasp that holds a belt together or perhaps it is what happened to person's knees or a carriage axle when put under too much stress and I move from being somewhat sad to very sad and confused. I feel as though I am shredding Van Gogh's "Sunflowers" to find out why he cut off his ear.

Lying in front of me now on the stainless steel table of my mind is what looks like the backbone of the dead bird poem. A whole sentence; SHEER PLOD MAKES PLOUGH DOWN SILLION SHINE, and I have always known just what that means: hard work makes even dirt clean! Each word is held to the next word by a thick nerve. I know by now that if I cut them apart there will be no backbone, just loose marbles rolling around my table. At the top where the nerves come down from the bird's brain and go off into his heart and wings, is a large nub, the likes of which I have never seen before: the word SILLION. I research everywhere in the library. This word does not exist anywhere else in nature or language. It has been invented, created by the poem's Maker and hidden in this place, a perfect place to trick the mind but not the heart. Created just like the poet was created by his Maker. I cry, pushing all the bloody parts to a heap. I want to see the bird soar, just 'the achieve of, the mastery of the thing'; nothing more.

Sean stared at the floor talking in a low monotone, the kind of voice that comes from a weariness that has overtaken pain. A weariness that comes after all the moisture has been wrung from the cloth of the soul. "It's like that, isn't it? Our life is a whole thing. Parts and pieces of it aren't who we are. I am not just the guy who could throw a strike on the inside inch of the plate. I am not just that guy who could climb a fifty foot rope with nothing but my hands. I'm not just that guy who got Popcorn blown to bits on my own hand grenade. I'm not just that guy who shot a farmer's daughter in their own little home. There has to be more of me than that. There has to be. I know that's what people see when they look at me, out on the street, taking me apart piece by piece with their eyes. That lump is a warrior, that lump is a murderer. But that isn't me. There's more. There's a whole me somewhere. I was a friend, I was a son, I was a brother and I know I still am. I don't know where, but I still am. I was only doing what they told me to do. They showed me how to do all those things and then they told me to do them. They told me to do all that and that was supposed to make it right. Why didn't it make it right? Why?" He looked up at his sister and she had the slightest of smiles on her lips and the biggest of smiles in her eyes. "Gwyneth, you are one smart little girl. Sister Mary Margaret can stick it up her arse." Sean said.

Gwyneth, sensing that a dribble of truth was better that a flood of self-pity, jumped up, put her hands on her hips, flipped her head back and said, "Guess what, Sister, my big brother says you can just stick it up your arse!" She hugged him and when his head was on her shoulder, beyond her face, he clinched his eyes shut tight and bit his lower lip to keep his chin from shaking.

Snow came. It came at night when Sean was walking. It started sparse. A flake here and there and then came thicker and thicker until the cold night air was full of flakes the size of thumbnails swirling the streetlights in dancing cones of virgin white. The amber lights from inside the Olde Dublin Pub spilled through the window like honey, beckoning. A stout man in his forties with his collar turned up and his white hair now whiter with snow, held the door open for Sean. "Comin' in?" he said. There was something familiar about this man. Sean went in, kicking the snow off his boots on the threshold and sat at the bar. "What'll it be m'boy?" the ancient barkeep asked. "Pint and a shot," Sean said. "It's on me." said the stout man as he sat in the stool next to Sean. "Too bad about old Weeksie," the man said to the bartender.

"Never felt a thing, they told me. Glad of a thing it is to go so quick. Thinkin' aboot a pint one minute, into the lovin' arms of the great hereafter the next. Pot o' gold, he was, that man, pot o' gold," eulogized the old man.

"You're Jimmy the Barber's boy, is it?" the man asked Sean.

"Yup, that's me. And you?" Sean said.

"That's a long story, son." He took a pack of Cigarillos from his shirt pocket, tapped them hard face down on the bar, pulled the cellophane band around the top, flipped the box lid open, pulled out the tin foil, wadded the refuse all up and put it carefully in the ash tray. Pulling two up, he asked Sean, "Cigar?" "No." Sean answered. The man opened his mouth, put the skinny brown cigar deep in between his lips and drew it out slowly, moistened. He put it between his teeth, clamped down and snapped his fingers. The old bartender stopped, frozen in time, then, as if the ice broke loose, started frantically opening drawers behind the bar, rustling things about, muttering. One drawer; rattle, rattle. Nothing. Two drawers; rattle, rattle. Nothing. The third drawer and there he had it. A narrow box as long as his hand, festooned with leprechauns and shamrocks. The old man, shaking from the elbows down, took out a long match, struck it on the side of the box and held it under the proffered end of the Cigarillo. Just like he had done every day until ten years ago when the man had gone away. The man was back now, on his stool with his Cigarillo stuck out, waiting for his match. "That's a long story," the man said again.

"Well then why don't you just give me the short version. You know, long story short." Sean turned in his stool, confrontationally.

"No," the man said, "A bald fact isn't worth telling. It's cold. No lyric to it. Scares people. Who I am and what I do is not nearly as important as who you are and what you do. I have seen you walk these streets night after night, talking to yourself, shaking your head, looking, looking, looking. I think you're looking for me and you just don't know it." He took a long drag on his cigar and blew the smoke in a thin plume out of a puckered side of his lips, straight to the face of the old bartender. The old man didn't move out of the way of the acrid smoke.

"You're a cocksucker, you know it? A real prick." Sean said.

"That I am, my friend. But I'm the prick at the end of your rainbow, sitting on your pot of gold. I know where you've been. I know what you've seen. I know how you feel. I know your family. I know things. Secrets. I can help you; you can help me." Sean could feel this man had spent his life accumulating power by hoarding secrets; like a cop, like a politician, like a spy. Secrets. Its glister outshines gold. Showing a hint of it, like turning up the edge of one card, will make a man fold his hand. Like pulling a skirt up to show a little slip will make a man go weak in the knees. Using a secret just a peek at a time is the craft of a master. It can cause a man to anticipate something that might not be real. To act irrationally.   To be like putty in another man's hands.   He knows things, Sean thought.   He's not going to tell me.   What does he know? About me? I don't care. Gwyneth? Something about Gwyneth?

Sean sat quiet.   He looked out the window and the snow was still falling.   Heavy now, heavy and thick.   He turned back to the bar.   The picture over the mirror of President Kennedy, now three years dead, was yellowing with smoke.   The stout man's face was coming back to him; a little more gaunt, a little less ruddy but the same curly white hair, the same cold eyes.   Just the face, not the body.   The body was under a robe. A white robe. Was he a priest? No, not a priest.   It was a barber's cloth.   Sean saw himself on a stool in his daddy's shop, a comic book in his lap. He saw the man leap up.   He saw his daddy turn his back and look the other way.

Sean swung around to the stout man, reached behind his hip and pulled his knife from the sheath.   Then, fast as a cat, jumped from his stool, grabbed the man by his throat and waving the knife in front of his nose, exploded.   "If you don't know what the fuck you're talkin' about, don't say nothin'. If you don't know nothin' about nothin', which you don't, just shut the fuck up!"   The ancient barkeep ran like a rat into the kitchen.   The Mobster did not piss himself.   He said, "Two hundred a week, one per cent of the take on the ponies. You just keep our end in the money."   Sean held his throat.   The bar clock ticked and ticked and ticked then he gave the stout man a single nod.   Whatever the man knew about his family, he'd have to find out later.

Sean knew nothing about horse racing but over the course of a few weeks that minor deficiency was corrected by two of the very best.   Wally Ennis and Charlie Markham were both graduating to the big money game; drugs.   Mostly marijuana and cocaine.   The three of them, Sean, Wally and Charlie spent days at the stables talking to the boys on the payroll. The trainers, jockeys, grooms, headers, farriers and stable boys. Suffolk Downs wasn't actually owned by the Spring Hollow Gang, but might as well have been. They traveled north to New Hampshire to Rockingham Park, west to Northampton. They talked to dozens of horse people in on the fix. Marcos the Mexican jockey described how he could imperceptibly straighten his legs as he rode down the last stretch so the horse would slow, thinking he was standing up at the wire. He showed Sean a battery powered shock box that he was tinkering with to strap under the blanket so he could jolt the horse as he came around the last turn towards the line. Hadn't tried it yet, but it might be a good one. Larry the trainer told him how a hose was fed down a horse's nostril and the stomach vacuumed clean, then a "milk shake" of water, baking soda, sugar and coca-cola poured back in just before the race. Jason DeWitt, the header, the guy who aligned the horses straight ahead in the starting gate said that if you set the head and front legs slightly towards the rail, the horse will come out of the gate crooked. The barrel-chested farrier could fit a shoe just ever so slightly off that it was sure to interfere with the thoroughbred's gait. The big payoff came when they had a horse that was sired by a champion but they lied on the papers so no one knew. They made him slow down, come in at the middle or back of the field in four or five races so when he got to the big money race; Blam! They got the right shoes, fired him up with a milk shake, set his head straight at the gate then juiced him with the shocker. He would run just like his daddy, ahead by a length. For the first four months, the winter months, Sean cut his teeth making book for the Florida and California tracks.

Steven's Grill sat on the corner of West Broadway and 6th Street. It had been serving burgers and beer for fifty years. The ceiling tiles and fluorescent lights were replaced ten years ago and sometime in the last decade a new ribbed metal edge had been put on the counter. Fat Mac, the owner and chief cook, had decided that the Formica counter top was fine for another ten years. The brown color had only worn all the way through to white at the corner where the beer taps were. The regulars sat there so they could talk with Fat Mac when he was drawing a Guinness or a Bass. It took a long time to draw a beer right so the head stayed small and conversations about people in the neighborhood would start, then stop while the beer was served, then take up where they left off when the next mug was put under the spigot. From the booth in the front corner, it was possible to look all the way down Broadway to Perkins Square. Almost everyone coming into the restaurant who didn't sit at the counter, chose that booth. On race day, an hour before the ponies streaked from the gates, Fat Mac would put a reserved sign on the table so Sean could sit there. He sat there so he could watch the front door of the tailor shop down the street. That's where Stitch made book on the horses. Suffolk Downs, Rockingham, Saratoga, all the New England tracks.

Sean set the fix for the races and collected the money from the bookies. He made sure there was enough money on hand for payout after a race, both to the bettors and the track people. Most of the money bet came back to the Spring Hollow Gang because they pretty much knew how every race was going to come out. He ran those profits from the bookmakers to Vannie Druggan. Once in a while, the payout on a long shot to guys who weren't supposed to be in on the fix was much bigger than it should have been. It was also Sean's job, and the main reason Druggan had hired him, to track those guys down, find out what they knew, how they got to know it and cause them and whatever poor stable boy sold out to never want to do that again. And get the money back. He watched the people going in and out of the tailor's shop, memorizing their faces and jotting down their license plate numbers so Sergeant

Danny Casey at the local precinct station could run the tags for him. Sean paid the Sergeant.

Gwyneth stretched out on her side of the booth, her school books on her stomach. She was eighteen, a senior at Notre Dame Academy. The same high school her mother had graduated from. The same high school her mother had gone to college from. Whenever she asked about college, she heard the same thing. It was as though her father's family had never sailed away from the potato famine. Work. Keep working. Scratch it out. Don't let nobody tell you you're no good. If you work, they won't think you're no good. You go off to college, we run out of money. Then we're poor. We're nothing. The rats'll come. People talk. You gotta go to high school 'cause they say you do. Finish that then work with your mama. Now get out here. I gotta go to work. "Gwyneth," her mother would say when asked about college, "don't put me between you and your father. Do what he says but keep your pretty eyes out for a good man, well off so you don't have to work every day of your life." Mary O'Neal knew that for Gwyneth to be able to go to college, she would have to leave her husband and take her daughter with her.

"There he is." Sean said. "There's that motherfucker. See the Caddy up the block. That's his car. Fake plates. Sarge says there's no plate with those numbers. This is the third time in two months this prick has done this. He's wiping us out and I can't get him. Nobody knows him. Who is this guy? Look at him, looks like a wop. But, shit, if he was one of Anguilo's guys he'd be busting up Stitch. He'd be breaking arms. But he isn't, he's just trying to bankrupt us. And doing a good job of it. I think he's got some other business going with Stich and that weasel is paying him out of the track money. Maybe Anguilo wised up, doesn't want a war, just wants to run us out."

Gwyneth was looking at the car, then at the tailor shop, then at her brother. "Sean", she said putting her hand on his arm, "You convince Dad I should go to college, and I'll get this guy to you. I'll bring him right to you. Wherever you want. I can do that. He'd be on to you, not me. I can do it. Please. Will you do it? Say yes, please. Just talk to Dad. I can do this."

"No," he said after a long silence, her hand still on his arm. "I can't let you get near these people. They're not nice. They're not good people. They're dangerous."

"Sean, I'm an actress. I can act. I know how to get people to say things. I know how to get them to do things. I know I can do this. I know I can. I can find out who this guy is!"

Sean thought. Looked at her, looked down the street. Looked back at his sister then stared down the street at the Cadillac. "OK, go do it, but don't let him touch you. Just get an idea who he is. Look at his rings maybe or in his car. Get him to say something. Listen to him. Is he a Greek? Is he Italian? What is he? Go! Be careful."

Fat Mac opened the back door. She stopped in the kitchen, glancing this way and that way. She grabbed a slice of onion from the counter. "Sean, take my books home!" she yelled as she bolted out the door across the side street and ran two blocks down an alleyway behind the houses. She stopped, pulled her skirt slightly sideways, pushed one sock down to her shoe, ripped the two top buttons off her shirt and smeared dirt on her shins, thigh, throat, cheek and collar. She disheveled her hair and squeezed onion juice onto her brow then crossed West Broadway, a block beyond the tailor shop, wiping the tears from her eyes and walking slowly with a limp, back past the blue Cadillac.

"Whadda happen to you? You OK? You donna look so good. Whada happen? Sweet Jesus, she donna look good," the tall Italian said to her as he came out of the tailor shop. His sidekick, an ugly man built like a refrigerator, just stared at her. The onion tears were gushing out of her eyes and she sobbed, pulling her shirt closed after she was sure they had ample opportunity to see her heaving breasts. "He raped me," she choked. "He raped me over there." She waved her hand towards a thicket of bushes on a vacant lot down the street. "He's going to come back. Please, stop him. Help me!"

The Italian, wearing a suit personally tailored and hand stitched for him in Palermo, opened the back door, put his hand on her shoulder and moved her towards the back seat. She straightened, braced, but his arm was firm. "We get you away from here." he said.

The square man got in next to her. After the door closed and the car swung from the curb, the square man picked a piece of onion skin off her forehead and smelled it. Gwyneth turned away, looking out the window. The square man reached over and yanked her school dress up to her waist. Gwyneth screamed. The tall Italian driver hollered, "Jesus Christ, Benito, whattaya doin' back there!" "Boss," the square man said, patting Gwyneth on her bare thigh, "She cry onion tears. Nobody rape her. She still got panties on. Nice and clean. Pink."

"Gwyneth, look at me. Look at me. My eyes. Look at my eyes. I'm your brother. Look at me, Gwyneth. You said the place they took you was near Angelo's restaurant. How near? Two blocks. You said two blocks. Is that right? On the right hand side? Yellow house. Big front yard. Steel gates. Right? Good. You said someone called the guy Benito. Is that right? Yeah, OK. Who called him that? The driver? OK. What did they do to you? I'm sorry. Gwyneth, you have to tell me. I'm sorry, but I have to know. What did they do to you?"

The front door to Steven's Grill was locked. Fat Mac had put up the "Closed" sign. He was in the kitchen. He had a meat cleaver and tapped it on the chopping block. He'd turned the water on in the deep sink so he could see Sean and Gwyneth, but couldn't hear their words.

"Who, which one of these scumbags made you do that to them. Who? The Benito guy? That fuck made you do that? That fuck is going to die. How'd they know? Oh my God, your school ID in your pocket? Oh, Jesus, Gwyneth, I never should have let you get anywhere near this. I am so sorry. Go home. Take a shower. Go to bed. Don't talk to Mom or Dad. Go."

"Seanny, m'boy, looks like they're looking for a fight."

"Fat Mac, they may think they want one but they don't want what they're going to get."

At Angelo's, deep in the North End at ten past ten on a Saturday night, Sean O'Neil walked down the alley behind the restaurant, around the dumpster, picked a brick out of a pile of construction debris and smashed the passenger side window of the big blue Cadillac. He reached in the hole, dropped an opened briefcase on the seat, a briefcase empty except for the sprinklings of a fine dust of heroin. He put the brick back beside the dumpster about ten feet away, took his gloves off and put them in his pocket. He checked his watch, walked out of the alley around front and into a very crowed, noisy and smoky Angelo's. The Italian mob owned the place. Every Saturday from nine to midnight, Don Anguilo would meet in the private room upstairs with his capos; "Dapper Dan," the drug man, little Silvetti "The Ant" Borsolino, the prostitution man, Johnny "Snubnose" Gibraldi, the ponies, rackets and extortion guy. People who heard Johnny's name but had never seen him thought the moniker referred to the type of gun he carried. Not so. "Snubnose" used to have all the fine aquiline features predominant among Sicilian males until his cousin, a wealthy viticulturist from the Piedmont region of northern Italy had come upon Johnny and the vintner's wife in the steel-wheeled wagon used to transport casks to market. The wine man's wife remained his wife but ever since that warm foggy morning, she wore her hair in a thick, bouncy American style page boy because she was missing the top half of her left ear. The men at Angelos, each with their own muscle man, would drink fine wines, most usually a Barbaresco from Cuneo in the same northwestern Piedmont region, an elegant powerful wine with bouquets of wild mushroom, truffle and a hint of rose. "Snubnose" eschewed these wines and usually, rubbing the callous nub where the end of his nose used to be, would order a bottle of Nero d'Avola, a stronger, more bitter variety from his native Sicily. They drank, they ate, they talked shop.

Sean, wearing a blue Red Sox hat with his hair tucked up inside, blue Red Sox reversible jacket and a fake black moustache walked into the crowded bar area and picked his way to the counter to the first guy that looked like a regular, tapped him on the shoulder and said, "I gotta pay my taxi guy but would you tell the bartender or a waiter that it looks like there's someone busting into a blue Caddy out back." Sean went out, walked out around the corner, into the "Reserved" parking area. He put on the gloves, picked a brick out of the pile and crouched in the darkness behind the dumpster. Two minutes later Benito, the square man, stopped on the street, pulled out his gun, looked into the parking lot, up the street, down the street and walked to his car. "Whadda Fucka!" As he stuck his head into the broken window, Sean brought the brick down on the base of his skull, kicked his feet out from under him and, as the square man slumped Sean jammed his knee between his legs, reached one forearm around his throat grabbing his jaw, the other locked under his shoulder. With a hard push and a yank, he snapped his neck. The square man wasn't square anymore. He was lumpy. Lying on the dirt like a sack of rocks. Sean threw the brick back in the pile, pocketed his gloves, walked out on the street to the phone booth on the corner and dialed the North End Precinct. Sergeant Ford answered. "Oh my God" Sean croaked, "there's a dead man in the parking lot behind Angelo's." He hung up, walked in the front door of the restaurant through the loud throng of drinkers and into the men's room. In a stall, he pulled off the moustache, reversed the Red Sox coat to the white side, put the hat in the empty inside pocket and walked back out to the bar. There were two bartenders. When he got the attention of one of them, he said, "Can I get another beer?" "What were you drinking?" The bartender asked. "Budweiser." Sean said. "Got it." said the bartender.

A few minutes later the two other muscle men came down the stairs through the restaurant section and out the front door. Sean was finishing his beer when they both came running back in bumping tables, spilling wine as they dashed by the diners. Sirens could be heard a few blocks away as the Don and his capos were rushing to the exit. Sean ordered another Bud with a Jack Daniels chaser and started chatting up Carl Yastrzemski and Tony Conigliaro with the guy sitting next to him. How the Sox might have a chance this year.

When the Boston Police detectives came to dig down to the bottom of it, no one said anything helpful. Neither of the bartenders, Benny Anguilo, the Don's nephew, nor Jason saw anything out of the ordinary. Nobody heard anything from out back because the place was really loud, jumping. Rico Pezzatti said some guy had told him somebody was breaking into a car in the parking lot and then the guy left. He had told Benny. Benny confirmed this and said he called upstairs. Rico said the guy had a moustache and a blue Red Sox hat and blue Sox jacket. The guy left to pay a taxi and he didn't see him again. Sean, when asked, said he didn't see or hear anything. None of the North End cops recognized him. The cops didn't ask anybody who they were. They knew better than that. It could be bad for business. After some brief questions with people in the bar and people on the street with no answers from any of them, the detectives left and didn't come back. The dead guy was definitely a mob hit man. The murderer was probably either a drug dealer or one of Vannie Druggan's guys. Edmund L. McNamara, Boston Police Commissioner, wanted nothing to do with this. It could easily end up as a murder investigation of some relative of his, a judge, a City Council member or the Mayor. So far, he had successfully steered clear of the war between the Spring Hollow Gang of Southie and the New England Mafia run by the Italians out of the North End and Providence, Rhode Island. On the hasty assumption that the murderer and murderee were in fact gangsters and therefore fell under federal jurisdiction, the Commissioner turned the whole mess over to the FBI, including a copy of one steno pad page of illegible notes. A few days later the front page of the Boston Globe ran a picture of a smiling Commissioner McNamara shaking hands with a stern faced Mr. Timothy Hancock, head of the organized crime unit of the New England office of the FBI under the headline, "Feds Take Lead In Gangland Slaying."

APPLE PIE

Special Agent Hancock was 39 years old. He looked ten years younger. Sandy brown hair neatly combed, parted straight on the right, short side burns. Not a buzz cut or a flat top like most of the Agents. Blue eyes in clear white eyeballs. No wrinkles, not even a crow's foot. He had been with the Bureau for ten years, the first four years in a six man field office in Lincoln, Nebraska. Now, he was in charge of the organized crime branch run out of the Boston office. Drugs, extortion, prostitution, race-fixing and all the related money and murder.

Hancock's black Ford Crown Victoria, unmarked except for federal plates, a long whip antenna and a set of removable red and blue flashing lights in the glove compartment, pulled into the garage under the Federal Building. It was 10 AM Wednesday morning.

"What do you have on the North End murder?" Hancock had a staff of twelve working with him in the organized crime unit. The unit hadn't existed at all until Bobby Kennedy became the Attorney General and dedicated himself to an all-out war on the Mafia and the Teamsters. Hundreds of full time agents nation-wide working to bust open the underworld.

"What happened?" Hancock asked.

"Anguilo and his top three guys are at Angelo's on Saturday night, just like every Saturday night. A man wearing a blue Red Sox jacket and hat, with a moustache, that's all we know, comes in and tells a patron at the bar that somebody's breaking into a blue Cadillac in the back parking lot. The guy says he's got to pay a taxi and leaves. Apparently he never came back.

"The bartender, Anguilo's nephew, calls upstairs and tells his uncle about the car. The blue Caddy is Daniello Capriati's car. It seems he sends his bodyguard, one Benito Romo down to check it out. Benito doesn't come back. Around about this time, ten sixteen to be exact, somebody calls the North End Station and says there's a dead man in the parking lot and hangs up.

"The two other bodyguards go down to find out what's happening. Presumably, they find their buddy Benito with his head caved in and his neck broken, his car window busted and an empty briefcase open on the seat. They come running back in. That's what the people eating in the restaurant said, 'running in'. The North End detail arrives just as Don Anguilo and his boys are coming out of the restaurant. They don't say anything about anything. Just, here's Robert Barone's phone number. He's their consigliore. The squad car guys call Homicide and two Detectives show up and take over. Nobody knows anything. The dust in the briefcase comes up heroin. There are no fingerprints on anything. Preliminaries are the victim never fired his gun. It was still in the holster. Ballistics is running it to see if there's a match with any other recent hits."

"There won't be," Hancock said, "they don't use the

same gun twice. They dump them after a hit. Who is this guy?"

"The dead guy is, or was, Benito Romo. He's the sidekick or bodyguard to Daniello Capriati, 'Dapper Dan' who runs the drug side of the Anguilo business from Rhode Island south to New York. Not much on his record. Brought in a few times for questioning but he doesn't seem to ever have been charged with anything. Honest to God boss, the arm muscles on that Benito guy were as big as my leg. He spent six years in Sing Sing for strangling a bookie in New York City. The bookie didn't die, but Romo was convicted of attempted murder. The DA actually got the jury to consider this guy's arms 'deadly weapons'. Whoever took him down and snapped his neck had to have been strong and fast and really know what they were doing. That was not an ordinary neck. That's why I'm not so sure it was just a drug transaction gone bad."

"What do you mean?"

"First, if somebody was breaking into the car, what were they trying to steal? These guys don't leave briefcases full of heroin in their front seats. Nobody saw this Benito guy bring a suitcase down the stairs. If the drug guy brought the dope, why'd he leave the briefcase? Second, drug dealers shoot people or they stab them. Has anyone here ever heard of a drug dealer killing anybody by snapping their neck? This looks to me like it was done by somebody who wanted the police to think it was a drug deal but that somebody actually had it out for this particular Benito guy."

"Like who?" asked Hancock.

"I don't know. Maybe the guy with the moustache in the blue hat. Maybe Romo's wife. Maybe a girlfriend. Maybe one of Druggan's boys. It sure wouldn't have been anyone who was upstairs. That wouldn't make any sense."

"Why would someone call the North End Boston precinct and not the main number?" Hancock asked rhetorically. "Because they know the phone number."

"How long has Vannie Druggan been back from Alcatraz?" Hancock asked.

"Since November. Six months."

"What's his share of the market look like now?"

"Pretty poor but getting better all the time. Nothing like it was when he left. Anguilo's got a grip on dope, girls, horses, protection; all of it."

"Go see Romo's wife. See if she'll talk to you. Look around for a girlfriend. I'll take care of the Druggan angle. Thank you all, let's get to work."

From the driveway at 348 Arlington Street in Watertown to the FBI offices at the Federal Building in downtown Boston was ten minutes down Memorial Drive along the Charles River, over the Longfellow Bridge, into the city on Cambridge Street. The Hancock's home was a modest but well-kept two story yellow clapboard house with a separate garage they had enlarged to accommodate his government issue Crown Vic as well as his personal car, a 1964 Ford Fairlane with red leather seats. The yard was large, bounded on all sides by a white picket fence. Rose bushes grew along the fence. A clump of lilacs and two apple trees, Macintosh, grew beyond the back patio. Each weekend from May to October, Timothy Hancock mowed the grass, collected the cut clippings into a sheet. He brought them in the trunk of the Fairlane to the Mt. Auburn Cemetery where Mr. Gribbs the caretaker would add them to his large pile. They talked about the neighborhood, talked local politics, talked baseball. The city collected all the clippings on Tuesdays, taking them to a landfill where they dumped them with all the other trash. When he got home he vacuumed the trunk of his car. Every other weekend he washed it in the driveway with the hose, soap, rags and a chamois cloth. Twice a year on Memorial Day and Labor Day he waxed the car and polished the leather seats.

Tuesday was Andy Griffith night on TV. After dinner, after the dishes were done and the kitchen cleaned, his wife Susan and his ten year old daughter Betsy sat in the living room sipping iced tea, watching the show as they did every week. Susan's iced tea only looked like iced tea. It wasn't. It was vodka, tonic water, ice and a splash of coca-cola to make it look like her daughter's tea. Before Betsy came home from school, she didn't bother with the Coca-Cola. Tim Hancock sat in his recliner, his wife and daughter on opposite ends of the sofa. Sheriff Andy Taylor had matured over the six or seven years he had brought Mayberry, North Carolina into living rooms just like this across the nation. When Tim Hancock and Susan first got married the Sheriff was a simple man, a rustic backwoods character with a strong hillbilly twang. Today, he was more thoughtful, patient, wordly-wise. Almost, but not quite, cultured. Almost Lincolnesque but clean shaven, usually smiling. All the people in town loved him. They trusted him. Probably all the people in the country had the same feeling. Deputy Barney Fife's bumblings brought laughter but no one was worried that his absurd shenanigans would cause things to go awry in Mayberry. There wasn't any crime there. There weren't any criminals. Just folks whose concern for their neighbor's wellbeing sometimes slipped a bit or their amorous emotions temporarily overtook their better judgment. Temporarily because the Sheriff, before the nine o'clock news, would smooth it out, right the ship. As an officer of the law, he embodied all of the traits Americans most revered. Honesty, toughness, compassion, simplicity and an abiding appreciation of a civil community. Susan, though she never told him, thought her husband was very much like Sheriff Taylor.

During the General Foods commercial break, Tim Hancock kissed his daughter good night and Susan tucked her into bed and read a chapter of *Johnnie Tremain* or *The Red Badge of Courage.* Susan volunteered as a children's librarian at an elementary school in Somerville. She told her husband, time and time again, almost every day, there was nothing more important than reading stories to your children, no matter what condition you were in. Hancock marveled that his wife, as drunk as she was each night, could read at all.

"Good Evening, this is Walter Cronkite with the CBS Evening News. Newark, New Jersey rioting continues into the third day. Snipers have been firing at police officers and National Guardsmen from windows and rooftops throughout the afternoon and early evening. The Governor's office has confirmed 18 dead and 287 people wounded. An actual count can't be made until the streets are safe for emergency personnel to enter. In Plainfield, New Jersey, eighteen miles away, what began as a minor disturbance involving a handful of angry youths has escalated into all out warfare between the residents of this town and the State and Federal authorities attempting to quell the violence. Local CBS Affiliate reports that 50 high powered M-1 military rifles with thousands of rounds of ammunition have been stolen from an arms manufacturer in nearby Middlesex and handed out to rioters; men and boys, they report, throughout the downtown area. 300 heavily armed New Jersey State Police and National Guardsmen have been taking up fortified positions throughout this city of 48,000 residents. Two boys have been taken into custody for the murder of Plainfield Police Office John Gleason. Youths allegedly beat Officer Gleason to the ground, stomped on him and executed him with his own service revolver. The FBI has been called in to assist in negotiations aimed at retrieving the stolen military style weapons. Sources in the Governor's Office have told CBS that the Attorney General has been asked to investigate allegations that the weapons were stolen by members of the Black Panther Party."

Timothy Hancock stared at the screen. Seeing the screen, hearing the sounds, but not registering anything more in his mind. Dumbstruck. Susan came back downstairs as Walter Cronkite reported that the 15th Artillery Regiment, the Indianheads, had for the first time in the war, fired heavy artillery, 8" Howitzers and 175 mm guns, in support of the 1st Air Cavalry along the Bong Son River in the Central Highlands of South Viet Nam. The massive guns had a range of nearly 20 miles and could reach well into Cambodia. The grainy film clip showed five or six soldiers, some bare chested with fatigue pants, boots and helmets loading an artillery shell the size of a man's thigh into the breech of the cannon.

"Well," she said, "itch good we finally got shome decent weapons for those shoung boys over there."

Her husband, still dumb and mute, looked at her as Cronkike said, "And that's the way it is on July 16th, 1967."

"Timmy, are you OK? Wha's the matter. Why are you looking at me like that?."

"This isn't 'social unrest', Susan, this is a war," he said staring back at the screen. A new episode of Bonanza had begun and Hoss and Little Joe were saddling up to track down horse thieves. Adam and Papa Cartwright smiled, leaning on the sturdy straight white fence, each with a cowboy boot up on the bottom rail, telling them to get back by suppertime. Their cousin Emmeline was due in on the 3 PM train. "These aren't random acts of violence. They are organized. They all have weapons. Big weapons. They don't just happen to be on some rooftop or end up in some apartment. They all know what each other is doing. They are fighting a guerrilla war, just like the Viet Cong but right here in our own country. This is a revolution. Good God is this ugly. Children executing police."

She hadn't seen that part of the news and had no idea what he was talking about. Even if she had seen it, she would still have had no idea what he was talking about. Not many people would. "Ish not like you to talk like that." On the screen, Hoss and Little Joe had the horse thieves tied up on top of the two spare horses they had brought along for this very certain purpose. The three o'clock train could be seen far off across the mesa, barreling along, belching smoke, right on time. "You're looking at me funny tonight. You're talking funny. Whatever it is, it'll be juss fine, juss fine. Sings get better. That's what you always say, Timmy. 'Just do what's right and be honest about it and everything will be fine' Isn't that whashu always say?" He looked at his wife, her flushed face, unfocused eyes, biting his lower lip nodding slowly. "Yeah, that's what I always say but Susan, honey, sometimes I don't know what right is." She lurched up. "I gotta go to bed now, Timmy. I'm really tired."

At five minutes past eight the next morning, FBI Headquarters called and said that Agent Hancock was to catch a commuter flight to Washington and be in David Meritt's office by noon. No message. No reason. Be there.

"Perhaps, just perhaps, Agent Hancock, you didn't hear what I said. What I said was that your office was going to participate in this program. That you were going to do everything necessary to achieve success in this endeavor. Is that clear enough?" Mr. David Meritt, assistant director of the FBI for counter-intelligence, leaned forward and glared at Timothy Hancock.

"Yes sir. I did hear you the first time."

"Hancock, let's get this straight. I don't give a damn about your 'lack of resources' or any other excuse you might have to weasel out of this. Maybe you don't like the sound of this program. You are an employee of the FBI and you do what I say or find some other job. Didn't you used to be a beat cop in some jerkwater town in Nebraska? Maybe they'll take you back. Maybe even a little promotion. Now are you understanding me?"

"Yes sir. I understand. Cooperate with the Program." Hancock got up to leave, thinking that was all there was. An order, a threat.

"Sit down. This will take a while. I'm going to tell why we have to do this and then, maybe then, it'll become a little easier for you to get on board."

Assistant Director Meritt had gone through this routine twice before over the last few days with two other Special Agents from two other regional offices. They both had reacted the same way Hancock was reacting. He knew they would. Nobody had enough money or people to do all the other things they were supposed to be doing and there were elements to this operation which might expose them to a nasty verdict being handed down from some jury somewhere, sometime. But that really was, as he had said, "tough shit." J. Edgar Hoover had personally ordered him to put this together. Never once had he failed to completely, thoroughly and, when needed, mercilessly execute the requests made to him by his boss.

David Meritt was a short round man who looked a great deal like his boss, J. Edgar, except that his head was almost perfectly round, not lopsided like Hoover's. They were about the same height, just over five-two but Meritt outweighed him by nearly a hundred pounds. He was completely bald. He had already started balding when he first joined Hoover at the Bureau in 1929. He wore wire rimmed glass. The temples, the thin steel arms dug deep into the flesh from his eyes to his ears. When he took them off, which was very rare and only to clean them, he looked as though he'd recently been garroted around the middle of his head. Meritt lived alone on the first floor of a two floor flat in a residential neighborhood two miles outside the center city. There were only two rooms in his flat. The bedroom was almost entirely taken up by a king sized, canopied four posted brass bed heaped high with embroidered pillows. The other room was huge. It had a bath, shower, sink, toilet, under-the-counter refrigerator, a single hot plate on a counter, a sofa, coffee table and open armoire when he kept his clothes. He lived in that room. There were no pots, pans, spatulas or any other accoutrements of a normal kitchen. He had never cooked food there. He ate every meal in restaurants, usually having dinner with his boss. His driver, a tidy and meticulous seventy year old Estonian immigrant, lived in the flat above.

How these two little men, Mr. Hoover and Mr. Meritt, stayed in absolute charge of the Bureau for so many decades confused and irritated many of the Agents. Neither of them could have apprehended a bag lady. There had always been height, weight and fitness requirements for every agent. 30 sit ups in a minute, 40 push ups (untimed), 200 yard sprint in 24 seconds, a one mile run in under five minutes, superlative visual acuity, average hearing loss of no more than 25 decibels. They had to look normal. No physical defects such as birthmarks, carbunckles, hair-lips or lop-sided heads that might be noticed then re-noticed by a bad guy. They had to also be normal. As J. Edgar himself put it, "No pinheads or people who look stupid, like a truck driver." In 1919, Hoover was hired as Special Assistant to the U.S. Attorney General A. Mitchell Palmer at the age of twenty-four for the express purpose rooting out and deporting anarchists, socialists and communists in the First Red Scare shortly after the Russian Revolution. He was appointed Director of the Bureau of Investigations by Calvin Coolidge at the age of twenty-nine when Henry Ford was still making the Model 'T'. He never retired and no President ever replaced him or probably ever even thought seriously about doing so. He died as the Director of the FBI, fifty-three years after his first appointment.

Meritt's office at 950 Pennsylvania Avenue in the Department of Justice building was on the third floor in the far western corner across the hall from the Director's suite. He walked to the high, small window behind his desk, put his hands on his corpulent hips, staring up and out.

"You know about Huey Newton, Eldridge Cleaver, or whatever his real name is and guys like Elroy Jenkins. You know about those guys and the Black Panthers?" Meritt wasn't waiting for Hancock to reply. Hancock did know about them and about the Bureau's plans to eradicate them from the American society. He knew about the CIA helping the Bureau with surveillance and tactical planning in direct contravention of the constitutional mandate to gather only foreign intelligence, not domestic intelligence. He also knew of Hoover's all-out assault on Martin Luther King. Hancock was sure that some of his fellow agents were going to be held accountable in a courtroom, somewhere, sometime. He knew that just because you are told to murder someone it is not OK to do it. But this he also knew. Whatever Meritt was telling him to do came from Hoover. It wasn't just that he would have to go back to Lincoln, Nebraska. It was that after he got there, the Chief of Police would find a photograph of him on his desk. A photograph of him doing something like having sex with a teenaged boy. That was Hoover's way and they all knew it. Great. Go with the Program.

"And you remember, Hancock, how the Director said publicly that this Black Panther thing was the greatest threat to America's internal security. You remember that? Well, let me tell you, it isn't. And let me tell you why it isn't. What I'm telling you to do is the only way to stop the complete destruction of our government, the whole social order of this great country." Meritt had turned from his window and was looking at Hancock over the four foot high back his $3,000 leather chair. The only parts of him that showed were his neck and head.

"This thing with all these Negroes; that's bad and it's dangerous. People get killed. Cops get killed and the good people of the country get really nervous and don't know whether it's safe anywhere. They don't understand why their government can't stop this bullshit. Things fall apart. Why can't we just arrest all these people, put them in jail or fry'em in the electric chair so our country can get back to how it was. And the hippies; they're not really a problem, they just look like one. Arrest them for having dope, which they all do, or arrest them for being naked in public or something. Don't kill'em. They may be mutants or whackos, but they're white. Just get them out of our sight. That's what people think. Probably in the long run it doesn't matter. Eventually they'll all look in the mirror and realize they look like morons and the whole thing will go away. But there's something out there that's a whole lot more sinister. What would be the biggest nightmare you could imagine? What would it be, Hancock?"

"Um, no idea, sir"

"We can eventually make this black thing and this hippie thing go away because of what they look like. Nobody likes Negroes, nobody likes hippies. They're different than everybody else. They look different, they act different, they talk different, shit, they even smell different. Hancock, the public opinion will always be against them. All we have to do is bust them up and we're heroes. That's all a temporary problem. But what, Hancock is a permanent problem?"

"Ah, still no idea, sir."

"The permanent problem, the thing that rips this country to shreds is when the captain of the college football team or the head cheerleader blows up a police station. When a white boy or white girl, college educated, intellectual clean cut kid who looks like everybody's son or daughter throws a bomb into a crowded courtroom. When thousands of everybody's children who look just like the sons of Mr. and Mrs. John Q. Public and all come from nice suburban neighborhoods start blasting away at police officers. Because then, Hancock, what do you do? You can't shoot them because when they're dead and just lying there in a casket they look like the little child mom and dad sent off to college and mom and dad are wondering what's wrong with the police. You can't try them and expect to get a decent sentence because on the stand they look just like every juror's kid. They got money for good lawyers and when they're acquitted, then what? You know how hard it is to make somebody who looks just like you," Meritt said coming around his chair and pointing at Timothy Hancock, "somebody who looks like you but is only nineteen years old, how hard it is to make them look like a vicious criminal? Impossible. The people; good people, white people, good citizens, mothers and fathers turn on their government when you kill their children. That's when the country is finished. Our Internal Security guys call it the 'Euro-American Youth Revolution'. It's not just us, it's international. Bring down governments around the world."

Agent Hancock was having trouble concentrating. He wondered what size the guy's pants were. Probably 48/24. And he noticed something he hadn't seen before. Mr. Meritt's belt buckle was his FBI badge. He'd had the goddamned thing made into a buckle like a motorcycle guy or a truck driver or a rodeo rider's buckle. And then he wondered what this fat little man would look like sitting on top of a giant bull whose balls had been cinched tight with a leather strap. He couldn't hold down a slight smile.

"So, Special Agent, I see you're smiling. That's good. I'm glad you get the importance of this. He paused. He waddled back around his chair again pretending to look out the window as if in thought. He was so short and the window so high all he could see was sky.

"I'm going to tell you what I know. I told Edgar I wouldn't divulge anything but out of fairness to you, to get you comfortable with doing your part, I'm going to tell you. Your region, the Northeast is especially important to this effort. And Boston in particular. Lot of college kids. And you also got the Anguilo gang and those Irish thugs all wound up in extortion and drugs. You'll see why when you know what we know and what we need to do. Directive number one. You are not to divulge this conversation to anyone. No one. Not your co-workers, none of them, and not your boss." Hancock's boss was Mr. John Grissom, New England Regional Director. "This is directly between you and me. The only other person aware of this is Bill Rayborn over at the Agency. It will stay that way. You report to me. Is that clear?" Admiral William F. Rayborn, Jr. was the Director of the CIA. The program, code named COINTELPRO, Counter Intelligence Program included specific directives to 'neutralize' American citizens. So far, only black ones. "Yes sir." Hancock said.

"OK, here's what it is. Somewhere, we think on a college campus, we don't know which one, but somewhere, maybe even in a student's house, we believe there exists a list of names of people who are organizing an army of clean-cut white kids to join forces with the Black Panthers to overthrow of our government. That's right, Hancock, they intend to overthrow our government. We believe it is an offshoot of the Students for a Democratic Society. SDS. You know of them?"

"Yes sir, I do."

"We have reason to believe that this group is not a part of SDS but perhaps affiliated with it in some way. A break-off. We've heard that folksinger Bob Dylan may have something to do with it so we're watching him real close. We know that this effort is being masterminded from within our prison system; from the Black Panthers we have put in jail. We believe, I believe, that those Black Panthers realize they can't win alone because no one cares if we shoot them. They need white kids on the front line. Then they can win. And make no mistake about this. They are right! We think a list of student organizers was smuggled out of a prison. We don't know which prison or by whom but our informant, who was in San Quentin out in California, told us that much in a first short interview. He gave us that information in exchange for getting a life sentence reduced to 20 years, out on good behavior in 12. Unfortunately for both him and us, an eight inch knife made out of a piece of bed frame was stuffed in his heart about an hour after he talked to us. Oh yeah, the other thing he said before his main valve got sliced open was their message in one sentence. Here it is. Quote, 'We are the incubation of your mother's nightmare'. End quote. How's that for apple pie, Hancock?

This we know. It's real and there is a list of people. This is sure; they are planning on blowing up this country." He put his stumpy forearms on his desk and leaned forward. "There is a list and we want it or a copy of it or an iteration of it or the names of these people as soon as possible."

"Here's the nut of it. We need people on some college campuses. Not a lot, just some. They have to be real kids. Long hair and beards are OK. Maybe some young guys in the gangs. Not agents posing as children. These kids are way too smart for that. We need real students being friends with certain other real students and finding out what they know. If they can't get their confidence, then they search through their rooms, through their papers until we get that list. We want to stop this before it starts. As far as resources, well you know how to do it. Look around and find some smart young kids that have done something really stupid that might get them a long sentence in a shitty government hotel. Maybe a big drug bust. Lord knows there's enough of those out there. Make a deal, Hancock. Make some deals. We'll talk about which colleges when you got some people, when you get some kids. You don't have 'limited resources.' There's a bunch of bright young resources out there just waiting for you to help them out. Kind of like; do this for me and you go free. Don't do it, or tell anyone you ever even talked to me, and your ass is in the slammer getting humped for the rest of your natural-born life. OK? You got it?" He stared at the young Special Agent. "Apple Pie, Hancock, that's what's on the menu. Call me in a week."

Hancock reached for the door knob. Meritt said, "Oh I forgot." He opened his desk drawer and pulled out a bottle of Smirnoff Vodka with a red ribbon wrapped around it. He held it out with both hands, tipped slightly like a bottle of fine wine. "A little present for your wife." His pig eyes smiled. Timothy Hancock left without saying good-bye.

THE LOBSTER TRAP

The summertime morning drive along the Charles River was peaceful, refreshing. The Harvard crew were often in their sculls rowing up river in perfect syncopation with the metronomic clacking of the coxwain's shell and rhythmic entreaties to the rowers through his megaphone. A few small sailboats would be out early for the morning breeze. This Monday morning, Hancock didn't see any of it.

"Brenda, I need to leave a message for David Meritt. I do not want to talk to him. Just a message. Would you see if you can get his secretary on the phone." The message he left for the Deputy Director asked him if he could get some cover for him from the United States Attorney General's Office. His people were going to be asking a lot of questions of law enforcement and state justice department people and he needed for them to say with some credibility who the request came from. Five minutes later Brenda came in and said that Meritt had responded. Quote, "No. Tell them it comes from the Director himself." Anyone calling Hoover had to go through Meritt first. Anyone except the President, Attorney General, Director of the CIA and a few of Hoover's favorite Senators. Now that McCarthy was gone there weren't many that he was close to. Just a couple that he would personally talk to, mostly Southerners; Strom Thurman. James O. Eastland. "The Southern institution of racial segregation is not discrimination, Mr. President, it is the law of God." James O. Eastland. Hoover liked him for his blunt talk.

When his staff had assembled for the morning briefing, he asked his secretary to brew a fresh pot of coffee. He began telling them what he wanted to happen. It was difficult not to mention Meritt or the instructions he had been given to keep the 'Program' confidential. Out the window of the conference room he could see the Mystic River Bridge and the Bunker Hill Monument. Hancock paced and talked. He told them he wanted status reports on all drug busts in which the alleged perpetrators had not yet been tried or had been found guilty and had appealed. Everybody who was out on bail or biding their time in a county jail. First time offenders only. No career criminals. He did not tell them that he was only interested in white people, nor did he tell them he was only interested in white people under the age of 24 or if they were 24 they had to look 20. He would sort through that himself. He told them he wanted the same information on all felonies which might have been committed against any government entities; local, state or federal. Any felony that carries a sentence of ten years or more. Most of these cases were being handled by state or local jurisdictions but that, he told them, doesn't matter. That's why you all have such good relationships with your friends in these other agencies. He told them he wanted the information on any case that comes from anywhere inside our region. Start with the people you know and trust the best but work your way up to the AG offices in Maine, New Hampshire, Vermont, Massachusetts, Rhode Island and Connecticut. Split it up by whoever has the best regional contacts. If you do this right, respectfully, professionally, nobody should ask why you want it. If they do and it's just curiosity, tell them we're trying to build a better base of information to be able to track first time offenders. If anyone seriously balks at giving you what you need, and you know they have it, tell them the request comes directly from J. Edgar Hoover and they should feel free to call him. Hancock said it deadpan, straight faced. They all laughed. "Get back here with everything you have next Monday. John, stay here for a moment. Thank you all. See you on this in a week."

"What do we have on Vannie Druggan? If we really wanted to bust him and send him back to prison, could we do it?"

"Probably so," Agent John Conrad answered. "On the horses and drugs we could probably muscle up an indictment. We might have to get one of his guys to sing, but if we got nasty, we could do that. Right now, the organization isn't real strong."

"John, you know these Mobs better than anyone. Figure out what I would have to say to Druggan to really, truly scare him. Don't answer now. Think about it. Come and see me before I go home today." That afternoon, after having heard what he needed to hear, Hancock told Agent Conrad that he wanted to meet with Druggan. Just the three of them in some place where no one would recognize any of them. Vermont maybe. Soon. Before Friday. Set it up. I need him working for us.

That evening on the news, Walter Cronkite informed Americans that the FBI had been unsuccessful at getting even a single person in Plainfield, New Jersey to give up their M-1 rifle and had begun a house to house search for the weapons. They didn't need search warrants, according to the FBI spokesman. All actions were authorized under the Governor's Declaration of Emergency. The NAACP had filed suit in federal court, alleging violation of the 'unreasonable search and seizure' provisions of the Fourth Amendment.

Twenty miles north of Boston, just past the last strip joint with the last moldy ten room motel tucked tight to it with the 'Rooms By The Hour' sign facing the main road, the neon finally gives way to the woods. Occasionally a small town could be noticed at an infrequent intersection but on the whole, the farm fields and timber stands were the same ones that have been there for a century or more. The people who lived there were farmers, fishermen, shoe and textile workers from the great brick factories built along the rivers where water could be dammed and spilled to spin the wheels that spin the machinery. Some factories were still like that. Most of the wheels had been converted to power generation. One condition was constant. The people were poor and had neither the means nor the inclination to travel into the maw of the indecent city. No one there was likely to have seen or ever even have heard of the Irish Mobster or Agent Hancock.

Jack's Clam Shack was perched on the edge of the Great Bay in Newington, New Hampshire, two miles inland from Portsmouth at the confluence of the Lamprey, Oyster, Squamscott and Bellamy Rivers. Rushing through the throat of the bay under the General Sullivan Bridge these waters join the Salmon Falls, Cocheco, and Piscataqua Rivers in a mighty rush to the sea. The tidal currents are nearly as strong as the Bay of Fundy. For years, Jack's had been just a shack at the end of a pier in a peaceful cove with clams, mussels and lobsters fresh caught from the cold Atlantic waters off the Maine and New Hampshire coast. The fishing boats, crews in yellow bib slickers and black gum rubber boots, unloaded at the dock and the catch was put in large open saltwater tanks. People picked the lobster they wanted by pointing at it. Buckets of boiling water sat under a tent on a large industrial gas stove. The seafood was boiled up and brought to an outdoor picnic table along with bibs, napkins, forks and bowls of melted butter. The white noise of the waves lapping the rock and eel grass shore masked all conversation. Mouths moved but nothing more than an undulating murmur could be heard. Hancock and Conrad had waited an hour for Druggan to show. When he got there, the three of them sat at the picnic table farthest from the pier, sipping bad coffee from Styrofoam cups.

"And just to what do I owe the great honor of the company of a couple of punk cops? You," Druggan said jerking him thumb at Conrad, "bark pretty loud for a dog that couldn't find his bone if it was up his ass."

Hancock said, "Did you like Alcatraz? I hear San Francisco is beautiful. Very, very beautiful. Peaceful. The Golden Gate Bridge and all those boats in the bay. Everything just as nice and pretty as you could ever imagine. Maybe you want to go back for another long visit or maybe you want to shut up and pay some pretty close attention to what I'm going to say." Druggan stared at them, his eyes shifting from one face to the other like a man in an alley sizing up two assailants. "You boys are closing The Rock. You ought to know that." he said.

"How about Sing Sing? Lot of Gambino boys up there probably like to have a nice long private talk with you. We didn't send you there the last time because we figured you'd be under a sheet in a cold steel drawer in about a week. But," Conrad said pointing both index fingers at him, thumbs up like a couple of pistols, "this is a new ballgame."

"OK," Druggan said, "I'm all ears. Talk."

"Vannie," Hancock said, "people don't like betting on horses then always losing money because you fixed the race. Your trainer blew a bad milk shake down the poor horse's nose and the blacksmith put his shoe on crooked. 3 to 1 odds comes in eighth. And you rake in the dough while Mr. John Q. Public goes home broke. That's enough for any good citizen on a federal grand jury to hand down a true bill indictment on you, don't you think?"

"That could be anybody you're talking about. Anquilos, Patriarcas. Anybody. So fuck off." Druggan got up to go.

Conrad pulled out a small notebook and flipped over a few pages. "Your Jockey Marcos didn't really have all his Mexican paperwork in order and, let's see, what do you call that guy? His real name is Thomas Coughlin but, but, but what? Oh, yeah, here it is, 'Stitch'. That's a good name for a tailor, especially one that hadn't filed a tax return for a couple of decades. That's a real stitch. People sing, Vannie. Maybe that's why they call it Sing Sing. Cause that's how they all got there. Somebody sang. People sing, Vannie. Now sit down and listen. You're going to learn something. Listen up."

Druggan sat. He didn't know how much they had. Probably not a lot. Probably not enough for an indictment, but he didn't know. So he sat.

"Oh, yeah, I forgot." Conrad said. "You're going to need a new horseshoe guy. What do you call them? A farrier. That's it, a farrier. You need a new one. It seems he took a swing at Agent Silver with a red hot poker. If Agent Silver hadn't spent all that time in Quantico learning about things like this, he might have gotten hurt. But he didn't. Mr. Farrier ended up getting all the tendons in his hammering hand burnt right through to crispy gristle. As my boss here is going to explain, you are going to need a new horseshoe guy. We're not here to drive you out of business. Honestly."

Hancock set up the deal. In exchange for staying out of prison, Vannie Druggan was to be an informant for the FBI. He could run all his businesses and the Feds would stay out of his way. Hancock wanted to know everything Druggan knew about the Italian mobs. Who, what, when, where and how. All of it. No cooperation, bad cooperation; back to prison. His whole organization busted up and all the pieces handed back to the boys from the North End. Simple as that.

"Why you doin' this? Why me? Why don't you talk to the wops? Get inside their shorts. Why should I do your dirty work for you?"

Hancock leaned forward, forearms on the picnic table, coffee cup in both hands. "Let's just say that if in time it turns out that you were helping us, then the world is a whole lot better, a whole lot easier for a lot of people."

Vannie Druggan's brother was the State Treasurer. "My brother. That's what this is. My goddamned brother shaking me down. You boys ought to be ashamed of yourselves. Tell Freddy to go shit in his hat. I'm leaving."

"I have never met your brother. I have never talked to him. Nobody in the Bureau has ever talked to him that I'm aware of. And if they had, I would know it. All I can tell you is, that's not it. Could have something to do with it, who knows? I don't think so, though."

Druggan leaned forward and held his cup just how Hancock was holding his. They stared at each other. Conrad got up and, after giving the waiter five bucks to get out of his way, took the whole pot back to the table and filled all the cups. The FBI man and the Mobster were still looking at each other. Then the Mobster smiled an Irish smile so wide it made his ruddy cheeks bulge out and his eyes crinkle with a hundred crow's feet. "Bobby Kennedy spent five years trying to cut the nuts off the Mob. Got somewhere with it too. Whatever it is the Gambino's are doing, you guys don't want them doing it. Or at least something of it that they're doing. The boys in Washington want help but they want to cover their asses. That's me. That's where I come in. That's why I'm drinking lousy coffee at a shithole clam shack in the middle of nowhere with a couple of goddamned federal agents. I hate clams, by the way. Little slippery snots make me sick; like eatin' giant boogers. OK, I get it now. Bobby Kennedy, Teddy Kennedy, John McCormack, Tip O'Neill. All powerful Irish Catholics from Boston. And my brother. They don't want to see me go down 'cause then everybody would think they were in it with me. Or on the take or stained somehow or helping them ship arms to the IRA or whatever people would think. So either I get out of the way and go back to the Big House so that 'justice is served all fair and blind' or they, those powerful guys succeed in getting me to be a rat, a mole, or as people like to call 'em; 'an informant' helping America bust up the Mafia and then everybody wins. Everybody except me and I got nowhere to go. How'd I do, Mr. Special Agent?"

Hancock said, "You ought to run for public office, Vannie. You have a real nose for it. Here's what we want. First, who killed Benito Romo and why. What's going on? Second, is the Mafia funneling any money to the Black Panthers? This is important. Maybe the answer is no. Might be we're crazy to even think of it. But maybe not. Anything you can find. You are to meet Agent Conrad here on the first and third Tuesday of each month at 1PM. That's right here again five days from now. Here, nowhere else. No phone calls. If a Tuesday comes and goes and you weren't here, we will come find you and we will have handcuffs and an arrest warrant. Clear?"

When Wally Ennis and Charlie Markham finished with Stitch he had completely filled out his 1040 IRS form, signed it and, after it had been rolled in a fresh fillet of raw pigeon guts they had sliced up in the park on the way over, he ate the entire thing. After they had pushed him down the cellar stairs, tied him in a chair and put gun to his temple, he told them everything. Choking and sobbing, he unloaded the whole story. Yeah, I skimmed the pony money, but I can pay it back. I can. I'll pay it back. Where'd it go? I used it to buy a little heroin on the side. I got a wife, I got rent, the tailor business ain't what it was. Yeah, I sold the dope to pay my bills. When Charlie and Wally had gotten everything they figured they were going to get, they pulled the trigger, yanked his teeth out with pliers so there wouldn't be any dental records down the road, rolled him in a rug and dumped the body deep in the mud of Dorchester Bay. Stich's confessions led them down the block to Fat Mac. After fifteen minutes the big man was bawling. Piss running down his pant leg all over his shoe. He was stripped to the waist. His enormous bare belly, broad back, arms and neck were smeared with hamburger fat. Each smack of the fire extinguisher hose made a sound like the crack of a towel snapped in a locker room shower. The barrel of a 9MM shoved so far down his throat he was choking to death on his own puke. He gave up what he had to give up to stay alive. He didn't want to give it up but he didn't want to die either. Not like this. Not in his own kitchen.

SLIPPERY, OILED BALOONS

Sean was in the Olde Dublin Pub when two men in gray coats and gray fedoras came in and told him that his sister was outside and she needed to talk to him. Ten minutes later Sean and Gwyneth were in Hancock's office alone with the Agent, the door closed behind them. Hancock explained what happens to people convicted of murder, whether or not the dead man had it coming. Maybe not life but surely a minimum of thirty years. Gangsters killing gangsters get the same as everyone else, sometimes more because the judges see them doing it again when they get out. Gangsters don't get rehabilitated. They just get bitter. And Gwyneth, it doesn't matter if he raped you. We can't arrest him. Your brother made sure of that. Now there is no perpetrator. All we have is that you aided and abetted a murder in the process of racketeering, bookmaking. A federal crime. Ten years minimum. Neither Sean nor his sister spoke. They looked at each other and both of them thought the same thought. 'Whatever this man wants me to do, I will do if it means my brother, my sister, will not go to a federal prison.' Hancock pressed the intercom and asked for an Agent to come in. Gwyneth was escorted out.

"When you walk out of this office you will either be remanded to the Suffolk County Jail to await trial for the murder of Benito Romo or you will be escorted to a safe house where you will be given a new identity and begin working undercover for the FBI. You will be assigned overseas, North Africa and the Middle East, where you will use your training in the Special Forces to find and neutralize enemies of our country. They are domestic enemies who have been given asylum in foreign countries to permit them to continue plotting the overthrow of our government. The danger is real. You would be doing a great service to your country. If you choose to do this, all records of your relationship to the Spring Hollow Gang including the death of Benito Romo will be destroyed and after your service, probably a year or so, you will be a free man with no record. You will also have the gratitude of many important people. Which will it be Sean, your country or life in prison?"

"I've already done my country. Some Major at Fort Bragg, I forget his name, said the same thing. 'You will have the gratitude of your entire country.' Didn't pan out that way, did it, Mr. FBI. People give gratitude when things work out their way. No matter how hard you try, if everything turns to shit, nobody's thankful about anything. I'm not looking for important people to think I'm OK. I'm looking for me to think I'm OK. What about my sister?"

"Same offer. She would likely be assigned to a college campus to find information about these people who want to destroy our country. You won't know where she is. You won't see her or talk to her until both of you are done doing what you agree to do. As a matter of fact, you won't see her again until then or, depending on what you decide, until she is done serving her prison sentence. This is how it works; if you both agree to do this, you're both free and clear when you're done. If either of you balks, you both go to prison. If you work with us, an Army Officer will tell your parents that you have been asked to re-enlist for a special secret assignment. You will be gone for a maybe a year. After you are out of the country, Gwyneth will receive a letter from a college admitting her as a full time student with a full scholarship. She will be instructed to 'turn radical' if you will, to drop out and have no further communication with you or her parents. Now what will it be, Mr. O'Neal?"

Sean remembered the swing in the backyard of the McKenna's house, two doors down the street. Mr. McKenna pushing him when he swung back down to the bottom of the arc. How he kept his little legs stretched out in front of him so his feet wouldn't touch the ground, so he wouldn't slow down and pulling hard on the chains as he swung up again to go as high as he possibly could. He remembered knowing that if he yanked the chains and let go at the top of the arc, lifting his bottom off the red wooden seat, he would catapult himself off into free space. The one time he did it, he broke his arm. Just like the Green Berets, Hancock was asking him to get to the top of the arc and let go.

Sean stood and extended his hand. "But you listen good to this, Mr. FBI. If anything bad happens to my Mother or my Dad or anything at all happens to Gwyneth...I don't care about myself, I don't care about prison and I really don't care about you."

"You will be given a birth certificate, social security number, driver's license and passport in the name of Joseph Ronald Cole, Joe Cole from Ashville, North Carolina. You will be given a written history of your life and your family's life. Read it. Memorize it. Destroy it. I will have one on file here. You are going to be sent to the border of Morocco and Algeria. When you get to Morocco, someone will meet you at the Hotel Al-Sakim in Tangier and brief you on what it is you need to do. Do you understand?" Sean nodded.

"But before you fly overseas, tomorrow actually, we need you to go to a house in the woods of New Hampshire to what will be a wild party. Two other undercover agents we've sent there to infiltrate these hippies have been fingered. They seem to be able to smell out government types. These people have been dropping leaflets about this party out of cars, for all we know out of airplanes, all over the southern New Hampshire area. We believe a lot of people we are interested in will be there. A number of different law enforcement agencies are going to help us out on this. The local authorities have been instructed to wait for our word before they even leave their stations. The only way we get access without everyone scattering is to have you there calling us when it's right to come in. Do you understand?" Sean nodded.

"Your name will be Joe Cole. Ingratiate yourself. There will be drugs there. There always are at those parties. Marijuana and LSD at least. God knows what else. Help yourself if you have to keep yourself from getting fingered. That's up to you. Good thing you haven't cut your hair for a couple of years. Fit right in. When there are just a few people left at the house, call us in so we can arrest them, get them out of there and search the place." He handed Jack a card with a phone number on it. "Throw that away too. Memorize it. Make sure a kid named Jack Duncan is there and is one of the people arrested. His mother is in Mexico. She's a poet. Goes down there for inspiration or some such thing. She owns the house so he should stay there until the party's over. He's got an older brother, Dwight Duncan who is doing three years in a Federal pen for draft refusal. We think this Dwight guy might have smuggled a vital national security document out of the prison. If he did, it's probably hidden somewhere in that house. We need to search the place when nobody is there. You'll leave for Morocco the next morning. You won't ever see those people again." Sean pointed at the photograph on

Hancock's desk. "Is that your wife and kid?" The stare that locked the two together didn't break until Hancock's left eye twitched.

Agent Connelly drove Sean out of Boston up the same highway he had driven with his boss to meet Vannie Druggin. He drove right by Jack's Clam Shack. He didn't say a word the entire trip. Neither did Sean. Connelly dropped him off on a lonely country road just outside the town of Madbury. "Walk a mile down this road. After you go over a bridge with a stream under it, go right down a dirt road. The house you're looking for is the second house. It's about a quarter mile down the road. You can't miss it. It's got a date painted on the chimney. Good luck. There's a phone in the living room. I'll wait for your call."

Sean got out and stood watching the black Ford Crown Vic drive off, fast and whisper quiet like a quick breeze. No wonder the hippies can always spot those guys, he thought. Only cops drive cars like that. Sean was wearing sandals, blue jeans, a black tee shirt, a necklace of shells, stones and beads and a tattered brown leather jacket. Sewn on the back was a smiling, bearded Zig-Zag man smoking a joint, wearing a stovepipe hat with a peace sign on it, pointing a stern finger. Over the emblem it said "Uncle Zig-Zag Wants You!" He wore a knife in a hand-tooled leather sheath on his belt under the jacket. Sean had toyed with the idea of asking Hancock to have someone get his Red Sox jacket for him but figured the woods hippies wouldn't even know who they were or, if they did, really wouldn't give a shit if they ever won or lost. It'd be out of place, like wearing a golfer's alligator shirt. He'd settled on asking for sandals, a string of beads and any old, ratty jacket from the Salvation Army. When Brenda, Hancock's secretary handed it to him she said, "My son would love this coat."

He hadn't walked far before a purple VW Beetle pulled over beside him, the front door swung open and a small man with small hands and wild hair said, "Going to Jack's?" Sean nodded. "Hop in." In the back seat was a man who looked just like the picture of Beethoven that Gwyneth had hung on the wall of her bedroom. Beside him was one of the most beautiful girls Sean had ever seen. Blond hair in braids hanging down with a fresh flower headband of daisies and dandelions, pink, pink cheeks and green eyes. She was wearing a white silk robe. Just a quick glimpse, but Sean was pretty sure she had nothing on underneath it. Beethoven was wearing a Red Sox Jacket, smoking a joint. He took a long toke and handed it up to Sean. "I'm Franz, ziss ess Susie Creamcheese und da little man driving ziss little car-car ess Voody the Voods Elf". "I'm Joe Cole. Pleased to meet you." Sean said, sucking deep on the joint.

When the VW pulled up to the house someone dressed in a Jester's outfit, stood up from his seat on a stone wall across the road from the house, walked up to them as they piled out of the VW. He stuck out his tongue and smiled. They smiled, nodded and did the same. Sean followed suit. The Jester placed a small stamp with the blue peace symbol on it on their tongues and Woody, Beethoven and Susie swallowed. Sean pretended to, turned around and unobtrusively let it dribble down his chin where he could wipe it off. "Peace Tabs," the Jester said, "Welcome to the party". Sean saw the man there all afternoon and as every car arrived and people got out, he walked up to each one, opened his mouth and stuck out his tongue.

Sean went by a huge beat-up rusted hunk of a car, much bigger than Eddie McKenna's Buick, probably an old Lincoln, he thought, and walked into the house. A dark-skinned girl in a stewardess outfit was on the phone. 'Good' he thought, 'the phone works.' Outside in the yard, there were twenty or thirty people standing around in two different groups. One group was in a grove of trees at the edge of a stream, stirring some kind of stone bucket with a branch, mumbling incantations. In the back yard there was a circle of twenty or thirty of people swaying and singing along to Bob Dylan's newest song: 'Lay, Lady, Lay'.

Some people were crying and others, like they had been born right there by Dylan's words, walked off into the soft moss and ferns in the woods. They're going to fuck right out there in the trees, Sean thought. Jayeesus! Two, dressed to the nines like Southern Aristocracy, were hugging each other in the center of the circle, rocking side to side, humming Ommm....Ommmmm...being married by a bearded fat man dressed up like a king. Most were in a costume of one sort or another. They looked like people out of a play. Velvet, lacey, puffy. Everyone was smiling smiles too big for their face that made their eyes crinkle and look old. Ten minutes there and Sean couldn't believe that the rest of the town, the rest of the world, didn't know that something was very awry in these back woods.

Sean wandered from clutch to clutch, hugging, laughing, talking small talk like what it's like to grow up in North Carolina on an Indian Reservation and how all the people in Washington were a bunch of assholes, murderers, ruining the world, always keeping an eye out for Susie Creamcheese. He noticed that the men who weren't in costume looked a lot like him. Boots, blue jeans, tee shirts and they all had knives on their belts and most had hammer holsters and a bandana either tied around their neck or hanging out of their back pocket. They were tanned; they looked strong and fit. Workers, he thought. These guys work hard outside. That's what they were talking about; knee braces, half laps, blind mortises and pegged dovetails. They're carpenters.

"Where's Jack?" he asked the group still stirring a big bucket at the edge of the stream. "He's down there with Susie," they said pointing to a vast thicket of poplar trees, "She's having a bad trip. Want some juice?" Sean looked in the bucket. It was a mass of dead bugs floating in water. "Not right now, maybe later. Thanks, man." He found Susie down by the pond. She had been swimming in her silk robe and he was right; she was naked underneath, lying across the lap of a young man. She was sobbing. Crying about a bald-headed monster in a black robe. He was stroking her forehead telling her it was going to be alright. It would end soon. Sean knew they didn't see him. So that's Jack Duncan. That's the guy they want. Duncan had long brown hair tied in a pony tail. He looked tall and strong, thin but sinewy. He looked at Jack holding that beautiful girl in his arms. Lucky man. Sean turned and made his way back through the woods to the house and yard. Ten or twelve were lined up single file about twenty feet away from what looked like a pig on a spit over an open fire. A huge tin of baked beans sat on the hot coals underneath. They were taking turns throwing a hatchet at the pig. When someone succeeded in sticking it in, they would walk up, lean over the flames, pull the hatchet out and dump wine from a big jug into the wound. Then they would slice off a hunk and put it in a tin bowl with beans using a fork and their own knife to eat it, their bandana for a napkin. The pig was half there.

Sean stood in the hatchet throwing line behind a tall and broad Scandanavian looking fellow. When it came Sean's turn, he threw the hatchet directly into the center of the pig, burying the head. The Scandanavian pulled it out and handed Sean the jug of wine. Sean took a long pull on the jug and poured some into the pig hole.

"Are you the Indian?" the Scandanavian asked.

"Cherokee." Sean said. "Are you a Swede?"

"Danish. I'm a Dane. I think we've known each other for many lives. I'm Troels."

"Joe Cole." Sean said and Troels hugged him.

They sat next to Beethoven and the Jester in the lawn where the "Oommmmming" circle had been, cross legged. Most people had left. The Jester's job was over. Beethoven was talking about language and how the limits of language were the limits of thought. That it was nothing more than a medley of language-games from which the meaning of words is derived from their public use in human activity. Philosophy, religion, ethics are nothing more that attempts to say the unsayable...the ineffable...the ineffable.

"The what?" Sean said. "My mother didn't like me using the effin' word either."

Troels leaned over and whispered, "He always talks about the philosophy of Ludwig Wittgenstein when he drops acid. Always. Do you have a favorite philosopher? Maybe we could veer him off this."

"No." Sean said. "I listen to the deer, the snake and the panther. And the bird. I listen to the chickapecker."

"Vas is dis?" I half never heard of dis 'chickapecker'.

"He's out there," Sean said, "deep in the jungle."

Troels took a knife from his sheath; a knife and sheath that were very similar to Sean's.   Troels unlaced his boot and held up the rawhide lace, then laid it across his knees. He held his left arm out, fist up and cut a thin line in his wrist just deep enough for the blood to trickle down the palm. Sean took his own knife out and cut the same line in his left wrist. They put their bleeding wrists one on top of the other and bound them together with the rawhide bootlace, swearing brotherhood. Forever. They sat, bound together as the sun dipped down below the peaks of the pines in the west. Jack Duncan and Susie came out of the woods and walked by them. The group that had been stirring the pot at the river came through the yard and walked by them. Beethoven and Puck got up and patted them on the head as they made their way to their cars on the dirt road. Puck shouted over his shoulder as he got into the little purple VW, "Going to Newmarket to see Ramblin' Jack Elliot." Troels unbound the rawhide. "I'm going in the house to check on Jack. And you, my friend?"

"See you inside in a minute," Sean said, "I left my coat at the river."

The living room was empty. The house was empty except for laughing, giggling, moaning and grunting coming from a room in the back by the kitchen. Clothes in a heap by the door. Scratchy music, classical music like a symphony, was playing on a record player in the corner. He had heard that music before. Music from Gwyneth's room. The same music. 'My God,' he thought, 'if she was cut loose from Southie, she would be one of these people. She would be here.' Sean went to the phone and dialed the number he had memorized.

"Connelly here"

"Joe Cole here. Now."

He took off his shirt and sandals, unbuckled his pants, stripped naked and went into a room full of slippery, greasy oiled balloons. Jack and the stewardess were in one corner, Troels and Susie, with another other girl, were somewhere in the middle. He slid into the balloons and closed the door behind him.

PART TWO

THE STUDENT

"The most perfect place to hide a revolution is inside the lines of a poem. The Chinese were masters at it. The French used it to perfection in anticipation of the guillotine blade slicing Marie Antoinette's head clean off from her body. Nobody truly understands a poem except the person who wrote it and the person or people it is written for. To them it is not abstract because they recognize the images as real. There is no blade sharper than a poet's word."

—Ray Meyerbach
Subversive Poet Provocateur

CATERPILLER PUNCH

For Jack Duncan, the day of the party could not have started more beautifully. It was a Saturday morning, the first weekend in August. The house and yard looked as though they had been kissed by the Goddess Persephone. Blueberries were thick in the bushes and grapes hung in great cone-like clusters. Acorns were in the oaks. Six friends had spent the night sleeping in the barn and on the floors. Early in the morning they all slid into Mother Mercury and set off to the University of New Hampshire to steal 5 gallon tin buckets of baked beans from the cafeteria store room, boxes and boxes of costumes from the school theater and pure grain alcohol from the Chemistry Lab in the new science building. To make room for this vast plunder, everyone but Bill Bear, the wheelman, had to hitchhike back.

By the mid-60's it was no good just to have a party. Any good gathering had to be an orgy. Bill Bear said that summer should be celebrated the same way the ancients would have celebrated this special season. The best orgies he said, are not planned; they emerge out of the sensuous goo of the communal psyche. To help everyone feel this need, he had printed up 500 leaflets that said only "SUMMER! SUMMER! ORGY! ORGY! AT THE DUNCAN HOUSE. AUGUST 5" and he threw them out the window as they drove through the towns of Lee, Durham, Newmarket, and Dover.

Troels, a tall, broad shouldered and fair Dane, the only one who had had a haircut since the 60's began, had arrived the night before with a whole pig tied to the roof of his girlfriend's Ford Falcon. He dug a roasting pit in the back yard, built a spit with metal pipes and coat hanger wire, gathered a great pile of stout dead wood and lit a fire. In the clean morning air, the smell of roast pork floated through the woods and down to the river. Jack had found a 20 gallon ceramic crock in the bushes behind the house. He washed it out and put it near the bank of the river in a little eddy. He filled it with fifteen gallons of fruit juice, then added the 3 gallons of research quality pure grain alcohol and stirred in handfuls of Owsley acid. The crock kept falling sideways so he put a large rock in it; a rock that was crawling with dozens of black and yellow caterpillars, all of whom died instantly and rose floating to the surface. Jack stood on the shore and bellowed through the woods, "Caterpillar Punch is Born."

Bill Bear had backed the car into the short stub of a dirt drive facing the hood to the south. She was a 1958 Mercury Monterey Phaeton. She was a behemoth. A monster of the road. One of the finest cars of one of the finest times in America. A twenty foot long four door with a wrap around front windshield, three speed push button Merc-O-Matic transmission and a 383 cubic inch 290 hp Y-block engine. Up front, the quad headlights were hooded. They made her look like a classy flat-faced whore. Along her sides she sculpted back in sensual curved crevices to the taillights; bulbous affairs with bright red thumb-like nipples sticking out the end. She had been blue with chrome trim when she came out of Detroit, zero on her odometer. Dwight Eisenhower was

President.   Everything was good.   The Industrial Machine hummed and ran and hummed and spun and churned out cars every day, all day and all night.   Lots of people had cars just like the Mercury.

Nine years later, after a murdered president, a murdered civil rights leader and 175,000 hard miles on her odometer, her paint had peeled down to the primer, her front end sagged; she wobbled like a drunk, like a lounge lizard, and belched noxious fumes.   Lyndon Johnson didn't want to be president anymore.   30,000 young soldiers had died, the ghettos were on fire. Children screamed in the streets. "Hey, Hey LBJ, how many kids did you kill today?"   El Presidente couldn't take it anymore. He looked like his dog; all droopy eared and teary eyed. He looked like Mother Mercury.

It was Jack's mother's car.   His mother did not drive this car. She never had.   She had sat in the driver's seat once. Anna Duncan was just under five feet tall and the man who gave it to her free of charge was a massive 300 pound industrial cleaning products salesman who had squished the seat down so far that Anna's eyes were roughly in line with the bottom of the steering wheel.   When she climbed out she said she had never felt so small and helpless.   The salesman, who lived a mile down the road, had been trying to woo Anna's affection with his gift.   For a while he stopped by to visit, humping himself onto her sofa, searching for something meaningful to say.   Anna would give him a cup of hot Cambric tea, Red Rose tea with milk and sugar and he would soon fall asleep, snoring like a thunder rumble.   Anna asked her son to get him to go away and not come back.   Jack waited until he was deep in his sofa snoring sleep, then sat down next to him wearing nothing but his underpants, leaned into his ham-hock shoulder and began softly singing, 'I Want To Hold Your Hand'.

Other people drove her places.   Handsome young men who she let live in her barn or camp in the woods, hiding out from the Establishment and its enforcement agencies. She had accepted the gift of the car because she had no money. Anna Duncan spent most of her days sitting in a high wing back chair in front of a fire in the brick fireplace, writing poetry. Poetry about love found, love lost, loneliness, desire. Poems about the ocean. About grey gulls flying into the fog; grey gulls flying out of sight. About losing love and things that slip away, like memories.

She was the elegant, charming mother lady of the destitute local intelligencia. Mostly college students, but all well read, anti-establishment and proud that they didn't prostitute themselves to the God of Capitalism in exchange for money thieved from the working poor. She had repeatedly asked that someone do something about the wobbling and screeching problems with the massive Mercury and Bill Bear had done that. He took her over to Dwayne's garage. Dwayne scooted underneath, scooted back out and said, "Frame's fucked. She's had the meat."

Four bare chested young men, all a few years out of high school, stretched out in the noon day sun. Luke, who'd just gotten a job driving an oil truck, and Jack, were on her roof. Troels the Dane and Bill, called Bill Bear because he was a big man with big curly hair, or sometimes called "wheelman" because whenever anyone had to go somewhere, to pick up a girlfriend, get sprung from the county lock-up or score some dope, Bill Bear was always there. Bill Bear was also the communal connection to the county bail bondsman. Every year the bondsman sent Bill Bear a calendar. It always had the same picture; a scrubbed, handsome young man, a real Todd Hunter, smiling and waving to someone as he walked a freed man out of the prison gates.

They were lying on her hood and roof with a case of Pabst Blue Ribbon. They loved this car. Everyone called her Mother Mercury and she was always referred to as "she" or "her", as in "Is she warm enough to lie on yet?" and, "You sure don't want to drive her when you're stoned." They had come to believe that being up off the ground on the warm metal of Mother Mercury imparted a magical ability to see the truth.

They talked about the Selective Service System. How there wasn't anything selective about it except that girls, morons and wackos didn't have to go. For everybody else, it was off to Fort Dix to get, as Bill Bear put it "mentally fucked all day every day by a monstrous muscle man whose name was "Sir!"

"How long were you in?" Luke asked.

"A month. Then they locked me up in the nut house," Bill Bear said.

"How come? What'd you do?"

"I wouldn't pick up my rifle," Bill Bear said.

"What do you mean, wouldn't pick it up?"

"Every time they shoved it into my arms, I dropped it on the ground. They figured I was crazy, not wanting to carry a rifle. So they locked me up for a long time. Then they let me out." He closed his eyes and drifted back to Fort Dix, the gray hood of Mother Mercury easing the memory to a mid-morning clearness.

"I said pick up your gun, soldier!"

The drill sergeant's face was an inch away from his. His eyes were a streaky yellow red with black dots in the center. His breath smelled of onions. His head was round and flat on top like a bucket and his neck muscles and veins bulged out, throbbing, pulsating.

"I can't, Sir."

"You can't, soldier? Yes you can. And you will! Now do it!"

Bill Bear looked past the man at the rows and rows of one story, white clapboard, tin roof shacks and heard nothing, saw nothing but the endless barracks in the blinding sun until a round-faced little man in a white coat with round spectacles asked him if he could hear him talking. The wooden edges of the narrow cot pinched his shoulders. It hurt. Yes, I can hear you talkin, he thought and closed his eyes so he could only hear the inside of his own mind. It went on like that for two months until the little man with the round face said to a nurse, "He's fine. Get him out of here."

"What was it like?" Jack asked from the roof of Mother Mercury.

"It wasn't like anything," Bill Bear said.

Somebody on the hood rolled a fat joint, lit it, sucked it and handed it backwards over their head to Jack on the roof. Bill Bear got everyone a cold beer.

"Woody didn't like it like much it either. I heard he just split," Troels said.

"Split? You mean he just left?" Jack asked. Woody lived somewhere far out in the woods.

"Yeah." Everyone was quiet for a while, realizing how dangerous it was to be AWOL and still in the United States.

Bill Bear didn't say anything. A few months back he'd taken Mother Mercury down to Fort Dix, fighting the slump, the shimmy and the wheel pull for six hours and pulled into the visitor's section on the pretext of seeing Ted, a friend who had enlisted so he could get away from his father. As he and Woody had arranged over the phone, Bill Bear went into the visitor's center and met with Ted. They talked, small talk, about the Army, about girls and parties. While they talked, Woody went to Mother Mercury and slid onto the floor of the vast back seat, pulling blankets over and about him. When Bill Bear got back, he got a basket of dirty clothes from the trunk, put it on top of the blankets and drove out without a hitch. Woody was sprung free.

Troels said, "When my brother did his physical he told them he really wanted to go to Viet Nam. Couldn't wait. They really got excited because they figured they got a good one. Then he told them the reason was, he wanted to go there so he could get everybody, including the Viet Cong, stoned on acid so they'd see the true meaning of the universe and they'd all stop fighting. Then he started shaking and jerking around. 4F. Basket Case."

Luke on the roof said. "1Y, me too. Crazy. Whacko, Mental Misfit. I hung myself."

"Hung yourself? Jesus Christ!" Jack said.

"They make you all strip down to your skivvies. Before I took my pants off I told them I had to pee and they let me go the bathroom. I went into a stall, shut the door, took off my belt, stood on the shitter, buckled it around the sprinkler pipe and wrapped it around my neck and tucked it in and waited till somebody came in. Then I stepped off the shitter and started moaning and groaning. The guy just pissed, flushed the pisser, and left."

"Probably thought you were in there pinching a big one." Bill Bear said.

"Yeah, probably. So I did it again. This time I left the door open. The next guy freaked out and screamed for people to come and they let me go. 1Y. Nut job."

Clouds gathered and a breeze quickened. A soft rain came.

Luke went on. "My brother's over there. I worry about him."

"He'll be all right. Your brother's a really tough guy." Jack said.

"No," Luke said, "my brother won't be all right. Even if he lives he won't be all right. None of the guys over there will be. And I'm not going to be all right either. Neither are you, or Woody. Nobody is. All right's something that used to happen before they shot Kennedy. All right," he said, getting off Mother Mercury and buttoning up his olive shirt that said Bingham's Oil Service over the pocket, "is something that doesn't happen anymore."

Two days ago, Luke Dickens went to pick up Bill Bear at the Boston airport when he got in from San Francisco. As they drove through their home town of Newmarket, Lester the Arrester, the lone local cop, pulled them over. He was looking for Susie Gallagher, who he thought was Luke's girlfriend. She'd run away from home again and her father wanted her back. As Officer Lester interrogated Luke about Susie's whereabouts, Bill Bear interrupted to tell the cop that he was just a hitchhiker on his way to Maine. Luke nodded. Bill Bear asked the Officer, "Can I just take my things and leave?" This was 1966 and Lester the Arrester really should have known better, but he said yes. Bill Bear reached in the back seat, took his suitcase, got out and walked off down the road. In the suitcase, wrapped in his underwear and t-shirts were two kilos of hashish and 5,000 hits of LSD. The hash was Lebanese, each half kilo sewn into a muslin cover, dusted with powdered vanilla bean and stamped with the infamous 'Red Lion'. The acid had been manufactured in a basement in Point Richmond in the San Francisco Bay Area by Augustus Owsley Stanley III, grandson of a Governor of Kentucky, soundman for the Grateful Dead and chemist par excellance. Each small dot was 99.9% pure lysergic acid diethylamide, aka 'White Lightening', each 500 microgram hit stamped with a light blue peace symbol. It had been a good trip to Frisco.

For the past year or so Lester had been trying to re-apprehend Luke. Three months ago Luke had taken up with Susie, who everyone called Susie Creamcheese because she was so incredibly pure and healthy. She was a seventeen year old cheerleader at the local high school. He had picked her with care. She had a bright face with high cheekbones, was tall and slim with breasts unusually large for her age. She wore her long blonde hair in braids tied with ribbons, a flat, silver circle virgin pin on her blouse, knee socks and wrap around plaid skirts secured with a three inch gold plated safety pin. Once a week or so, her father, owner of a furniture factory and also a Town Councilor, would call the police station and tell Lester to go find his daughter who was missing again. Lester very much wanted to please the Town Councilor. Luke had been arrested the year before in a marijuana bust at the Salamander Saloon and Lester the Arrester never understood why everyone else got at least six months and Luke went free. Unbeknownst to everyone except Luke, Susie and dozens of their friends, the good judge had offered Luke probation if he could do some acting work for him. He gave Luke some specific qualities of a co-star he wanted him to find. The whole town, the whole county, maybe even the whole state was lucky Lester never found Luke and Susie together; they met at their weekly meeting with Judge McFife at his home, in his living room, in front of his great stone fireplace. The judge, a huge jowly bald-headed man, had typed the day's script with his usual care, demonstrating a judicial command of detail. Luke lay naked on his back on the thick white shag rug while Susie, with nothing on but her knee socks and a cowboy hat, braids slapping against her breasts, rode him, moaning and urging on her stallion stud.   The judge, in his black robe, naked underneath, filmed it all for his private collection and paid them each ten dollars a session.

    The rain stopped at noon. It smelled of wet leaves and moss. Moss that grew in shadows on the north side of a stone or a tree where the summer sun couldn't dry it out. Often, as summer moved towards fall and the days became shorter and began to hunker in for the certainty of winter, Anna Duncan thought about moving on, making a new life. Maybe finding a man in Mykonos or Santorini.   Ten years ago, on the winter solstice, her husband had died, and now each year, she waited through three seasons for that bleak, cold time to come again. And it always came. The memories of her husband were hard for her. This summer she decided to go with her best friend to Mexico. When there were no other tourists there. To wash it all away. To write new poems. To watch the Mexican men.

The house in the woods of New Hampshire, built in 1699, had, except for a bathroom and a small kitchen with a huge soapstone sink, never been altered. Painted on the chimney was, "circa 1699". The house had been built with hand hewn pine posts and beams, now hard and dark red with age, scalloped. Large brick fireplaces in the living room and dining room were back to back under a four foot square central chimney, each with a hand pounded wrought iron bar swinging free in the middle of the fireplace for hanging pots to cook stews and soups. The floors were pine boards as wide as the length of a man's forearm, worn thin where people had walked from room to room for almost 300 years. Every time the water faucets were touched there was a shock from a frayed light cord wrapped around a water pipe in the crawl space. It was like that for years until someone finally took a flashlight, crawled over the furnace and unplugged it.

Behind the house was a small ramshackle barn, crooked and leaky. Below the barn was a pond and at the head of the pond on the banks of the river were stone abutments where a saw mill had stood hundreds of years ago. The millhouse, which had spanned the river on deep wood beams from abutment to abutment and would have held the stones rigid and straight, was gone. The stones had shifted crooked out of place from the push of ice and rush of spring floods and some had tumbled into the river. Above the mill site was a pond with thick ferns around the edges and a fine, powdery green scum floating thin and fragile as though sprinkled on the still surface. They called it the leech pond and Jack left jars of salt with tin foil covers by the big diving rock to dry up and shrivel the long leeches that sucked blood from the legs.

Cars began arriving in the early afternoon when the sun was high and hot, on its way to the west. Bill Bear had given some of the acid to Jack for the punch concoction and some to Robby to give out to everyone as they arrived. He'd eaten a couple. Jack had laid out the pile of theater clothes, mostly from Shakespeare, but a smattering of Ibsen, Albee and a tight black, low cut dress and a white linen suit from Tennessee Williams.

"Hey Robbie, if you're going to be the prankster who gets everybody stoned, why don't you wear this one?" Jack held up a costume for Puck from 'A Mid-Summer's Night Dream'. Robby stripped naked in the road and wiggled himself into the outfit. The buttons on the pants popped off when he tried to fasten them. Jack brought him a hank of rope from the barn and he tied them tight. He filled an Altoids tin with acid tabs and sat himself on the stone wall across the dirt road, sipping a Pabst, awaiting his mission. Serena was among the first to arrive. She spun up in her Sunbeam Alpine convertible and slowly, gracefully, with great presence, got out one long dark leg at a time, allowing her short blue skirt to ride all the way up, winking at Jack and Robby. She tucked in tight her short sleeved blouse emblazoned over the right breast with wings and 'Eastern Airlines', reached in the back and took out her blue cap with silver wings and with a curtsy, set it on her head in such a way as to not muss-up her long, long curly black hair. A Jamaican Stewardess. She gave Robby a kiss on the cheek and he stuck out his tongue, raising his eyebrows. She stuck out her tongue and Robby put a small tab on the end. She swallowed. 'Jesus God is that a long, pink tongue,' Jack thought, 'Holy Mackerel!'

"Jack, don't forget to remind me to call in sick for tomorrow," she said giving him a kiss on the lips, "I'm supposed to fly Boston to Nassau. Hate that flight. Bunch of drunks going on vacation." She walked past them, bent over and smelled the daffodils.

"Yikes." Puck said.

"Holy Mary Mother of God." Jack said.

Bill Bear directed traffic, getting people parked along the dirt road in such a way that they might, depending upon their mental acuity three or four hours later, have some chance of driving away. Forty of fifty or sixty people came. Jack knew most of them or had at least seen them in the coffeehouses near the docks in Portsmouth or in the bars in Newmarket. He didn't know them all; didn't even recognize some but that didn't matter. Unlike backyard barbeques in suburbia where friends and neighbors shared afternoons, gatherings of the counter-culture were open to all, to everybody in the vast karass who shared the communality of the times. When Bill Bear first arrived, when the crock concoction had been stirred, Jack drank one glass. In the woods, each tree became alive. Alive so when he tickled the bark, the tree giggled.

An acid trip doesn't have a beginning. At some point, you're in it. It's in you. You are it. You don't realize that any other condition had existed before. It is irreversible. Not like sipping whisky where you can stop at any time and ride it out from wherever you are. Once that little dot slides down your throat, your whole being has slid through the rabbit hole. You are in. All in. At some point, some small time after the acid has seeped its way into your brain, you feel the smile on your face almost wider than your face can take and you've been staring at a leaf for a long, long time. Not that you know you have been staring at a leaf for a long, long time because there is no time and it is not a leaf. It is undulating, shining, sparkling green and yellow and rose and it is huge and the water droplets on it are the water from the beginning of creation and it is all there is because it is all there is. The entire universe is one thing and now it is this thing and there are no things other than that thing which there are no things other than. It is all one. Bill Bear is as tall as a tree, his smile also as wide as a river is long and you tell him that all the universe is in that leaf and it is so beautiful you cry a little bit. And you hug him because you know that he knows all the things that you know and he says, "This is really good shit, man!" You nod and nod and nod now wandering away while everything undulates, streaking pulsating rainbows of colors until the touch of a branch on the bare skin of your shoulder is, once again, the entirety of the universe.

Jack went to the river to stir the pot. Luke was still working on "Macbeth." Early on in the party he'd had it all down. By now, he could only mumble "Trouble, Trouble" but he still stirred and stirred with the stout poplar branch Jack had skun for him with his Buck knife. A handful of others milled about, laughing, talking, kissing, reciting Shakespeare. Susie came down to the river, slowly, barefoot floating on the fern undergrowth, silk robe wide open, eyes wild. When she saw Luke, she froze. She put two fingers in a cross and screamed , "NO! NO! NO! She jumped and pranced around like a deer and then pivoting with arms held wide like in crucifixion, face to the sky, fell flat backwards in the stream. Jack bolted in and picked her up in his arms, nodded to the knot of wide eyes staring and carried her off through the woods to the edge of the pond. He pulled her silk robe about her, stroked her head and told her he would get that mean, mean man. And tomorrow, Susie, you will be the same Susie you were yesterday. It's all OK. It's all OK. It's not Luke's fault. It's the judge. He is a monster. Tomorrow you'll be the same girl you were before you met that man.

Jack had gotten Susie to stop her moaning and walk with him from the pond back to the Caterpillar Punch crock on the river bank. Now his mind was focusing sharper. "Luke, Susie's got to stay here. She needs to come down easy. I think, maybe tomorrow, you need to go see the Judge. Scare him and walk away. He doesn't own you, he doesn't own Susie and he doesn't own the law. He's a pervert."

In the yard he saw Troels, bound by the wrist to a copper skinned man. They were staring into each other's eyes. By early evening the party had thinned to just a few. In the house, the door to the living room was closed. Jack had never seen it closed before. Serena's Eastern Airlines uniform lay on top of a heap of clothes and underclothes. He could hear moaning and giggles from inside. He knocked on the door. "Hello?' Everybody OK?" After a bit it opened and a balloon spilled out at his feet. Green and slimy and greasy. Serena's long brown arm reached out and her oiled hand found his cheek. "Jack, I've been hoping you'd find us. The oil's on the stair. Strip down, oil up and slide in." He peered around the door. She was standing chest high in red, blue, yellow and green balloons, her bronze skin glistening with oils, rubbing her breasts, eyes closed and licking her thick pink lips. Jack went to the phonograph and put on his favorite piece of music; Vivaldi's Concerto #1 in E Major, La Primavera, Spring. The first part of the *Four Seasons*. He stripped and oiled himself with Santini extra virgin olive oil from a gallon tin that had been heated on the fire. He slid Susie's silk robe off her slender shoulders and oiled her up from her feet to up to the nape of her neck. They eased into the room, fought the door closed behind them and slithered through the balloons. It took slow care and planning for Jack to move gracefully into Serena's arms and breasts and straight deep into the sweet softness between her legs. There were others behind him in the room, he heard the Ahhs and Ohhs but he didn't know who they were. Someone else came in but he didn't know who that was either.

Jack stopped moving. The music had stopped. Somebody had taken the music off. Who would do that? There was a crisp rapping at the door. When Jack slid his way back out; naked, slippery and still engorged, he looked straight into a big brass badge. "Captain Henderson, State Police." the man in the uniform said. "Everybody out. Keep your hands above your head and move slowly." He backed up across the room to keep himself from being engulfed in a sea of balloons. Jack came out first and an officer took him into the living room. "Put your clothes on." He struggled slippery, sliding, off balance into a pair of jeans and a shirt. Then they handcuffed him. "Take him to Rockingham. Everybody else goes to Strafford."

The yard was empty and still when Jack was led out the door, put in the lead cruiser and driven off. Serena, Susie, Troels, Joe Cole and another girl came out the front door in handcuffs. Bill Bear watched it all from a crevice behind the stone mill abutments where he had hidden all the acid and all the hashish. Their clothes slid around on their bodies from the still warm olive oil. Susie's white silk shift turned transparent where her curves pushed against the fabric. "Yikes! An officer muttered. "Shut up, Gleason." Captain Henderson commanded. Troels was singing the Village Fugs; *Comin' down, I'm comin' down*".

Jack was booked on drug possession charges. Two local cops, two State Policemen, an FBI agent, a DEA agent and four Sheriff's Deputies searched every square inch of the house, the barn, the cars and the woods. Across the river behind the stone abutments, Bill Bear watched; crouched, silent, and careful. They found no list nor anything that looked like a list. They thumbed through every book, all of Anna Duncan's poetry and all her poetry anthologies. They shook out every volume of the Encyclopedia Britannica. It took them hours. They found nothing. The only drugs they found, which

121

were in the bathroom on the shelf by the sink and which the local cops were sure was heroin, turned out, after the DEA agent licked his finger wet, put it in the little Mexican ceramic dish and tasted it, to be baking soda that Anna Duncan used to brush her teeth. Sure there was nothing there, the FBI called the jails and had everyone released, including Joe Cole who had never actually been arrested in the first place. He disappeared and never came back.

SWITCH-WHIPPERS

A fire burned. Mostly maple with a few apple branches that sweetened the smell. Red-orange flames filled the fireplace, bending back to the throat of the chimney, the smoke pulled straight up through the flue and out into the warm, black midnight air. Serena, in Anna Duncan's bathrobe, her hair wrapped in a towel, sat cross-legged on the edge of the hearth. It had taken a half hour's soak in a bubble bath in the claw foot tub to wash off the oil and the leering stares of the policemen and jailers. Jack had felt his way along the path to the pond with a towel and a bar of soap.

They sat on the sofa looking at the living room strewn with papers, unzipped open pillows and an upended chair. They looked down the hallway, impassable now with all the books and encyclopedia from the bookshelves lying haphazard on the floor and they looked through the door to Anna Duncan's bedroom where the all the clothing from her dresser and closet lay in mismatched heaps. "What do you suppose they were looking for?"

"I got no idea." Jack said. "It couldn't be drugs or they would have come much earlier. It looks like they wanted some kind of paper. They went through every book in the house.

They even went through the cookbooks in the kitchen." He snaked his finger through the glass hoop on the top of the gallon jug of Vino Fino, nestled the bottle on the crook of his arm and took a long pull. "Let's clean this place up, then talk." He got up and set the right the chair in the corner. "Serena, could you straighten out my mother's room? Bill Bear, there's Murphey's Oil Soap in the kitchen. Could you try and get the balloon oil off the walls and woodwork in the back room? I'll work on this mess."

"Your mom's not going to like this." Bill Bear said.

"The only thing my mother is not going to like are the little round oil smudges on walls. Use a lot of Murphy's Oil Soap. The rest of it she won't mind. Anna, in her own way, is an anchor to the underground. She likes it that way."

"Are we the underground? Is that what we're doing? Is that what they think? I don't feel like I'm underground. I feel like I'm me. Right out in the bright sunshine. Here I am."

At three o'clock in the morning the house was clean. Cleaner than clean. Cleaner than it had been since the day Anna Duncan bought it. Serena, still in a bathrobe, had lit candles on the mantel and window sills. She had taken a bronze sculpture off the mantel to wipe it clean. It was not attached to the base. The base was a shiny, lacquered box the size of a fat book. She sat cross-legged once again on the hearth in front of a fully stoked fire, now all apple wood. In her lap was the opened box.

"They didn't find this. Look at it. It's full of poems and photos, letters and this little book; *The Prophet* by Kahil Gabran"

"That's my stuff." Jack said. "Wow, they didn't find it. I wonder if what they were looking for is in my box. Something about my dad or maybe my brother."

"Jack, look at this." Serena pulled a letter out. "There's no postmark on these letters. The return address is just

25730, Box No. 1000, Milan, Michigan, OFFICIAL BUSINESS. POSTAGE AND FEES PAID FBP' "What's FBP?"
        "It's addressed to me, care of my mother. She never opened it. She forgot to give it to me. FBP is, I guess, the Federal Bureau of Prisons. It's from my brother, Dwight. Open it, Read it." Serena opened it and read.

"Dear Jack,

Eight years ago on my 19th birthday I was working in Washington for Uncle Sam, living in Georgetown and attending the concerts at the Phillips Gallery. I was still dutifully registered for the draft, was living on my own for the first time, had never dabbled in politics and had not been out of the country for one day. In other words, I was still wet behind the ears. It wasn't until a year later that the Eisenhower era was over (you were 11 at the time), the sit-ins had begun, I was about to be arrested for the first time and a new phase of our history had begun. Nobody thought about the draft, everybody loved Kennedy, Diem was ruling Vietnam with an iron hand and "beatnik" was a new word.

*   When I became 19, we waited for the old golfer to leave the White House so we could join in new programs sponsored by the government. Now you are 19 and people spit out the President's name and call him a murderer. When I became 19 we talked about an Alliance for Progress and were glad that Castro had overthrown Batista and nobody knew where Vietnam was. Now you are 19 and nobody loves us but South Africa and Chiang-Kai-Shek and there is a boy from every town in Vietnam.*

*   I guess you're aware of all of this. Eight years ago I worked for the government, just two blocks from the Capitol. Now I am locked up by the government. The real question, of course – must you play by the Marquis of Queensbury rules when those you oppose pay no attention to them in the war? As one minister said last night, "This is a time when justice is more important than order." If the war is illegal, does that condone illegal methods of opposing it or is that a repudiation of democracy? Anyway, I assume you are in more or less danger of joining me in prison. Don't get a martyr complex because*

125

resistance to the draft is not so much heroic as it is the ordinary duty of anyone who doesn't wish to become a latter-day Eichmann. From what mother tells me, the things you've done and seen ought to prepare you well for making these hard decisions. As W.H. Auden said, 'If we want to live, we'd better start at once to try, If we don't, it doesn't matter, but we'd better start to die,' Love, Dwight."

"Jack, your brother is amazing. He's in a federal prison because he chose to go there. He actually decided to go to jail instead of going to war. He's not a draft dodger, he's a draft resister. My God, he must be on the bottom of the pecking order." Serena folded the letter and put it back in the box.

Who's this?" She held up a picture of a man in a bow tie with his hands on his hips, staring out at a bleak desert. It looked like Mongolia. She flipped it over. *Feb. 1947. Greystone Duncan at Los Alamos. AEC.*

"AEC means Atomic Energy Commission. That's my father. 1947. That picture was taken after the Atomic Bombs were dropped on Hiroshima and Nagasaki. He must be looking out at the site where they were going to build a bigger site to make shit for the Hydrogen Bomb."

Greystone Duncan, Jack's father, was born in a working class town on the banks of the Ohio River twenty-five miles outside Pittsburgh, Pennsylvania. His parents, grandparents, uncles, aunts, cousins, brothers and sisters were all Presbyterians of the Calvinist bent. Devout believers in the Total Depravity of Man and the Complete Ruin of Humanity's Ethical Nature. Greystone's father, John Duncan, a church elder and a clothier whose own apparel seldom strayed from black, relentlessly drove this message of worthlessness into his children. The older children, two boys and a girl accepted this notion wholesale. Stoic youths, seemingly unaffected by pleasure or pain. Greystone, the youngest child, did not like being told

126

what to think or what not to think. He was given to doing things he knew were blasphemous, such as peeping through the key hole on the bathroom door when his sister was undressing to bathe or singing to himself while he worked. Laughing at a joke he might have heard at school. He wasn't devious about his sacrilege. He always got caught.

A great willow tree in the back yard of their modest home provided an endless supply of switches for the purpose of John Duncan's repeated attempts to teach this young lad the evils of emotion. He would break off a branch, strip the leaves, strip the little branch shoots until it was a narrow whip, then stride into the house and point to the stairs which led to Greystone's bedroom. God will save you if He so chooses. There is nothing you can do to cause His favor except work, work, work and wait for His Grace.

By age eleven he had come to conclude that there was no proof whatsoever that any God existed or, if He did, the statistical likelihood that He would ever get around to noticing him was, year by year, month by month, day by day, approaching zero. One fall day, after school when his chores were done, when yesterday's ashes had been shoveled out and today's new coal had been loaded into the stove hopper, he told his sister that the notion of God was something people had invented to feel better about all the things they were afraid of. He said it in a serious but friendly way as if to invite a conversation. The sister told the brother and the brother told the mother and the mother told the father and the branch stripped from the willow tree that day was frightfully long and stout. The bugaboo oozed straight out from the foundation of their home, and, like a liquid vapor, settled in every room, every nook and every cranny. The lashing he got that evening was epic. From that day on, not a word could be spoken, not a pot of water boiled, not a simple chore done without screamed incriminations, dire forecasts of certain doom, beseechings of the Lord to drive the Devil from their home. Greystone left that house a week later at the age of twelve. As he walked down the road carrying his canvas satchel with a few clothes and a bedroll, the bugaboo slithered back into its hole. The boy didn't say good-bye. He didn't look back over his shoulder and he never returned. His mother and father were glad of it. They never again mentioned his name. Not once.

He went north, picking up odd jobs along the way, staying out of sight of the Constables. By spring, he was in Lowell, Massachusetts, a place where there were shoe mills that always needed young, strong boys to work twelve hours shifts, six days a week. He found a friend, an older man, a bespectacled, bald, chicken-like little man who played the violin and owned a store in town called 'Greenberg's Fruit and Real Estate.' The store sold neither fruit nor real estate. It sold used books and sheet music. His name was Morris Greenberg. His grandfather, Simon, had been a fruit merchant. His father, Benjamin, had amassed a fortune selling land and buildings. After they both died, Morris played his violin and sold old books, mostly mysteries and romance novels.

Morris became a mentor to Greystone, arranging a night time job for the young lad in the bookkeeping office of a shoe mill, adding and subtracting numbers. He enrolled him in a local private academy. Five years later, Morris paid for his tuition to study engineering at the Massachusetts Institute of Technology. After graduation, Greystone received a request from the United States Army. Would he consider enlisting in the Corps of Engineers?

Paper-clipped to the back of the photo of Greystone Duncan was a picture of him in a full suit, with a bow tie, his arm around a woman, in a bridal gown, laughing, coming down the steps of a church. "Is that your mother?" Serena asked. "My God, she's beautiful."

Anna Hinckley was the daughter of a doctor, a General Practitioner who treated the ill at any time day or night, at any place, his house or theirs. He often took payment in food or goods like bolts of damask cloth. The doctor lived alone. His wife, Anna's mother, had died of pneumonia when Anna was young. Over time the doctor became addicted to his own prescriptions, dying of an overdose when his daughter was away at Rhode Island College for Women. She became a nurse and took a job in the cancer ward of Massachusetts General Hospital attending to the dying needs of the very poor, like Johnny Pratt who had been found near death on a bench in Boston Common and the very powerful, like a Mayor. She said that by the time these men were in her care the differences between a life of begging for scraps to stay alive and a life of riding about in limousines and eating foie gras meant nothing. Whether they were atheists or God-Fearing parishioners meant nothing. They both needed their bed sheets changed and a cool cloth on their forehead.

Greystone Duncan and six other engineers recently discharged from a four year stint in the Army Corp of Engineers, had met in Boston to celebrate their freedom at Wally's, a pub at the foot of Beacon Hill. It was 11:30 PM on a hot August night. Six second shift nurses at Mass General had just gotten off work and were walking up Charles Street on their way to their apartments on the Hill. Greystone Duncan lurched out of the pub to hail a cab, tripped on the threshold and fell into the arms of Anna Hinckley. Her cropped auburn hair, long thin fingers and big hazel eyes in a deftly sculpted face drew men to her like the moon draws the seas. She squared him up, straightened his skewed cap, adjusted his expert marksman badge, giving it a little imaginary polish and propped him up against the brick storefront. The girls walked on, laughing, their white starched skirts swishing side to side in the warm night air. Three months later Greystone Duncan and Anna Hinkley were married by a Justice of the Peace on the front steps of the Boston Public Library between the two stone statues; one representing Art, the other Science. Morris Greenberg, then eighty-five and a month away from death, made the journey to be with Greystone at his wedding. One year after their wedding, Anna gave birth to their first child, Dwight Greystone Duncan. It would be eight years before she had another child.

It was 1940. War was on in Britain, in France, in Finland and Norway and Russia. All over the European continent and into North Africa. Japan was amassing her troops and air force for a full attack in the South Pacific. Greystone Duncan had been asked by the government to go off and help figure out how to split an atom. "Anna, I don't want another child until this is over. Who knows where I might have to go and who knows if I would even come back. Nothing is certain. Nothing is predictable. It is all chaos. Madmen are everywhere." Anna neatly folded her nurse's uniform, put in a few mothballs, wrapped it in a fine piece of damask her father had left her and packed it away. She began spending her days alone, writing poetry.

A second son, Jack Duncan, named after the Presbyterian switch-whipper, was born in 1948, eight years after the first child, Dwight. The Eisenhower Era, a time of security and prosperity in a more ordered world, was around the corner. The international balance of power, in a macabre paradox, hung in a political stability created by a fundamental physical instability, the radioactive isotope. The madmen had all been murdered or committed suicide. Things were on an upswing. The war was over. We won.

THE STAR OF BETHLEHEM

Jack didn't remember anything that happened to him before he was ten years old. There were snippets of scenes that sometimes came to him, without action or color; silent, stopped in time like cropped photos. They must have had a trigger, like a smell or a touch, but when he tried to piece them together to make some memory whole, they'd dart away. Dart like minnows dart past a pier post. Gone. These recollections were without context. They came to his mind randomly or were brought to him by others. He had been told of a mischievous child in Dr. Denton pajamas, the soft cotton ones that zip up the front with plastic bottomed feet attached to them, running through the back yards of houses on their block in the early-early morning, turning on all the neighbors' sprinklers. He's heard that story and heard the laughter and seen the smiles when it was told, but when it was told he couldn't feel the dampness on his pajama bottom feet, he couldn't smell the wet grass or hear a spigot handle creak. Jack was told he was there but there wasn't any part of him that was still there. He could see a boy running. He could see little legs moving fast and an impish smile and he was happy that people thought he was mischievous but that boy could have been any boy. He could only see him, he couldn't feel him.

He was ten when his father died. He remembered that day. He could hear a voice, feel a wetness on his hand, water dribbling over his knuckles down his wrist. Dew on the inside of a cold window in the back seat of a military car. He didn't have to be told what happened because this time had stayed as a part of him. It had left a mark. The first one. Jack didn't remember the year leading up to his father's death, but he recalled voices talking about a long, painful dying. A cancer caused by exposure to radiation. He remembered his brother Dwight telling him how sick father was. A sickness that came from uranium. A sickness that couldn't be fixed.

It was Christmas break. Dwight, eight years older than Jack, had come home from college. The chasm between them was so wide they could have come from different families in different parts of the world. They had nothing to say to each other. When Jack was in the third grade, Dwight was on the high school debate team. Not an ordinary student, but one of the best in the country. Perfect 800's on his SATs. When Dwight was at home he lived in the attic in a foul smelling landscape of dirty clothes, half eaten food and volumes of encyclopedia. His ears stuck out, he had pimples and no girlfriends. Dwight delivered speeches to various intellectual groups, like historical societies and book clubs. His first speech, when he was twelve, was about the history of the Mayan calendar delivered at a monthly meeting of the Philosophical Society. Dwight was home from college for the holidays. At the dinner table, no one was ever allowed to speak unless asked a question by the father. Various vestiges of the Presbyterian tradition from the coal mining country of Pennsylvania eked into their lives from time to time. Anna always held her tongue. Dwight and his father seemed to be the only ones who ever spoke, involving themselves in long discussions about things no one else either understood or cared one whit about. When Dwight wasn't there, the table was silent. "What, Dwight, is your opinion of Adlai Stevenson?" his father might ask. "Which one, Father, the man who was defeated by Eisenhower or his grandfather who ran as a Vice-Presidential candidate with William Jennings Bryan in 1900? Their philosophies had a few significant differences."

On Christmas morning, Anna and her two sons slid the spangled, bobbled, tinseled Christmas tree, blanket, presents and all, across the living room floor and into Greystone's room. They sat on his bed and handed him a box wrapped in red tissue paper with a gold ribbon and bow tied around it. He nudged it off the bed and onto the floor. He told his wife to put the tree and presents back into the living room. "Please don't make me celebrate this holiday. The birth of a savior has done little to make this world a better place." He rolled over and nestled into his bed sheets. Anna and her children pulled the tree and gaily wrapped boxes back to the living room. Just as he had on the way in, Dwight reached up and pulled the top of the tree down just a bit so the Star of Bethlehem could leave the room.

"Anna," he said to his wife when she asked why he had done that, "I have tried to understand God all my life, but I can't find Him. I have tried to provoke Him into showing his face. It didn't work. I have come to realize that you can't make an atomic bomb that incinerates innocent children and still believe that God has time for you. To him, you are not worth his Grace. My father was right. God won't come to me."

A few days later on a cold, cold morning, Jack's mother had told him he didn't have to go to school. He was to go visit with the Perkins and stay overnight. Mrs. Perkins had come over to pick him up. His mother opened the door to the sick room and told him to go say good-bye to his father. Jack was going to ask his father why he had to go to the Perkins if they didn't have any kids he could play with, just two old people, but as Jack went into the room, his mother closed the door behind him and his mind went blank. His father lay still on the bed, his head turned away from him, silent but for short gasps, the intermittent squeak of sucking air. Jack walked through the room, looking out the side window at the Greeley's house next door, looking anywhere but at the bed. Jack didn't know if his father even knew he was in the room.

Jack turned away from the window and back into the room. He saw his father with the sheet pulled up only to the middle of his bottom. Jack was a skinny boy but his father was now skinnier than his little son and his arm, yellow-gray like a skun stick, was laid across a pillow. Jack moved beside the bed and his arm nudged the white steel tray set on shaky fold out legs. Glass jars and vials with pink stoppers in the end and marks on them like a round ruler, rattled. Jack stood with his arms down at his side, fingers fidgeting the seams in his pant legs. His father's eyes rolled up slowly his son's face. "Good-bye, son" he said. "Bye, Dad." "Good-bye, son," his father said again. A whisper. Jack left the room, looking down, around the foot of the bed straight to the door and out.

Jack was standing on the front step watching his own breath. Mrs. Perkins came out, put one long arm around his shoulders and led him to her station wagon parked in the driveway. Jack sat in the front seat. Her husband was John Perkins, a General in the United States Air Force. Jack's mother came out and handed Mrs. Perkins a small duffle bag. She said, "Here's some clean clothes and his tooth brush," and Mrs. Perkins put the bag between them on the seat. Jack didn't know where anyone was that night he went to the Perkins's. He didn't know anything when he was put to bed that night.

The next morning after General Perkins had gone off to the production site of the nuclear aircraft and Mrs. Perkins was downstairs in the kitchen, Jack went across the hall into their bedroom and put on the General's clothes. The dark blue jacket covered his whole body and hung near the floor. It had three stars on each side of the collar and rows and rows of red, white and green bars pinned to it. There were tassels hanging from each shoulder. His hat, like a policeman's hat, was twice as big as his head. It had a huge brass badge on the front and the bill has hard, black and shiny. Jack was standing in front of the mirror holding a bronze Air Force Cross medal with his thumb and finger cocked like a pistol. Pow! Pow! Pow! he shot at an imaginary enemy. Mrs. Perkins came in. She began to cry. She took the coat and hat off, put them on the bed, then knelt down and wept, hugging him. Her face was wet and a bracelet dug into his neck. She took him by the hand, down the stairs and out the front door. It was raining and there was a black car with black windows parked in the driveway. She opened the back door and Jack climbed onto the seat. All she said was "312 Grant Avenue." The seat was leather, slippery, cold and hard. It had stitches in it that made it look like pillows sewn to a sofa. The seat was as big as a sofa. It was cold like the gloves his father wore when he took Jack's hand on a winter's day. He felt small. His feet couldn't touch the floor. The man driving the car had on a military coat and hat just like General Perkins's. The window beside him was wet with fog, thick wetness. Jack wiped his knuckles across it and the fog felt like rain inside. The window fog dripped across his knuckles, inside the cuff of his shirt over his wrist and down his forearm. Jack and the man sat in the car for a long time.

The man, looking straight ahead out the windshield finally said "Your father died." That was all the man said. "My father?" the ten year old said. "Died?"

On that morning, Jack's mother had talked to her husband's doctor. She put the phone down slowly, very softly then breathed deeply, eyes closed, head tipped back. She found her nurse's uniform wrapped in her father's damask cloth, put it on, went to the sick room, kissed her husband on his forehead and gave him his pain medication, his morphine, by syringe, ten times the prescribed amount and he died in her arms. Peacefully. No more pain. Gone. Gone off to meet the God who wouldn't come to meet him. Within a month of her husband's death, she had found a new home in a small town a few miles from the University of New Hampshire, near where she had been born.

Bill Bear drank some of the wine, wiped his mouth on his sleeve and handed the jug to Jack. He reached into the black box and took out a picture of Jack, bare to the waist, hanging from a cross on the front of a little church, his feet resting on the top of a ladder. He handed it to Serena. She looked at Jack, looked at the picture, gave it to Jack and said, "I really think you need to talk about this. Maybe we'll all get a better idea about why all those cops are here if you can explain just what in the name of the Good Lord you're doing in this picture hanging on a cross on the front of someone's church."

"Jack," she said, tapping her finger on the cross, "talk."

"That was a couple of years ago. The Quaker school I went to sent a bunch of us kids down into Alabama and Mississippi to help out in the Civil Rights movement. Darleen, or somebody, I can't remember who, snapped this picture of me on the cross about a minute before this fat redneck tried to kill me. He shot at me with a rifle. He missed. We'd been run out of Selma and gone way down into southern Mississippi to help re-build bombed out churches. Something happened there. Something happened to me. I got scared or mad. I don't know. I chased the redneck into a river. I threw a hammer at him. I think he might have drowned."

The fire had burned to embers. Bill Bear and Serena were nestled together on the sofa, snoring softly. Jack watched the rose of the morning sun slide through the summer leaves, just rubbing the window panes. He wondered what it was all about. What they wanted. I don't have anything they could want. We didn't do anything. We're not the underground. We're not traitors or thieves or subversives. We're just different. Is it something about the bomb? Is it something about Dwight? They want to get him for something? Did I kill that guy in Mississippi? Somebody here at the party was a cop. Had to be. He remembered Luke Dickens saying early that morning, stretched out on Mother Mercury, 'All right is something that doesn't happen anymore.' In a week, he had an interview for admission to Deakins College. He put *The Prophet* in his back pocket where it fit perfectly, pulled a blanket over himself and stretched out to sleep. 'All right' he thought, is something that better happen.

HIGHER EDUCATION

Jack was sure the interview was going well. The questions seemed to come right from his college application so the answers were easy. "How long have you been writing poetry?" Since I was twelve, he said, explaining how his mother would often leave her *Anthology of Modern Verse* on the coffee table in the living room book marked to a different poem for him to find after school. He would read the poem by Yeats or Eliot or Hopkins and then, inspired, write one of his own. "Has it been difficult growing up with an older brother in jail?" No, he told them, I'm very proud of my brother and the stand he took against the war. The sneers from the people in the local country store can hurt sometimes, but I've learned a lot about courage, both from him and from the Quakers at my high school. How you have look hard into yourself, and stay true to your beliefs. "The unexamined life," he told them, "is not worth living." Since he couldn't remember who said it or even what century it was, he just left it like that. The interview went on for almost an hour. Softball. They were in the college president's office. President Richard Binder. He said please call him Dick and that he personally interviews each applicant who makes it to this final stage. They were sitting in a semicircle of black lacquered arm chairs with leather seats. Copies of *Ramparts*, *Evergreen Review* and the *Village Voice* were neatly placed on a coffee table in front of them The man to Jack's right looked nearly seven feet tall and thin with long blonde hair and a very long blonde moustache. He was dressed in motorcycle boots, leather motorcycle pants with zippers from the cuff to the knee and a wrinkled blue work shirt. He looked about thirty-five. He was Grant James, professor of mathematics. Beside Jack, on his left, was a student, Gwen Anne Ahern. She had thick curly red hair that hung half way down her back, a small nose and lips that seemed to always hold the hint of a smile, even when she frowned. She had asked him, "Do you think marijuana should be legal?" "No," Jack had said and she frowned at him but still with that hidden smile, "not until the peasant farmers in South America are given something else to grow. The price would plummet and they would starve." The philosophy teacher nodded and she looked at Jack as if to say, "Well aren't you a Mr. Smarty-Pants."

President Binder asked Gwen to show Jack around the campus. Deakins College was only four years old. It was the most radical college in the country founded by ex-Berkley professors as an experiment in education. Gwen told him their idea was to see how unstructured a school can be and still have students learn. Does education necessitate any structure at all? "I think we're all guinea pigs." she said, laughing. The campus had been a millionaire's horse farm high up in the Adirondacks overlooking the Lake George valley. The mansion was the college offices, library, some of the classrooms and a student dormitory. Servant's quarters, barns and stables had been converted to student housing, a dining hall and more classrooms. There were tennis courts and a swimming pool. Gwen introduced Jack to students as she led him around the campus. Almost all the boys had long hair, beards and bellbottoms. The girls wore either very long skirts or very short skirts. None seemed to wear a bra. Gwen didn't either. Her skirt was long and white with tassels on the bottom. She took Jack to every building, saying "Hi" to most students, hugging some and kissing others. The students were mostly in small groups. Jack had not seen even one sitting at a desk, writing on a notepad or reading a textbook. Some were lying on their bed reading but not reading the thick hard bound books that are bought at a campus bookstore at the beginning of the year. Jack sensed a hierarchy. The small groups seem centered around a person, usually one who was more striking than the others; the longest hair or the tallest or the one with the guitar. "Lee, this is Jack. He'll be coming here next year," Gwen said to a young man sitting cross legged with a guitar in his lap, surrounded by six or seven other students. Lee lifted his head slightly up towards Jack, looking at him through small perfectly round red sunglasses, nodded and looked back down at his guitar. "He's the campus guru," Gwen said. Dink was in his room drilling a small hole in a carrot sized piece of wood. His desk was strewn with files, drill bits, sandpaper and a soldering iron. On a shelf laid out on a velvet cloth were dozens of dope pipes, beautifully crafted. Most were a dark wood with silver inlay. Dink handed Gwen a long curved pipe with an ivory mouthpiece and ruby-like stones set around the bowl. She handed it back. "Dink, you sell these, don't give them away." She kissed him on the cheek.

In the first classroom they peeked into an Hispanic student was talking about the similarities between Merlin, the wizard of ancient lore and Gandalf, the wizard in Tolkien's `Lord of the Rings` On the walls were taped up pages from comic books and posters of Thor and Beowulf. "Medieval Literature" Gwen whispered. Down the hall a classroom door was open. A short bald man standing in front of ten or so students seated at traditional schoolroom desks was spinning a plum sized steel ball on a long string over his head. Gwen nudged Jack into the room to a seat in the back. This is dangerous, Jack thought. If the string broke or slipped out of his fingers it could crush someone's skull. "The faster this ball swings the more energy it gathers. Where does that energy come from? Is there more energy in this room now that the ball is accumulating it? No!" The portly little fellow was shouting. "The more energy the ball gathers, the less energy something else has in this room or in this universe. Energy is never created or destroyed, it just changes form, changes place." "Atomic Physics." Gwen said. "Donald Phelan. He worked with the British on the nuclear bomb. He's brilliant." Yeah, Jack thought, brilliant but not smart enough to know what a horrible idea it is to build a nuclear bomb or hurl a steel ball around people's heads. Brilliant, not smart.

Gwen and Jack walked into a room bigger than most people's houses. It used to be the ballroom of the mansion with high arched Palladian windows and a wall of French doors leading out onto a flat stone patio. This professor was clearly popular. Fifty or so students sat in a haphazard ensemble of chairs, comfortable, legs stretched out, some with note books in their laps. The professor, James Henry Lodge, a watered down relative of the Cabot Lodge cross pollination and one of the four founders had just begun his weekly soliloquy. He held forth dressed in a New York Yankee's pinstripe uniform.

"The New York Yankees," he boomed, "are a winning team. A storied franchise," he said. "Season after season, year after year, they stand atop the heap of all the teams. They get to raise their arms in exuberance, they get to smile every October in a snowstorm of confetti. Once again victors in the world series of sport."

"What's up with this guy?" Jack asked Gwen.

"Listen to him." she said.

"But are the managers, the coaches and the players who are riding and waving in the motorcade the same ones who rode this route a decade ago? Who here knows baseball?" he asked the students. A few raised their hands. "Are they?" Most kids shook their heads, sensing where this was going. "No!" he boomed again, "they are all different. Not even related. Most have never even seen or met the great ones of the past. Heard of them? Probably. Maybe even, when they were teenagers a couple of years ago, idolized them but did they ever sit knee to knee in a dugout and soak up their wisdom, catch the intricate stories of strategy, cunning, strength, camaraderie and teamwork that welded together that magnificent fighting force? No. They didn't. The Yankee managers certainly are good fishermen. They know how to cast their lure into the right part of the gene pool and to yank it just so but that is only a small part of the science of winning at sports. There are lots of good fish and they don't catch them all. There is something else with this team that binds the winning ethos of the past to the winning ethos of the present. Some strong communal string that ties them together from generation to generation with a constant certainty of victory. Who knows what that is?" Nobody said anything.

"That's right," he said, "It's ineffable. It can't be said in words." And then he went on to say it in words. "And so it was with America. We were the same kind of winning franchise. Oh, we didn't win every year, not even every other year. Neither did the Yankees. But always after short episodes of watching other countries' achievements, we'd be right back on top."

He went to the blackboard and wrote with a flourish. After each statement he turned back to the class, held his hands up, raised his eyebrows as if to say, "everybody knows that." "Napoleon codified law, Garibaldi unified Italy, England and France set new standards of urban decency with subways and parks and sewer systems but time after time America won it all. We won the Revolutionary War. In 1812 we beat the British again. In 1848, the Mexicans. In 1865, the Confederacy. In 1890 the Indians were finished at Wounded Knee. In 1898, Spain. In 1918, Germany, Austria, Hungary. In 1945 we buried 25,000 people in Dresden as Germany collapsed, Italy gave up and the atomic bomb obliterated 100,000 Japanese in 30 seconds. In 1952, China was stopped in Korea. That's everybody who is anybody except Russia and France and their time would have come, except, something happened to us."

He left the front of the room and began walking through the students, putting his hand on some shoulders, standing looking down at others, eventually ending up with his back to the class, looking out on the vast patio.

"There began a time when everything was so good, so sure, that no one bothered to check and see whether that communal string still had the right tension. Dwight Eisenhower had been president for eight years. Then Jack Kennedy got elected. Youth and Hope. Everybody had big cars. That is, everybody that anybody could see. Or bothered to look at. They didn't realize the string actually went through the whole country and in some places it had gotten a little too taut. Some had begun thinking that wherever there is a victor, there has to be a loser and lots of people began to see themselves as the losers because they didn't have a big car. They didn't know how to play golf. They couldn't even vote."

"When things start to go badly, it always happens from inside your own team. Discord. Arguments. Some get a lot of money, others get almost none. Some get to play, others always sit on the bench. Negroes sitting on the benches began fretting with the string, rubbing it, worrying it, yanking it until little fibers sprung free and it started to fray. Music turned inward, not out to all like a soothing balm as it always had been, like Frank Sinatra, but raw, accusatory and, like the art and poetry, sung in a syntax that only the disenfranchised could understand. A great portion of the nation's children began to dislike victory. Hundreds of thousands of fish began to see the lures for what they really were; sharp barbed hooks. They wouldn't bite. They dove deep and gathered in schools, out of reach where they couldn't be caught. Then on November 22, 1963, in Dallas, the string snapped. America hasn't won a game since. Nobody remembers how."

Nobody moved. A girl wearing lederhosen shorts and a Mexican peasant blouse cried. Her mother had been a secretary in Senator John Kennedy's Boston office before he became President. Her mother revered him. The girl still cried whenever people spoke of his assassination.

Gwen led Jack past the tennis courts to the swimming pool. "Want to go in?" she asked. Jack looked at her from the top of her head, slowly down to her sandals. She raised her eyebrows and smiled. "No," Jack said, "maybe when I live here." She led him to a hiking trail. "Down this path it turns into a forest of oak trees where the rich guys came to shoot the birds. It's really beautiful. Do you want to see it?" she asked. Jack nodded.

The path became soft with leaves. Gwen leaned back against a tree trunk, took a joint and matches from her skirt pocket, lit it, took a long drag and put it up to Jack's lips. He inhaled deeply. They smoked most of the joint leaning into the tree, not talking. When they got to a small clearing she lay down looking up into the branches of the huge oaks. Jack lay down beside her, asking her questions about the school. He asked her if she thought he would like it there. She answered by nestling her head on his chest and talked to him about how her family came here from Ireland when she was six. How they lived in Brooklyn and how much she missed her older brother. He was her best friend. He was drafted into the Army, sent to Viet Nam and died the week he got there;

145

crushed to death when the Jeep he was riding in rolled over on him. She despises our government, she said, for what it did to her brother. Senseless and unnecessary. Two years later, she told Jack, her father was dead from drink. She was glad about that she said. He was a hateful man. Gwen unbuttoned his shirt and waved her long hair over his chest, slowly rubbing his stomach, then unbuckled and unzipped his pants. She took him in her mouth and her mass of red curls bounced up and down and up and down and up and down. She stood, hiked her dress up and straddled him. She slid him all the way inside her. She was kneeling, leaning over him now, eyes closed, arms splayed beside his shoulders, rocking. She rocked and humped slowly, deep, shallow, deep, smiling. Jack heard the low throaty purr of the motorcycle as it came down the path. He couldn't see it, it was behind him. She could see it. He could tell that in her eyes, now wide open, staring. It was close, he heard it very close, idling. She was looking right at it and her rocking, her humping got faster until she clenched tight down and began a long slow shaking, her mouth wide open, coming. Jack heard the motorcycle rev, turn around and purr back off to campus.

Grant James derided Jack's application. "He's too much of an intellectual. He needs to go somewhere and study the classics." he said. "He won't fit here." Gwen was adamant. Jack was perfect for the school. He wanted to attend and he would be good for Deakins. It took a unanimous vote of the president, a teacher and a student for an applicant requesting full scholarship to be admitted. President Binder thought Jack Duncan was one of the best applicants they'd interviewed. Gwen stared at Grant James from her chair. Then she stood up and glowered at him. He knew that never again was she going to ride up to his mountain cabin on his BMW, drink his wine, take his mescaline and make love. That was over. That's alright, he thought, lots of other girls here. "OK." he said.

"Thank you," she said too quickly. Dick Binder looked back and forth between them. "I take it your walk around campus with Mr. Duncan went well," he said to Gwen.

The road to town was damp with spring rain. Soft rain that washed the fresh smell of new green leaves into the air. It was a narrow road, just wide enough for two cars to pass with no center stripe and the pavement was rough like black popcorn. There were seldom any cars on this road because it didn't go anywhere, just from town to the school and, a few miles on, to a dairy farm and then circled back through dense woods to the highway, two miles north of Deakins. It was not a shortcut to anywhere. As the rain let up, Gwyneth pulled her windbreaker hood back off her head and shook her mass of red hair. She loved this half-hour walk. Once a week in the mid-morning she walked into town. Alone. It didn't matter if it was raining or snowing, she walked anyway. Sometimes friends would ask to walk with her but she always said no; she needed this private time to center herself.

In the Dunkin Donuts, she ordered a cup of regular coffee, milk and sugar, and picked out a blueberry muffin. She sat in a booth by the window, looking out across the road at the Catholic Church, collecting her thoughts, thinking about confessions. She couldn't confess anymore. Never again. She wanted to confess, to tell a father everything so he could give her punishment and she could accept that punishment and be whole again. But she can't confess. She could never talk to a priest again. Gwyneth knew this. She finished her coffee and muffin, went outside to phone booth on the corner. She put in a dime and dialed a number. The operator told her that will be fifty cents for three minutes. She put in four quarters. The phone at the other end rang ten times before a woman answered. "Federal Bureau of Investigation. Drug Enforcement Division."

"Agent Hancock, please. This is Gwen."

"Hold, please," the woman said.

"Gwyneth, how are you? What do you have?" Agent Hancock asked.

"Two things. I'm pretty sure a shipment of LSD is coming from Toronto on Friday morning. It's not coming to the college. It's going to the Swiss Inn hotel at Jasser Peak ski resort and from there to Brooklyn. There's supposed to be ten thousand hits. I don't know the guy who's bringing it in from Canada. His name is Kevin. He's not from the school. I'm not sure who is going to pick it up at the hotel, they're still talking about that, but the car will either be a green, 1966 Pontiac GTO or a really old convertible Citroen".

"How do you know that?" Agent Hancock asked.

"They're the only cars here that could make it from here to Brooklyn." She said.

"Is any of it going back to the school?"

"Well, sure some would, but I got the feeling it was going to get sold in New York."

"OK, Gwyneth, thanks. Let me know when you find out more. What else?"

"Jack Duncan, the kid from the Quaker school that you said you hoped would get in here, he did. He got accepted. I got myself on the interview committee. What do you want me to find out? He doesn't seem like he's into either drugs or money."

"Good work. You're right. He doesn't deal drugs. This request doesn't come out of this office. The Bureau wants to know about AWOL soldiers and anything about a group that might be calling themselves 'The Weathermen.' Somewhere in his papers he may have a list with names or places on it. See if you can find it. That's all I can tell you. Just listen, listen to anything he says about his brother, the one in prison, maybe ask some roundabout questions. See what you can find out but don't ask anything direct. OK? Sign up as a member of that group, Students for a Democratic Society, and let me know what they are doing. That's important. They are tied into this 'Weatherman' thing. And Gwyneth, this guy Duncan, he's your assignment. Get to know him."

"I have."

Special Agent Hancock smiled to himself. The kid had only gone to his college interview. She seems to enjoy that part of her work. Really good at it, too. He knew that from the Bureau's de-briefing documents. A Mobster and a Catholic priest, who, after his indiscretions had been whispered to Richard Cardinal Cushing by Vannie Druggan, had been reassigned to be a chaplain in a federal prison. He knew from Druggan that Gwyneth had become despondent after her brother left and she had sought him out, thinking that her copulation with the priest was the cause of her depression. She thought also that revenge might fix it. Maybe neither of those trysts were her idea. He had thought of rejecting her as an informant because of her libidinous proclivities but then figured, given the culture she was going to slide into, it could be an asset. Agent Hancock also knew that if he ever tried to find out firsthand if what those men had said about Gwyneth was true, her brother would slit his throat. Federal agent or not. He wouldn't even see or hear him coming. Sean O'Neil was a very dangerous kid; Viet Nam Green Beret, Special Ops. And, like Sean had told him, she keeps her head even when she's stoned. Valuable girl.

"How's my brother?" Gwyneth asked, reading his thoughts.

"Your brother's fine. He's overseas. You wouldn't recognize him. He looks like the Zig-Zag man."

"I would recognize him. I miss him. I'd like to see him."

"Someday. Not now, not for quite a while. I have to go. Thanks."

*   *   *

Ted Hilliard brought the axe all the way from the ground by the back of his boot heel in a long arc up over his head, down and right through the ten inch diameter oak log on the stump, splitting it cleanly in half. The Long House dorm had a wood stove in the communal room at the far end. The forestry class had pruned, thinned and cut three full truck loads of oak, maple and beech from the from the hardwood stands all along the ridge. They had cut it into two foot lengths and left it in a pile for Ted to split. He said he wanted to. He wanted to split it all by himself. With each swing he sang, *"I can hoist a jack, I can lay track and I can swing this hammer, too."* Each time he sang he drove the axe harder and faster into the logs making sure that even as he tired he would never have to swing twice to split one log. John Henry died swinging his hammer, one swing for each spike, each swing a nineteen foot long arc from his heel to the railroad spike. Ted wasn't quite a big as John Henry, but just about. He figured his swing was sixteen feet. John Henry died swinging his hammer in a race with a machine and Ted thought that would be right for him as well. To die in this meadow from a busted heart racing against his father's machine, the United States Military Machine. Ted hated his father. The hatred wasn't new, it was just worse than it used to be. Worse now that his father, Army Col. Richard Hilliard, shut off all payments to the college and sent President Binder a letter saying that his son was no longer a student there and if the college didn't like that or tried in any way to intercede with his wishes, he would have the 'Authorities' start investigations of the school. Somehow his father had caused Ted's student deferment to be terminated even before the college received his letter.

The letter, registered mail, had not been sent to the college mail room. It had been hand delivered to President Binder personally by the local Postmaster accompanied by the local Police Chief. He had to sign for it in front of them. In it were Ted's military service induction notice stamped, "Physical Examination Waived', a curt, hand written note demanding that his son be notified that it had been delivered and a scathing letter from Benjamin R. Johnston, MD, on Englewood Memorial Hospital letterhead, copied to the director and commissioners of the New York Board of Health and the state's Republican Senator.

Colonel Hilliard had not called his son, had not informed him that he was going to do this, simply ordered President Binder to carry out those duties. Ted was to report to boot camp at Fort Dix on January 15, 1968 on or before 0800 hrs. His birthday. That bastard, Ted thought.

It probably wouldn't have happened this way if he and Jack hadn't shown up at Ted's home in Englewood, New Jersey on Christmas day, each of them with a case of gonorrhea so bad that Ted's mother had to take them to the emergency room before anyone had sat down to eat dinner. "There's a clinic in town for pregnant girls," Ted had said as they were driving down Interstate 85 two days before Christmas. "We can go there and get some shots before we go to my house. We should be OK." Ted thought that Jack looked, spoke and acted more normal that anyone else at the school so he had asked Jack to go home with him to prove to his parents that not all of his fellow college students were freaks. His mother would cry on the phone when she told Ted what his father was saying about his school.

Dink wasn't going anywhere for Christmas vacation. He had lots of pipes to make for presents. He loaned them his 1956 Citroen Deux Cheveax with a shifter that came straight out of the dashboard and a full top canvas roof. The car began acting funny around Kingston, New York, belching occasionally, losing power. By the time they got to Poughkeepsie, the engine was banging, huge clouds of smoke came out the rear end until finally there was an explosion and a fist-sized piece of metal ripped out of the engine, through the car hood and flew off into outer space. The car was small and very light. Ted and Jack pushed it down the highway, off an exit and into a gas station. "What the hell is that?" the mechanic asked. "A Citroen Deux Cheveau." Ted said. "Sorry," he said, "you'll have to push your douche bag chevy or whatever it is somewhere else. We don't work on those things."

That night, after pushing the car to three gas stations, they found one that had gone out of business but had left the bathroom doors unlocked. Jack took the ladies room, Ted the men's room and they each curled up on the floor out of the cold drizzle and tried to sleep. In the morning they found a young, energetic mechanic with a slight German accent who promised to find a used engine from a friend of his in White Plains who had a whole field full of oddball cars; Borgwards, Bandinis, Fauves, you know, he said, sheet like that. He would also fix the hole in the hood. They gave him $110, all their money except a twenty dollar bill, got his phone number and said they would check in after New Year's. They hitchhiked through New York City to Englewood. By the time they got there it was afternoon on Christmas day and the clinic was closed. Neither of them could pee without screaming. Ted's eyes were red and puffy. "Goodness gracious!" Edna Hilliard exclaimed. "What in Heaven's name happened to you boys?"

"I think it's something we ate, Mom. Can you take us to see a doctor?" Ted said.

The turkey had been stuffed, the table set and Ted's cousins were arriving. A station wagon full of scrubbed and well-dressed people with arm loads of wrapped presents had parked in the circular drive. Colonel Hilliard was bellowing from the doorstep about hippies and cowards as Edna Hilliard drove Ted and Jack off to the emergency room of the local hospital. In the waiting room, a nurse asked them what the problems were. Ted told her that they had been helping out on an Indian reservation where the health conditions were deplorable. He thought they might have got something there. Jack passed out in the hallway when he saw the nurse preparing a very large hypodermic needle. Both were kept overnight for care and observation.

"So," the doctor said to Jack in the morning, "what have you been doing over the last few weeks?"

Jack knew what the doctor was thinking. "I've been on an Indian Reservation teaching English. It was really unsanitary. I must have picked up something there."

"Yes," the doctor said, "I've heard they're like that. What reservation was this?"

"An Apache reservation in New Mexico." Jack said.

"Let me get this straight." the doctor, Benjamin R. Johnston, MD said, "You have a very serious case of gonorrhea infection in your urethral canal. Very dangerous. Your friend has the same serious infection in his urethral canal and in his eyes. You got yours, you say, on an Apache reservation in New Mexico and he got his on a Seminole reservation in the Everglades. Can you explain that?"

Jack was on the maintenance crew on weekends and vacations as part of his tuition payments to the school. He had decided to surprise the few students still at the college over Christmas break with a beautiful, mid-winter frolic in an outside heated swimming pool underneath a December full moon. He had found a manual in the maintenance shed that told how hot the water should be so no one gets scalded. He had turned on the pumps, the valves part way and the heaters full blast and slowly filled the pool to 104 degrees. It took a day and a half before it was full and hot. Almost thirty people showed up, some not even from the college, friends from town who had heard about it. Someone brought mescaline, many had smoking dope and a few kids dropped acid. As they swam and babbled and laughed and coupled in the polygynous way of youth, the gonorrhea bacteria blossomed in the giant hot Petrie dish, darting about and nestling deep into every available soft mucous membrane. Jack had forgotten to fill the chlorine hopper.

"Who was Cassandra?" Gwen sat cross-legged on the foot of their bed, reading his poetry. They lived together now, boyfriend and girlfriend at college in the same dorm room. "She was a girl who refused to have sex with a God and so the God gave her the gift of prophesy and cursed her at the same time by making it so no one would ever believe her." Gwyneth shuddered. I'm just the opposite, she thought. Nothing I say is true and everyone believes me. Peter Putz, Jack's physics professor and his advisor, walked by the open door, smiled and tossed them a short wave. "Class in ten minutes, Jack."

Gwyneth, alone in the room, had finished reading every poem and looking at every piece of paper. Nothing. No list. Nothing that looked like one. The next day she walked alone down the hill to town and called Agent Hancock. First, she told him, Eldridge Cleaver and David Dellinger are coming at the invitation of the Students for a Democratic Society to give lectures and to focus the 'radical energy' as they are calling it. Lists of names in Jack Duncan's papers? Nothing, she told him. Keep listening to things Jack talks about, he said. I can't keep listening, she told him. Jack is leaving for India in a week. Where, Gwyneth, in India is he going and why is he going there? He is going to Coimbatore as an exchange student. I don't know why. When you're our age, Mr. Hancock, there is no why. There is no because. Things just are.

154

President Binder had found Jack after class and, in his office, had told him that the school was going to close. Various investigations were beginning concerning health issues, political activities and drugs. There was no way the school could withstand the scrutiny. It was simply far too radical for the politicians to tolerate. He told him that Peter Putz was setting up a 'student exchange' status for a college in India for him but if the school closed first, his student deferment would be terminated and the Selective Service would come after him. He told him Ted Hilliard had been inducted but he suspected if he looked around overseas, he might find him. Israel, he thought. "Go," Dick Binder said, "you're a good student with a great future. Go find an education." He opened his personal checkbook, wrote Jack a check for a thousand dollars and said, "Don't tell anyone I've done this, especially my wife or your girlfriend."

Jack and Gwyneth's parting that night had been like a piece of whole cloth ripped into two parts. Tearing sounds and bodies pulling in opposite directions as fibers of friendship separated until there were two cloths. Each piece, after the anguish, was a fine piece of fabric by itself, if a bit tattered and frayed at the edges. They both knew it.

IN THE BIGG HOUSE

The prison cafeteria was as loud as a rock concert. Steel tables, steel trays, steel bowls clanging, sounds banging off the solid concrete walls in the milieu of two hundred men out of their cells, barking, laughing, growling almost as one multi-headed beast.

Dwight Duncan was in the last year of his three year sentence. Elroy Jenkins, Popcorn's older brother, had twenty four more to go. Elroy didn't look at Dwight when he was talking. He looked straight ahead or down at his plate of food, talking with his mouth full. Once in a while he would look across the lunch room at Fred Johnson, a black man from Chicago, a literate saboteur as he liked to describe himself. Fred was sitting next to Jeremiah Pickford, a University of Michigan English student, son of a millionaire oil baron, arrested for throwing a Molotov cocktail into the file room at the Selective Service Office in Ann Arbor. Occasionally, Fred would nod to Elroy.

"When I'm on the outside, I'm doing things. I'm organizing. I'm talking. I'm loving and I'm trying to keep from getting my ass shot off by the pigs. My mind and body are working, pulled along by my soul. But you know what? When them great steel doors slam shut behind me and my body's locked in here, those dumb sonsabitches think everything about who I am is going to shut down; gonna stop and I'm gonna lie around wishing I hadn't done any of things I did. Oh how wrong they are. When my eyes see those thick steel bars, my spirit soars because I know that whatever I did pissed them off and that means I was getting' somewhere. So I keep working, I keep talking and I keep organizing right under their goddamned noses. You get me?"

Dwight, sitting next to Elroy, didn't look at him either. He just kept eating his rice with spam chunks and gravy, drinking his glass of powdered milk. "What do you want?" Dwight asked.

"I'll catch you tomorrow. You working in the library?" Elroy asked.

"Yes, I am. Two to five." Dwight said.

Warden Hughes had heard that Dwight had defended himself in federal district court and, without notes, with extraordinary recall of the law, had presented a powerful defense. He knew he narrowly lost in the Supreme Court. Out of deference to Dwight's clear intellectual capacity, and because the warden secretly agreed with the young man's position, he was assigned the plum job of "campus librarian" working under the watchful eye of the local pastor.

The prison library was a twelve foot square alcove off the hallway beside the clinic, originally designed, but never used, as a "waiting room." The alcove had bookshelves on all three walls and a small desk with two chairs facing each other in the middle. Dwight had taped a hand lettered sign out front that said "The Bigg House" because the pastor of the jail had found money from the Ford Foundation to buy books and put up shelving. His name was Fr. Robert Bigg, a former Jesuit priest who had been relieved of both his collar and his parish in Boston for serious transgressions of the holy vow of celibacy. Excessive and persistent fornication with various wives and daughters of upstanding, often well connected, tithe paying Irish Catholic parishioners. He had been instructed to lead non-denominational prayer meetings and administer counseling of the spirit to the inmates of this prison in exchange for room and board. Somehow the warden, a practical man, a man good with a tight budget, a Methodist on Sundays, had, after a phone call from Archbishop Cushing of Boston, managed to submit the application to the Department of Corrections omitting the banished part, actually omitting the entire Jesuit part and only including all of Father Bigg's extensive religious education and immensely important social work. His efforts in providing help and solace to the disadvantaged; like Thelma Byrne who confessed a desire to commit suicide because she couldn't get on the high school cheerleading team, to the suffering, like Gwyneth O'Neal who carried the hideous burden of passion clamped tight down by a strict society, to the lonely, like Mrs. Bridget O'Malley, who was perpetually distraught because her husband was always away on business and to the deformed, like Eloise who had never heard any admonitions pertaining to weakness of the flesh because she was stone deaf. Everybody liked Father Bigg. He would articulate, or in the case of Eloise, gesticulate, how important it was to effectively use the tools God gave us to relieve the suffering of others. Those girls and all the other girls would giggle at this.

For the good Father, his job at the penitentiary was to have been a short penance. "I am a sinner, Dear Lord, punish me so that my soul might once again be clean." But these adjurations to God were always in the present tense. There had been no measurable progress. His philandering continued nearly unabated except for the eight hours a day he was inside the walls of prison. When he stopped by the library, he and Dwight would play a game of chess and test each other on their recollection of historical data. Dwight still bore the blight of youthful acne. Serious, like an American Strelnakov. Father Bigg was quite the opposite; round and ruddy red-head, startlingly blue eyes and a thick lipped mouth. However different they were in demeanor, bearing and belief, they shared a great respect for each other. He confided in Dwight, in considerable detail, both his transgressions and his deep desire to return to the fold, to once again be wrapped in the pious cloth. But, in a strong punctuation to his confessions, he also noted he thoroughly enjoyed his escapades and if he could put off an irrevocable renunciation of this bestial behavior until the last possible moment that his entreaties might still receive divine forgiveness, all the better.

"My goodness," Dwight said, "you're the modern day equivalent of Saint Augustine, the 'Pious Procrastinator.' Also referred to by qualified historians as a notorious sex-addict. Wasn't it Augustine, talking to his God, who said, 'But I, a wretched young man, even more wretched than in my youth, begged you for chastity, yet said, 'Make me chaste but not yet! Give me chastity, Dear God, but not yet!"

"Yes, yes, yes, he did say that. And yes, he had the same problem I have. How astute of you to recall Saint Augustine. The Temptation of Passion overpowers our Faith. We, me and the Saint, that is, keep putting off our inevitable chastity until the last pollen has been sucked from the earthly flowers and then, and only then, become chaste and pious once again." the Father exclaimed, clapping his hands. A prison guard walked by, listened for a moment, shook his head and walked on.

Dwight said, "Augustine also opined that we are in the same class as beasts. That every action in animal life is concerned with seeking bodily pleasure and avoiding pain. I am locked in this prison for three years because I find it more pleasurable than being free as a result of hypocrisy. You,

Father, must simply find young girls sweeter, more tender, more succulent than God." Dwight smiled at his own wit.

"Blasphemous!" he shouted, "But....but.... do continue."

"All procrastination is nothing more than a subliminal assessment of pleasure versus pain. Perhaps," Dwight continued, "you might want to consider, if you'll pardon the pun, gradual withdrawal. You know, slow down a little. Some moderation. Start getting ready to do, in the near future, what your soul knows you ought to do today."

"Humm, Humm," the priest considered. "No....Nope.....Augustine also said that complete abstinence is easier than perfect moderation. You're right, Dwight, I have enjoyed enough of the pleasures of passion. I am going to schedule a talk with God in the next few days. That's exactly what I'm going to do." His burden lifted, his eyes twinkling with a mixture of mischief and promise, he patted Dwight on the shoulder. "But don't you mention this or any similar recantation you might to make to God before I do. That might spoil it." he laughed.

"Father, you forget, I am an existential atheist. To me, there is neither a yesterday nor a tomorrow. There is only now; you and me, here. And me talking to God? I can't talk to someone who doesn't exist. People might think I'm crazy. And, I would guess that with all the murder and mayhem going on in Viet Nam, your God might be quite busy."

"By Jove, you're probably right about that. Thank you Dwight. I'm going to give it couple of weeks," he said walking out into the hallway with a definite bounce to his step. He bumped into Elroy as he stepped out, his round head bouncing off Elroy's chest. "Oh, I'm sorry Elroy, I apologize. I was just caught up in thinking about Saint Augustine."

"My," he said looking up at Elroy, "you are quite large." Father Bigg bounced a bit down the corridor, then stopped. He cocked his head as if in thought, then inched his way back towards the alcove, listening.

Elroy liked the library because there were no cameras pointed into the alcove and the guards in that wing were inside the foyer of the clinic. He came to talk to Dwight about smuggling a verse out of the prison.

"Why don't you get Jerry Pickford to do whatever it is you want me to do?" Dwight asked.

"Cause ain't nobody never come see him. His family lives in Texas. He don't have no brothers or sisters. He's got no relatives to come see him. His father is a Texas millionaire who thinks his son is a communist. Jerry's been helpin' us out though. He's a hell of a writer. He knows a lot of people out there but they can't come here cause they're on the bad side of the law. But you, Dwight, your mama comes to see you. By the way we figure, she comes the first Tuesday of every other month. She does, don't she?"

"Yes, she does," Dwight said.

"You got a good mama. That means she'll be here tomorrow." Elroy said.

"That's right. Now just what exactly do you want me to do?" Dwight asked.

"Your mama writes poetry don't she?"

"Yes, she does, Elroy. What are you getting at?"

Elroy leaned across the table, his voice low. "You been a member of the Students for a Democratic Society when you was at college. That means to me and it means to the other brothers in here and in prisons around the country that you and other smart white boys ought to understand the troubles we Black Panthers have in our struggle to bust off the racist chains of the fascist state. You ought to understand that and we think you probably wouldn't mind helpin' us out. You followin' me?"

Dwight was seeing the beginnings of a trap. He and Jeremiah Pickford and five or six other college educated radicals sitting in the jail cells at the penitentiary were treated well by the black inmates. Hands-off. That was definitely not the case with rapists and kidnappers; not even drug dealers or whoremongers who made the mistake of taking advantage of black women and children. If they crossed the Panthers, they ended up getting hauled down to the infirmary on a gurney. But the "goodwill" the radicals enjoyed could evaporate very quickly. "What do you want?" Dwight asked.

"We have a poem, just a little poem that needs to be delivered to a friend of ours on the outside. A friend of ours who loves poetry. Reads it and writes it all the time. Loves the shit. That's all. Just a little poem. We want you to get it to your mama so she can mail it for us. You know nobody in here can mail anything out unless it's a letter all about how sweet the guards are and how God-Almighty tasty the spam is. So we gotta have your mama mail it for us. She's a poet. The guards checkin' her in and out won't ever even know what it is. That's not much, is it Dwight? Just a poem." Elroy smiled.

That was it. Just as surely as if he had put his foot into jaws of a bear trap. "What's in this little poem that you can't put in a letter?" Dwight asked.

Elroy stared at Dwight. Far off down the hall a steel door opened and clanged shut. A basketball thumped on the concrete court outside and a netless hoop rattled. The shot missed. Somebody in the clinic screamed "Jesus H. Christ" when a doctor stuck his rubber gloved finger in the guy looking for an enlarged prostate. Then it was quiet. "If I give you a general idea of what it is, you gonna help us?"

"No. Not with my mother." Dwight looked straight at him. Not blinking.

"You fuckin' coward. You fuckin' white boy coward." Elroy growled.

"No, Elroy, I'm not a coward. Neither are you. We, you and I alike, didn't get in here by being cowards. The cops don't put cowards in jail. What's in it for them? There's no statement of justice there. They slap them silly, beat them up and make them work for the man. Tell me what's in this poem, generally, if that's all you feel you can do. Tell me that much and I tell you if I can help you get it out of here."

"Names," he said, "Names of people who we think can organize a white movement to work with the Panthers to achieve our shared goal, a common goal. That's what it is." Elroy's black slang, his Ebonic grammer was gone. Dwight realized he was talking to a very bright, very competent man. "I'm not showing it to you until you agree to get it out of here. Because if you read it, if you know what's in it and if they find that out, they will beat it out of you. Then they will know what's up and our friend out there won't ever get it and our shared goals will get seriously derailed. Capiche?"

"I'll do it. I'll ask my younger brother to come see me. He's also a poet. I'll make it so he can get it mailed."

"Whole damn family full of poets, huh? Smart bunch."

Elroy took a sheet of paper out of his shirt pocket, unfolded it and handed it to Dwight.

164

THE POEM

BRINGING IT ALL BACK HOME

there is no
weather where i am, deep down
underground in a bomb bunker
hunkered below my parent's home,
incubating my mother's nightmare.
never again will i care to sleep upstairs
in the mansion of my childhood
or hold my favorite bear,
a round brown
teddy, gold buttons for eyes,
silk shirt.
the spell of china's finest,
the damning spell cast on western greed
by the silk of ancient
cathay will curse on and on and on.

can our land be fresh again?
will airs from the east
blow soft and clean or will a northern
gale howl and

tear robins red-breasted
from their ancestral nests?
i am subterranean,
sick at heart for my home now lost to greed
i sing loud,
i envision stars above me.
i clutch a makeshift
mike, clone sky above me,
circle plastic icons
of contemporary culture
in a round ring about me and
ignite them singing
jimmy d! jimmy d! as I
burn a dean down and elvis melts.

even the temple of
diana oughten possess the power
to wash our monstrous guilt away.
but i climb out now
into the fray
like the beanstalk man
jack, jacob's ladder up and out
to find my path, to
mark ruddy roads ahead

i need sun to see it right
i'm off to spain for boots
of spanish leather.
i need to eat with
estefano, tappas in a bar
and then to france
to stroke the sculpted bronze of maceo
jefferies joans of ark and jesus
and then back here
to fight, to free my home of fear.

"Odd poem, Elroy. Sounds like it was written by a depressed teenager who listens to a lot of Bob Dylan. I don't see any names in here." Dwight got a book off the shelf and handed it to Elroy. "Make it look like you came here to do something in the furtherance of your education."

Elroy grinned. "Don't see any names. Listens to a lot of Bob Dylan. Damn! Looks like we got ourselves a real pearl here. How long will it take you to memorize it?"

Elroy didn't know about Dwight's perfect 800 scores on both the English and Math SAT tests in High School. He didn't know about the speeches delivered at age twelve with no notes to serious historical societies on the social organization of the Mayans. He didn't know Dwight could read five hundred words a minute nor did Elroy know that he had memorized the entirety of the Declaration of Independence in an afternoon. Dwight still knew it all. He hadn't forgotten any of it. Elroy didn't know all of that but, when they were searching around for the right venue, Father Bigg had told him that Dwight had the finest mind and best memory of anyone he had ever known.

"Give me twenty minutes." Dwight said. Elroy leaned back in his chair and began reading Machiavelli's *The Prince*. Ten minutes later Dwight handed him the paper back. "Got it." he said. "Who's it get sent to?"

"Gail Howland, care of, Hotel Gulhane, Istanbul, Turkey."

"OK, Elroy, I got it." Dwight recognized the name Gail Howland; northern gale howl and....and then....Mark Ruddy roads ...Mark Rudd. He got it and didn't say a thing to Elroy.

Every other month on the first Tuesday, just like Elroy had said, Anna Duncan would drive with her friend in her VW Beetle from New Hampshire, across Vermont, New York, the top western corner of Pennsylvania, Ohio and up to the Federal Penitentiary. Her friend's aunt lived in Toledo and she would visit there while Anna went to prison to see her son. They always stayed in the same hotel, The Lake Erie Inn, halfway through the trip. On the porch overlooking the wide water, it smelled a little like dead fish but that was OK. It reminded them of the ocean.

On this visit, Anna told Dwight that his brother Jack had been accepted into a college in southern India as an exchange student. He was going to study linguistics. He was leaving in a week or so. Dwight said, "Mother, please tell Jack to come see me. I really want to see him before he goes." he said. "He might be gone a long time. Tell him to bring all his poetry so he can read me some. I really, really like his poetry," he said. He asked her if she could call Jack tonight from Toledo so he had enough time to hitchhike here and back before he went overseas. "Yes," she said, "I'll do that. I'm sure he will come. He loves you." That was something mothers always said about their children with the often vain hope that it was true. In Dwight's mind, there was no genetic disposition towards love, whether it be for a mother or a father or a sibling. It wasn't that he and Jack didn't like each other, they just didn't know each other very well. Mother didn't need to know any of this and even if he had told her his thoughts, she wouldn't have heard them. That's how she was. Mother never wanted to hear anything that made her world less perfect.

"Hey, Dwight, how are you?" Jack asked. Jack thought it a stupid question because if the answer was anything other than "I'm good," there was nothing anybody could do about it.

"I'm good." Dwight said. "Did you hitch hike?"

"Yeah. It was good. Three rides. The last guy I think was a pervert. He had a pink Cadillac with those things that hang on the mirror that smell like perfume. I didn't tell him exactly where I was going and when he drove by the main gate to this place and I said, 'This is good.' he let me out and sped off. He was a fat bald guy who kept looking at me. Creepy." Jack said.

"I can't even remember what it feels like to be out there, going wherever you want to go." Dwight said.

"I wasn't going wherever I wanted to go." Jack said. "I was coming here because you asked me to."

"Right. Sorry." Dwight looked at his brother and smiled. The kid was tough.

They sat in plastic chairs leaning their elbows on a stainless steel window sill, separated by a solid bullet proof glass panel. There was a telephone on either side. A regular black telephone that they used to talk and listen to each other. The room was pastel green, like the whole prison, like all government buildings. Supposed to be soothing but actually created a strong feeling of nausea. Like nobody cared. Like this particular color of paint was cheap. No one cared at all whether or not anyone liked the color. "Do you think the government owns a giant green paint factory?" Jack asked looking around.

"Did you bring your poetry?" Dwight responded.

"Yeah, I did. Mom told me you wanted to hear some of it. That's really nice. I appreciate that." Jack said.

"Did they search you when you came in?" Dwight asked.

"Yeah they did. They thumbed through it but when I told them I just wanted to read you some, they said fine."

"Do you have a pencil?" Dwight asked.

"Right here." Jack pulled a pencil out of the folder of poetry.

"Read me a couple, would you?"

"What do you want to hear? Some of it has heavy Greek Mythology woven through it. I call that the 'classical stuff'. Others are more like free verse. I call those the 'modern stuff'. I've never been really comfortable with them because it's so easy to write a bad poem, a poem that doesn't bring up in the reader's mind the image that you intended. It's too loose for my taste. Some others are constructed to be sonnets or sestinas. Almost like an exercise in structuring, like a verbal painting. I call those the 'method stuff'. What do you think?" Jack had his poetry, all hand written, bundled in three parts with big paper clips.

"Whatever you want," Dwight said. "You choose."

Jack was wondering what was going on. Why he had to hitchhike six hundred miles to read his brother poems that his brother, it seemed, didn't even care about. He picked two. One called "Cassandra" about a girl who wouldn't sleep with Apollo so he gave her the gift of prophecy and cursed her because no one would ever believe her. And he read another, a sestina about the waves pounding on the beach. Like horse's hooves.

"The horse's hooves, the pounding," Jack said, "that reminds me, I forgot to tell you. We had a big party up in Madbury. The cops came, pounded on the door and hauled us off to the jailhouse. They didn't find anything so they let us go but, here's the weird thing, when we were getting booked, they searched the whole house, every single piece of paper in it. I don't know if they found anything but they wrecked the whole place."

"Did they show you a search warrant?"

"No."

"Feds." Dwight said. "FBI. They seem to think the Fourth Amendment doesn't apply to them. Are you going back there before you to Europe?"

"No. My college is closing and my student deferment is going to expire. I'm hitching from here to New York, sleeping somewhere overnight and flying to Luxembourg in the morning. Then, I don't know where. I'll see what happens. Think about what I need to do about the Army. I need time.

Do you have any idea what the FBI might have been looking for?"

Dwight paused for a long time, looking at his brother through the bulletproof glass, tapping his fingers on the stainless steel shelf. "No, no idea. Now I'd like you to write down a poem that a friend of mine wrote. If you could write it down and, when you're over there, mail it to his girlfriend, that would be great. We can't send any stuff out of here except censored letters to relatives and those two had been writing poetry for each other for ten years before they locked him up. I guess that's how they say 'I love you'. Would you do that for me?"

"Sure, Dwight, I'm happy to help your friend." Jack turned over one of his poems to the blank side and said, "Shoot." Dwight recited the poem slowly and distinctly, giving his brother ample time to write. When it was done Dwight said, "I don't want you to write this down. Just remember it. This is who it gets sent to. It goes to Gail Howland at the Hotel Gulhane in Istanbul, Turkey. Gulhane. G.U.L.H.A.N.E. Can you remember that? Say it back." Jack said it back. "I can remember that. Pretty dismal love poem. There must be other reasons they like each other." When he left, the guard thumbed through his papers and asked him what he had been writing. "A love poem." Jack said. He pulled the poem out and showed it to him. "Oh." the guard said and pushed the buzzer lock on the steel door. The names the FBI was searching for had been sprung free.

PART THREE

ON FOREIGN GROUND

"Courage is a special kind of knowledge; the knowledge of how to fear what ought to be feared and how not to fear what ought not to be feared."

—David Ben-Gurion

THE CASBAH

Sean O'Neal, now Joe Cole of Ashville, North Carolina, had been driven from the Strafford County jail in New Hampshire to Logan Airport, given a shower in the security officers' locker room and put on a plane to Madrid. He took the train, the Estrella de Estrecho, The Star of the Straits, to Gibraltar and ferried across to Tangier on the North Moroccan coast. He had checked into the Hotel Al-Sakim a day ahead of his planned meeting with someone, he had no idea whom, someone sent by the FBI. The hotel, on Rue d' Marcel overlooked the beach on the Atlantic shore. A clear day and the Rock of Gibraltar could be seen fifteen miles across the Straits. On the portico off the reception area, nestled around the Moorish columns under the clay tile roof, Berbers sipped mint tea poured from elegant Moroccan pots and linen clad tourists sipped gin and tonics. The atmosphere was largely unchanged from the not too distant days when this portico, as well as most others in Tangier, was a viper's nest of international intrigue. The legendary home of smugglers and spies; watching the lips of Nazis, listening to the mutterings of gun runners, plotting the assassination of Franco. Ginsberg, Kerouc and Burroughs concocting magnificent literature of

175

disaffection. Jean Genet, poet, playwright, deviant, thief and vagabond is buried in the Spanish Cemetery south of town. All of this around these columns.

Sean sat alone, comfortable, drinking cold Heineken beer, wondering what it was that Special Agent Hancock wanted him to do. He had no choice but to do it, whatever it was, lest his sister, mother and father suffer harm. He could run and hide if he did it now because he really didn't know anything yet. Maybe they would let them be. But not likely, certainly not after tomorrow. Tomorrow he would know enough to be dangerous.

At precisely noon, Sean was drinking a cup of strong North African coffee called 'Moroccan whiskey'. He had walked through the town from daybreak, watched the boats at the port ready for debarkation, listened to the Berber vendors set up their wares at the bazaar outside the Casbah, the old center of town. He had showered, shaved, eaten and readied himself to meet whomever he was going to meet at noon. He was unaware that he had been followed the entire morning by a retired CIA operative. The Agent had retired from the Agency two years ago and moved with his wife, Virginie Deneuve, to her family's home near Marseille on the banks of the Durance. From time to time he did favors for his friends in the States or in the French Government but he mostly tended the family vineyards.

"Mr. Cole?" The man was tall, tanned, well built, in his seventies with close cropped white hair and a hard stare. "Yes, I'm Joe Cole," Sean said rising, extending his hand. "Please sit down." The man shook his hand, sat, signaled to the waiter and asked, in French, for a glass of tonic water with lime and ice.

"Agent Hancock has asked me to deliver something to you. He has asked that you unseal it, read it, memorize it, reseal it and hand it back to me. I will destroy it. I have no idea what its contents are, what it pertains to, nor do I want to know. If you could simply read it and commit it to memory without making any comments, I would appreciate it. Agent Hancock said that if you speak to me or anyone else about the contents of this envelope, in his words, 'your deal is off.' Is this acceptable to you?"

"Yes," Sean said returning his stare. The retired agent reached in to the inside pocket of his white linen suit coat and handed Sean an envelope.

Typed on blank paper.

"In Tangier, purchase headwear, cloaks and sandals similar to those worn by the Berbers. Take the train to Oujda. Arrange for a room by the month on the southern side of town in the Hotel Royal. Room with a phone. From this hotel you will be entering Algeria. Do not cross the Algerian border with your American passport. Do not bring it with you. Take the train (Casablanca-Algiers Express) to Algiers. Return the same way. There are three Black Panthers that we know of in Algiers. We don't know where they are. Find them. Neutralize them. 1) A Sub-Saharan African, short, bald, goatee, very dark, almost purple skin with a large head, an attorney. 2. A Black American basketball player, full beard, very tall, very deep voice. 3. Black American, thin, pronounced scar on right cheek, Afro hair, talks with a lisp, an author, playwright. Do not stay long on each trip to Algiers. It is dangerous for us. Return by train every few days. It may take a while to find them. Keep at it until you succeed. Call Tuesdays, 8 PM your time. Your sister and parents are fine."

He read it again, folded it and handed it back. The retired agent put it back in the envelope, took out a lighter and lit it on fire, got up, dropped the burning envelope in a large brass ashtray at the outer railing and watched it burn. Then he poked the ashes around with his finger. People looked, waiters looked, no one said a thing. They had seen this before. Hundreds of documents had been burned in that urn. That's probably why it was there. When the agent came back he handed Sean another envelope and left. No good byes. No good lucks. In the second envelope was a French passport under the name Jacques Botier. It had a picture of Sean taken before he went to Viet Nam. The photo had sat framed on his sister's bureau.

So that it what it is. I am a murderer. I am a murderer of black people. My government trained me to kill the Vietnamese and I did that. Then I killed an old man and a little girl and they made me go away. And then I killed a man who raped my little sister and they had me. They had me. Killing for them on their terms is fine. Killing for me on my terms is not. They own me. There is no arguing that and there is no way out of it. But who am I going to be when this is all done? Will it ever be done? Will they ever trust that I won't tell and let me go back to where I came from? How could they trust that? Does that mean that if I do this, if I kill these people, they will have to kill me? Maybe so, maybe not. They have my family, maybe I need their family in the same position. You told me to do this. I did it. Anything bad happens to me, something really bad happens to your family. Even Steven. Walk away. Go back to what I was. Go back to who I was. I was a baseball player. I just wanted to help my country. Popcorn was a baseball player. He just wanted to help his country. What the fuck happened? Can anybody ever go back to who they were. No. No they can't. No more than a duck can go back to being a duckling. I wonder, is one of these people I'm supposed to kill Popcorn's brother? Would Popcorn have a problem with that? Maybe, maybe not. He seemed to think, just like the FBI guy, that they were going to kill a lot of innocent people and try to ruin the country. I'll never know. Popcorn won't either. So screw it. Do it. My country will be proud of me. Right. Sure they will. If my country is proud of me for doing this, I need a different country. "Waiter, a Heineken beer please."

On a silver tray, with a fancy white linen napkin draped over her arm, pretending to be the highest class waitress of all, a girl brought Sean a cold Heineken beer. She flicked the blond wisp of hair from her eyelash, tucking it behind her ear. "Thirsty?" she asked. "Very." he said. "I've been watching you. You're brooding. You're all inside yourself, looking off at nothing with a scowl on your brow. The afternoon is too beautiful for that. Nothing can be more important than a bright sun, a beautiful ocean and a soft breeze, can it?" She was still standing. Sean pointed to the chair. She sat, crossing her legs allowing her skirt to ride up on her thighs, leaned on the table putting her chin in her hand, looking straight at him. "You are too young to so disturbed," she said, adjusting her bra strap at the shoulder. "How old do you have to be for it to be OK to be disturbed?" Sean asked. "Old enough to never be able to make right the things you've done wrong." She shook her head a bit, quickly, then smiled, the lock of hair falling back from behind her ear. Dimples and a long narrow neck. "Want to take a walk on the beach?" she asked. "Are you picking me up?" Sean leaned forward, his eyebrows up. "Yes," she said standing up, offering her hand.

They walked hand in hand, barefoot on the sand, saying nothing. Then Sean stopped. "Why are you here? What are you doing?"

"My husband brings me here once a year or so for a 'vacation'. This time he's gone off with a Bulgarian to Israel to buy guns for tribes in the Congo, or some such thing. Or maybe the other way around. Maybe he went to the Congo with an Israeli, I really don't know. But he is definitely old enough to be disturbed, and goddamned well ought to be. I am his fourth wife and I married him because he had lots of

179

money, two beautiful houses and led an exciting life. So exciting there was no room for love. So I'm here, with you, and I'm lonely. What about you? What are you doing here?"

"Well, I sold out to a man a while ago and I'm just here to see how much it might cost to buy myself back. That's all."

For such a thin thing, she was a tiger. Sean got up before sunrise. His back had scratches from his waist to his shoulders and bite marks on his chest and neck. There were even deep tooth marks on his kneecap. He vaguely remembered pain in his leg about the time someone in the adjoining room was banging on the wall and shouting angrily in some Slavic language. Her ornately carved onyx dope pipe, inlaid with gold, sat on the dresser beside a fist-sized hunk of hashish. His head hurt. He left for the early train to Oujda before she awoke.

At the border, the soldiers came. On each car on the train they checked passports then stationed themselves in front of the sliding steel doors that led to the next car. They wore green battle fatigues, jack boots and carried submachine guns held chest high. Around the waist was a leather belt with handcuffs, an eight inch knife and a 9MM Soviet made holstered pistol. The revolution establishing independence from France was over. The government was military. Algeria had sent soldiers to fight Israel in the six-day war and expelled all the Jews from their country. Some had made their way to the Promised Land. Some to Morocco. Most had gone to France where they had been offered automatic citizenship. The French had remained neutral in the Six-Day War but had given tacit approval of Algeria's position and tacit disapproval of the United States and Israel. Even though Algeria had recently, violently thrown off the French colonial bonds, the countries remained close. Not so of any country which had lent support to the Jews in 1967. Diplomatic relations with the United States had been totally severed.

There were only four Americans in all of Algeria. Three Black Panthers and Sean, traveling as Jacques Botier. He looked every bit like a French ex-patriot doing business in an Arab land. He wore a simple wool djellaba, the traditional hooded cloak, and a pair of soleless goat skin shoes, ankle high. He, like most foreigners, did not wear a turban.

From the station, on this first day of hunting, Sean walked to the French section then down a wide boulevard by theaters, museums and cathedrals. He was the assassin looking for his prey in a city of one and a half million people. Where were they? On the train he had framed four possible questions that might lead him close. Might lead him to the area or neighborhood in which they lived. Then it would be a beggar or a child or a neighbor who might tell him more for a small amount of money. All three Panthers spoke English; they might have needed something translated. One was very tall and might have bought some western clothes. One was a playwright and might frequent a theater. One was an attorney and might have bought books or newspapers.

"Excuse me," Sean spoke to the clothier in French, "I have a friend who is very tall. 210 centimeters. He asked me to buy him a pair of dress slacks. He said he had bought clothes here before and you might be able to help me. He is a black American. Do you remember him?"

"No Monsieur, your friend must be mistaken. We have no clothes like that." He laughed. "Those trousers would come up to my neck."

"Maybe he got the wrong store. Is there another clothier here who might have this apparel?"

"Yes, you might try 'Le Monde d'Vogue. It is two blocks on the right."

The last train to Morocco left in an hour. He would come back and start again.

Two days later a young clerk remembered selling not a pair of pants but a pair of shoes to man like that. He remembered because it was the biggest pair of shoes he had ever seen. The shoes weren't in the store, they don't sell shoes of that size. They were in the window as a sales gimmick. European size 51 dress shoes, made in South Africa he told Sean with his hands held out eighteen inches apart. He whistled. Miraculously, they fit the man perfectly. And yes, he had been with a short, bald very dark man with a goatee. He didn't know where they lived. He had never seen them again.

A week had passed but Sean at least knew they were there. Day by day, week by week he would dig away at the dirt until he found the bones.

"Le Negres" by Jean Genet was playing at a small theater in an alley off the main boulevard. It smelled of lamb or goat. The seating was pews, like a church and the stage was framed by a Moorish arch, garishly tiled in pinks and oranges. Behind the stage in the changing room, Sean found a man; young and muscular, bearded with a shaved head, full lips and large black eyes. He was striped to the waist sitting in a small alcove by a lead-glass window counting a pile of coins, putting them, plink by plink into an earthen jug.

"Yes, I have seen him once or twice. He sits in the back by the door, always looking this way and that, never sitting still. I don't know his name. He doesn't speak French or Arabic. When he speaks, he speaks in English. I don't know what he says. He always gives me twice the admission fee. I don't know where he lives but when he leaves I have watched him walk that way down the alley and up the hill," the man said gesturing up towards the old city, the Casbah. "Why do you want to know?"

"I am a friend of his wife. She asked me to send him her love."

"I am sorry I spoke to you. You are a liar. That man would not have a wife."

'Watch him walk down the alley'. No wonder he looks this way and that way, never sitting still, Sean thought as he walked up the hill into the old city. A homosexual in a Communist Muslim country. It could hardly be more dangerous. The government must be protecting him, but only to a certain extent. If he were found cavorting with an Arab boy he would surely be staked spread-eagle in the desert, covered with honey and left for the ants and buzzards. Or worse, put in prison.

Three weeks, dozens of beggars at the bazaar, dozens of children, dozens of shopkeepers and two thousand dinar later, Sean began to find them. The big guy was first. He was easiest. Nobody who had seen him forgot him or his feet. The little man with the goatee also made an impression on the children. They were afraid of him. The homosexual playwright was the hardest. He was secretive and very seldom walked the streets. It turned out he had a passion for candy; baklava and sweetened citrus rinds that he would buy from a cart that came through the neighborhood early in the morning. It was a huge cart, six feet long with racks and racks of candies and a storage bin underneath. Everything in the Casbah was delivered by cart. The streets, built five hundred years ago, were too narrow for cars or trucks. Sean watched the men. He followed them. He knew where they ate, what they bought, who they talked to. He knew that the young, blond Slav who went into the playwright's house at midnight and left before sunrise was a clerk at the German embassy. Every evening at about seven a soldier would come to each house. The soldier would knock, go in for a minute or so, then leave. They each had their foible. The playwright had his German boy and his candy. The basketball player had girls down in the port at the seamen's bars; the bars that were cordoned off from the rest of the city, left only to the sailors and stevedores who came from around the world. The attorney had his communist friends who met in cafes in the French section. They talked into the early hours of the morning; mostly in French, sometimes Russian, sometimes German, translations going every which way. Then they walked home, stern faced, clutching manuscripts. Sean knew where any one of them would likely be at any given time.

In his hotel in Oujda, Sean called Hancock at 8 PM every Tuesday. Finally he could say, 'I have found them. I have found them all but there are still too many people nearby for me to do anything. There have been some kind of disturbances and the streets are full of soldiers. I'll go back, but I'm all set up now'. Good, Hancock said. Do it. Get it done.

ON THE STEPS OF THE MOSQUE

The day after leaving his brother in the federal penitentiary and saying good bye to his mother, Jack paid at the counter with traveler's cheques for a ticket on Icelandic Airways out of JFK, bound for Luxembourg. Most of the passengers were young. Most male passengers had scraggly beards and long hair. The girls wore sandals and long wrap-around skirts. After the plane had been airborn for an hour or more, the kid sitting beside Jack asked the stewardess what laws applied when an airplane was in international air space. The laws of the country in which the plane is registered, she told him. In this case, Iceland. He asked her if marijuana was legal in Iceland. She nodded. Can I smoke? She said she'd have to ask the captain. When she came back she told him the captain said small amounts for personal use are not prosecuted. Just don't sell it to the person sitting next to you and go to the smoking section in the back. She was Nordic beautiful; blond hair braided and wrapped up on the top her head held in place with a large fish bone, pink complexion, wide eyes, full lips, an embroidered blouse and a tight white skirt slightly slit up the side covering a mere fraction of her long legs. She looked as though she had just emerged, mermaid like, from a pristine glacial pool. An hour later, most of the passengers, including Jack and two businessmen in suits, were totally stoned. There is, it seems, a significant difference between smoking dope with your feet on the ground at sea level and smoking dope at 30,000 feet in the air in a pressurized cabin. Totally stoned. Laughing uproariously, hugging strangers and wolfing down whatever food they brought on board and whatever goodies the stewardess would bring. Two young boys had brought their guitars in carry-on. They tuned up and played "Puff the Magic Dragon". The whole plane sang about Little Jackie Paper and kids waved their Zig-Zags.

Customs in Luxembourg was sobering. Not that the Luxembourgies were mean-spirited; they weren't. If a bit staid and formal in their actions, they were quite liberal in their social outlook but an entire plane full of young Americans stoned on marijuana was somewhat appalling to the round-hatted, blue suited officials. They were stern and curt. "What are you going to do in Luxembourg?" they asked Jack. Something needled in the back of his mind about Istanbul. "I'm going to hitchhike to Paris and then take the train to Istanbul." he said. "Good, do that today if you don't mind." Jack actually had no idea what he was going to do except to get to an Indian Embassy to find his visa for India. Istanbul sounded good as it rolled off his very thick, very dry tongue. The love letter from his brother's friend in jail. That was what was supposed to go to Istanbul. I'll take it there, he thought. Why not?

Jack walked out the airport doors, around the curved access road and stuck out his thumb. The first car by was a little blue Peugeot. It stopped. The Icelandic Airways captain opened the passenger door. "Hop in." Jack slung his backpack into the rear seat and got in.

186

TONY IRONS

"Where are you going?" the captain asked, putting his hand on Jack's leg. "Paris. It's really important I get there," Jack responded stiffening at the touch. "Well, you're welcome to come to my place tonight; shower up, get some food, get a good night's sleep and head off in the morning," he said, patting Jack's knee and smiling. Jack was about to tell him to pull over and let him out; that he liked girls, not boys, when the captain said, "My wife will be happy to have a young American visitor. She wants to know about all the demonstrations." His English was perfect, his accent slightly German. "She is Czechoslovakian. They want to have their own revolution." Europe. Different. "OK, thanks." said Jack.

They talked until midnight. They talked about change. About why it is that governments won't let go of the people when the people don't want them holding on anymore, as though the government is a thing that is different than, more than, the officials who run it. "It's like a web," the pilot's wife said, "a sticky web that catches everyone in it. The police are the spider that feels the web jerk when any one of us flutters. The Secret Police. They're not called that just because we don't know who they are, they're called that because they have all our secrets. They know things about us that we don't know about ourselves." They talked about revolution.

In the morning, Jack hefted his backpack on the train bound for Paris. He changed trains at Guar du Nord and boarded the Orient Express bound for Milan, Bucharest, Sofia, Istanbul. Three days of knees, thighs and shoulders pressed tight into strangers who mostly smelled like salami and stale clothes. Three days of the thunder and scream of steel wheels on rails and the endless fight over whether the window should be open or closed. Jack had never decided what, in the long run was worse, the smell or the noise, but when a little German man with a sharp red goatee knifed his way between Jack and a fat Italian women, unwrapped and bit into a fist

187

sized hunk of Limburger cheese, Jack had barfed up into his throat. He opened the window, the little man closed it, Jack opened it, the little man closed it, Jack opened it and the fat Italian lady smiled at Jack and he figured she was on his side so he picked the man up by his shoulders and stuffed him half way out the window, hollering, "If you touch this goddamn window one more time I'm going to throw you out, you understand me little man?" "Ja! Ja! Ja!" the little man screamed. He didn't touch his cheese or look at Jack for five hundred miles.

Jack Duncan might have been raised a Quaker but found out early on that the ways that normal people handled tough situations was often more effective. He probably wouldn't have actually let go of the little man, just held him out there long enough for him to change his mind about things. He thought about how it came to be that a good Quaker boy enjoyed a good fist-fight. Would never turn the other cheek. Once he had turned the other cheek. It was at an anti-war rally in New York City. He'd been standing at the edge of a crowd with a picket sign that said "Peace Cannot Be Kept By Force". It was a quote from Albert Einstein. He liked that quote and he liked it that Einstein was opposed to war and opposed to using the bomb that he had made possible. A mailman had walked up to him in his mailman uniform with his leather satchel of letters slung on his shoulder and spit in his face, all over his cheek. Jack had looked at him with whatever little sympathy and understanding he could muster, rotated the sign so the mailman could see it was a quote from Albert Einstein, pointed to Einstein's name and turned his head. The mailman spit on his other cheek.

Jack thought about this for hours as the train lumbered out of Trieste and on to Bucharest. He opened his poetry file and leafed through it. The poetry was, as always, neatly arranged in three bundled categories. It was in the free verse section. There was the poem his brother had asked him to mail. To a girl....to a girl named....named what? Howland. That's it. Gail Howland. In the Hotel Gulhane. I'll probably be in Istanbul before the mail would have gotten there anyway. At noon on the third day, he hefted his backpack out of the aisle of the economy car, bumped his way through a knotted string of tired travelers, stepped off the train in Sirkeci Station and wandered aimless into the blare and spangles of the ancient city.

Jack stood off to the side of the entrance to the Blue Mosque watching hundreds of the faithful rise up in almost in perfect unison and leave the cathedral after their afternoon worship. Incredibly, they all found their own shoes or sandals or slippers among the thousands laid out amidst the columns on the wide polished stone entry. No one seemed to hesitate or even look. They walked straight to their pair, put them on, then down the path and back to work. He watched a person in a black cloak tip-toe barefoot through the shoes, pick up a pair of hiking boots and walk far off to the edge of the plaza around the corner of the mosque. He sat on a stone bench, pulled a pair of socks from a pocket, laced up his boots and laid a shawl on the bench. He wasn't a man. He was a girl about Jack's age, twenty or so with a long black braid. She pulled her cloak off over her head, rolled it into a ball, put it in the shawl and tied the whole thing around her waist. She jogged off down the hill.

The wailing minarets were silent then giving back the cacophony of the beautiful Old City. Car horns, wooden wheeled carts on cobblestone and barking of the hawkers in the bazaar a few blocks away. Maybe the sounds never stopped but standing here by this mosque, Jack felt that when the prayers came, the city was unplugged for fifteen minutes, then plugged back in. Nobody knows I'm here he thought, smiling to himself. This is the other world.

Gail Howland was no longer a guest of the hotel. The desk manager had said, somewhat obtusely, that she had gone off with a large group of people two days ago. He wouldn't say what group of people or where they went. He said, "Check with the police." The lobby of the hotel was crowded with young people with backpacks, the kind with padded shoulder straps and wide belts and buckles that cinch around the waist. They were mostly from Europe; Danes, Brits, Germans. Most of the backpacks had flags of their countries on them. Skinny kids with thin beards and girls with long India print skirts and Byzantine bracelets bought, no doubt, earlier that day. The decade of the sixties was not particular to America. The raucous disregard for tradition and authority could be found everywhere in the "civilized world" and in all places to which the children of that world now chose to wander. There were sit-ins and be-ins and concerts and demonstrations in every country that allowed people to congregate without the police having a need to shoot them. Much of the ballyhoo had to do with America's war in Viet Nam, but even beyond that, a sea of change was flooding through the world.

Jack didn't have much with him. He had his sleeping bag, pocket sized book *The Prophet* with a photo of Gwen stuck in at Poem #13, "Freedom", file folder of his poetry, some socks, underpants, an extra pair of jeans, a few shirts, his beret and black leather motorcycle jacket. He thought he'd get a Canadian flag somewhere and have somebody sew it on his knapsack. Fly the Canadian flag everyone said, not the American. Everybody loves Canada, everybody hates America. Then he'd go to the Indian Embassy and see if his travel visa had gotten there yet. In Boston they had said if he didn't want to wait, if he wanted to leave for Europe right away, he could pick it up in any embassy. They could call Boston after a few days and receive authorization to issue the visa. That was ten days ago.

Through the clutch of youth in the lobby of the Hotel Gulhane, Jack saw the girl with the braid from the mosque sitting in an overstuffed armchair in front of an ornately tiled fireplace in which sat a three foot tall statue of Ataturk. She was reading a worn out copy of Paris Match.

"Excuse me," Jack said, "do you know where the embassies are?

"Which one are you looking for?" She asked.

"The Indian Embassy."

"Let's see, go down the hill three blocks, turn right and go straight maybe six, wait, one, two..." she counted on her fingers, long fingers, Jack noticed.... "eight blocks. You won't miss it. It looks like a little Taj Majal. But it's not an embassy. It's a consulate. Embassies are in the capitol, Ankara."

He thinks her accent is French but she looks like a tall Oriental. Black, shiny hair, long legs, high cheekbones and smooth amber skin. How, Jack thinks, could such a low lyric voice come from a neck that thin and a mouth so small and round?

"Are you staying here?" Jack asked.

"No. I just came over to see if my friends are here yet but the clerk says their boat doesn't get in until morning. I'll come back then."

"Well, OK, maybe I'll see you tomorrow." Jack said extending his hand, "my name's Jack."

"Marie." She said shaking his hand. "Maybe we meet again tomorrow. And Oh, I should tell you. Here, they think it is very bad manners to watch them pray."

Jack showed his passport to the man at the consulate counter and asked for a visa to travel to India. The man asked Jack to return in the afternoon after he had called Boston to check on his visa status.

"Mr. Duncan," the man said that afternoon, "I am so sorry to inform you that you cannot receive a visa to enter India. It is not possible."

"Why? In Boston they said there was no problem. Just pick it up at any embassy."

"Mr. Duncan, this is not an embassy. This is a consulate but that is not the problem. Your application says you will be studying languages at the university in Coimbatore. There is right now great problems with language there. There are many riots in the streets and many people hurt. We cannot approve you to go there."

"What if I change the purpose on this application and just go visit?"

"Mr. Duncan, this is your application," he said putting a blank application on the counter in front of Jack. Nothing was on it but his name. Across the top in red block letters was stamped something in Hindi and beside that, in English, 'DENIED'. "You cannot change this. We are sorry, Mr. Duncan."

It was getting dark when Jack got back to the hotel with no idea what he was going to do or where he was going to go. Nobody knows I'm here he thought again, I guess I can go anywhere I want. I can get visas at the borders of most countries. He zipped up his leather jacket, first checking to make sure his passport and a thousand dollars in traveler's checks were in the inside pocket, put on his black beret with a small red star sewn on the front and walked out into the night. He loved doing this. Being somewhere he had never been before. Free to follow whatever he saw, whatever he smelled or felt anywhere it took him and find out what is out there. What people are doing. How they live. Usually he gravitated toward the poorer, more dangerous parts of towns because there, nothing is structured. Nobody has planned what anybody should do or see. But be careful, Jack thought to himself. Careful. Don't get hurt. Watch out. Careful you don't roll the fat man all the way over. Things can get ugly down in the barrios.

He remembered hitchhiking to Boston from the Quaker school and that night going alone into the Combat Zone, going from bar to bar and at the corner of Tremont and some dark alley littered with a dozen bums and empty pints of Old Overholt coming to a plywood box with a roof on it, a green box about six feet square with a plywood door that was ajar and he went into it. It was two parts, separated by a plexiglass window and below the window was a hole about the diameter of a man's cock and in the other compartment a naked young girl with little blonde pigtails and a mat to kneel on. "Five dollars." She said. Jack couldn't do it. He turned to leave. "A pint of gin?" she asked. He remembered buying a pint at the liquor store down the block and giving it to her through the back door, her door that was locked from the inside. Jack remembered being drunk and crying about the girl on the way back to school. He was sixteen and she wasn't anything more than an eighth-grader.

On the narrow stone streets Jack watched men sitting at small tables in wooden chairs smoking short cigarettes pinched between thumb and forefinger, sipping thick coffee or bitter tea from tiny cups and slamming the flat backgammon stones back and forth into the rails. Sometimes they shared a hooka with water cooled tobacco and maybe some hashish inhaled through long woven hoses. It smelled good. The farther away from the center of town he walked, the more lamb was being roasted on vertical spits on the street or in little nooks between the buildings. Sliced lamb and cous-cous on paper plates. The women were inside, only men on the street. Jack walked, thinking about college, how he got here. Why did President Binder give him a thousand dollars to go "find an education" as he had said. Why him? Strange. Maybe my education is over. Nine months of college and that's it. Jack walked downhill turning this way or that way, whichever seemed more interesting, livelier. He headed for the harbor where the ferries cross the Bosphorus to New Istanbul. Old Istanbul, Constantinople, is the last city in Europe. New Istanbul is the first city in Asia. That's where all the maps have the line drawn. He rememberd that from Mr. Dickman's high school geography.

Jack found a bar full of men and laughter, shouting stories to each other. The whine and cymbal of Turkish music was deafening and blue smoke of cigarettes so thick it was hard to see the end of the room. "Beer," Jack shouted when he got up to the bar. Jack pointed to a bottle of something the guy next to him was drinking and the bartender brought him one. It wasn't like any beer he had drunk before. It was warm and it tasted yeasty but it was the only beer they had. It was called Tekel Birasi. It wasn't good but it was beer. The men in the bar were not dressed in Turkish clothes. Western clothes, mostly uniforms. Jack drank his beer quickly and got another. Looking at the pin-ups of belly dancers behind the bar, he wondered why men in the Mid-East like their women to have fat bellies. Jack sipped this beer then sipped another, listening to the laughter, the shouting, back slapping, looking at the men, table by table. Jack had been there for almost an hour. The bar had thinned out. Only a few men remained. He ordered a fourth beer, got up to find the bathroom and realized as he bumped into a table that he was lurching. He sat back down. A man in full dress uniform with ribbons and badges and wings came up behind Jack and put his arm around him. "American?" he asked. Jack considered lying but didn't. "Yes,' he said.

"American fight." The man said, shadow boxing in the air. He looked as though he was an Air Force pilot with all the silver and brass wings. It wasn't nasty yet. He was smiling.

"No," Jack said, "I don't fight." The pilot put his elbow on the counter, imitating arm wrestling. "Yes?" he asked.

Jack had made money before in bars by challenging men bigger than him to arm wrestle for five bucks, sometimes ten bucks. Easy money usually. "Sure," he said. The pilot took off his jacket and shook his arm to loosen it. He put a Turkish bill on the counter. Jack didn't know how much it was, what it was worth, but he fished through his pocket and pulled out one that matched it, carefully laying it down on top of the other. Jack stood, took his motorcycle jacket off, laid it on the stool and rolled his right sleeve up over his bicep. The men were about the same size, Jack slightly taller, the pilot slightly wider.

They went to a small round table, adjusted the chairs a little in, a little out, a hair sideways, a just a bit in, a bit out until they were just how they wanted them. Jack clasped the pilot's right hand, the pilot shook his head. No. He locked thumbs with Jack and Jack nodded OK. He didn't like it as much that way but if he could turn the guy's wrist at the same time he brought it towards him, it will be alright. The pilot grasped the table edge with his left hand. Jack shook his head. No. He laid his left arm flat down on the table. The pilot nodded and did the same. They stared at each other, wiggling their fingers to the best fit. A man slamed his palm down on the table, shouted something and they pulled and pulled and pulled. An inch this way, an inch that way until Jack got his fingers inside the soft muscle between the pilot's thumb and first finger. He squeezed and felt the pilot's hand begin to twist and Jack knew he had him.

The bartender clapped his hands and motioned for everybody to leave. Closing time. Jack took the money from the bar and shook the pilot's hand. They put on their jackets, slapped each other on the shoulder and left the bar. The pilot and two men got into a car outside and drove off. It was late and finally quiet. Jack walked hunched against the chill, hands in pockets, alone in the city, street after street of smooth cobblestones slippery with night dew singing over and over to himself *"Won't be water, be fire next time, little darlin', when the world's on fire."* He thought about Marie, the girl with the braid who'd been at the Mosque, been at his hotel, hoping he could wake up early enough to see her. Jack found the hotel at two o'clock in the morning.

THE AMERICAN CITIZEN

L ight and noise outside. It was eight o'clock in the morning. "Oh, no! Oh no! this is bad." Jack whispered to himself, "They have to be here. Where are they?" Jack went through every pocket in his motorcycle jacket again. Then again through every pocket in his pants, all his pants, his shirt, all his shirts. He was getting frantic. He looked again through everything in the knapsack. He looked in the bed, in the sheets, in the pillow. He ripped the sheets off the bed and tore the pillow out of the pillowcase. He leafed through every poem in his poetry folder. Nothing but paper. He checked every inch of the floor. Nothing. No passport. No money. His mind raced back. Did I have them when I went out last night? I had them at the Indian consulate. Yes, I had them when I went out last night. He remembered stopping outside the front door as he left the hotel and making sure they were in the inside pocket of his motorcycle jacket. "Oh my God! Oh, my Jesus Christ! They stole them when I was arm wrestling in the bar. Oh no! Those Fuckers!!" he screamed in the small room. Down in the lobby, Marie was sitting in the same chair that she had been sitting in the day before.

"Your friends not here yet?" Jack asked.

"No, they aren't coming," she said. "Good," he said, "please come with me. I need some help." Jack took her hand, pulling her up from the chair. He started talking as they went out into the late morning heat and noise. Jack told her what had happened. He told her he wasn't sure where the bar was but he was sure they stole his passport and money. Every few blocks he stopped. He looked around, feeling the night before. He made quick decisions. Sometimes they backtracked but after an hour they were standing in front of the bar. On the door taped to the inside of the window was a hand lettered sign in Turkish written on paper with a magic marker. The door was locked, the front curtains drawn. They decided to find somebody who could translate for them. Marie told him English, French or German would do. She pulled a pencil and a small note pad out of her pocketbook. She wrote the Turkish letters with all the curves and swirls and dots. It looked right. Two blocks down on the waterfront they found a booth that sold tickets for passage on freighters bound for Europe, Africa and the Mid-East. The girl in the booth spoke some French. "Closed for one month" is what it says.

"Jack, sit down. You need to think. You need to get your passport back," Marie said. Jack was looking at the necklace she had on. It is a string of small sea shells strung on a very thin rope. Nautical, he thinks. Her braid is tied at the top and bottom with the same kind of thin rope wound around and around and tied with a simple knot. She smells like the ocean. She is wearing blue jeans and a man's button down white oxford dress shirt with the top buttons undone so the necklace can hang loose, exposed. Beautiful.

"Jack, listen to me. You have to go right now to the American consulate, tell them what happened and get them to give you a temporary passport today. Now. You can't be here, especially here in Turkey, without a passport. It is very dangerous. And you can't get your traveler's cheques back until you have a passport."

Jack was entranced with the low throaty timbre of her voice. "How do you know so much?" he asks. "Let's go," she said, standing up, "it's about ten blocks that way. Not with the other consulates."

"Marie, did you have any friends who were coming here to meet you?"

"No. I lied. I only wanted to meet you. I followed you from the Mosque to the hotel."

The consulate had wide stone steps leading up to a columned portico. Two soldiers stood sentry just inside the huge brass entry doors. Jack and Marie stood at the counter talking to the receptionist; a warty, sallow woman. "If you don't have a passport, I can't verify that you are an American citizen, can I?" she said. Jack explained that he lost his passport last night and that is why he is here. To get a new one. You know what I mean? I am here because I don't have a passport. Do you understand what I mean? She was in her sixties, brownish gray curly hair, flabby, flaccid face with a mole the size of a raisin on the side of her nose. Her dress was a green and white checked sack. Her eyes, Jack thought, look like little brown rabbit turds. He showed her his driver's license, his social security card and his student deferment card from the draft board. OK, she said, you can see Mr. Bigelow, but you, she said pointing to Marie's French passport, you are not an American citizen and you, she said in an aggravating whine, must either have a referral from your embassy or an official request for amnesty to be admitted to see an officer in this consulate. Marie wasn't listening anymore. She walked away while the woman was talking and sat down in a lobby chair. She waved the back of her hand to Jack. `Go talk to the man yourself. These people are morons.' She taps the top of her head. The woman called a Mr. Bigelow and told him that

Jack was there, why he was there, what papers he had and that there was some French girl with him.

Harold "Harry" P. Bigelow, Consul General, Department of State, United States of America. Except for a photograph, the ornate brass sign was the only thing on his vast polished desk. No calendar, papers, not even a blotter. The photograph was of a handsome young man in uniform wearing a green beret with a red and gold insignia. The young man was smiling, happy and his eyes were confidant. Mr. Bigelow was a corpulent man, thick necked with a graying military brush cut. Jack felt a visceral hate coming from Mr. Bigelow. This man's son died in the jungles of Viet Nam. Jack was sure of this. Sliced to bits by little yellow people in black pajamas skulking through the underbrush in silent, ruthless stealth, stalking his son in the night and ripping the life right out of his throat. The gulf that separated Jack and this man was not chronological. It was not generational. It was not philosophical. It was not even a gulf. A gulf implies distance over tranquil water. It was a wide and deep chasm filled with fear, with anger, with pain. A chasm of demons. His world on his side, my world on my side. And nothing, nothing but the fact that we both exist, is shared in common. Jack rememberd Marie patting her head as he turned from the counter to walk the long hall to Mr. Bigelow's office. He reached up and took off his beret, stuffing it in his back pocket.

"What do you want?" the Consul General demanded. Jack began to tell him the story of how he lost his passport. "Where are you staying?" It was almost a hiss. Jack said he was at the Hotel Gulhane. "Get out of here you filthy coward, goddamned draft dodger, drug addict. You didn't lose you passport. You sold it for drugs. You sold it for heroin. You are lying. You don't deserve anything from your government. Get out!" he snarled. Jack stood rooted, fixed. I can't leave. I have to have a passport or I'll end up in a Turkish jail. This man knows that and might even make it happen. Turn the other cheek. Don't run, don't even walk away. Turn the other cheek. You are not a coward. Jack turned his head slightly sideways and began to apologize for all the inconvenience, but the chasm was far too wide. The sounds from his mouth couldn't travel that far, couldn't move through that much dead space. Harry Bigelow stood and punched the intercom button on his phone. "Get the guards in here."

Marie watched the two Marine guards stride down the hall and come back a minute later with Jack between them, each with a white gloved hand jammed under an armpit. They opened the front door, pulled Jack across the portico landing and threw him down the marble stairs.

Jack heard Marie scream, "You barbarians!" She dragged Jack up, put his arm around her shoulder and walked him down the street. He dragged one leg. Marie was tall but not as tall as Jack. It was hard for her. Three blocks away they stood in front of a building flying the French flag. She hollered in French for help. A guard trotted down the stairs and helped her with Jack, bringing him to the front lobby. The receptionist hugged Marie and they talked. Soon a man came to the lobby, sat them all down and talked quietly, in French with Marie. He nodded when she asked him a question. Marie and the man went off into an office. The receptionist brought a damp cloth, sat next to Jack and wiped blood off his forehead. Jack thought he looked worse off than he was. His knee hurt, his head hurt but everything else seemed OK. He was not shocked at what happened at his consulate. He was sure something like that was going to happen as soon as he saw the man and the photograph of his son. Jack wondered again who Marie was and how she could just get all these people to help. Maybe the French are nicer than the Americans. That's probably true. Maybe they always help pretty girls. That's probably also true, he thought. Maybe she knows them. That seemed most likely.

After a long time, Marie and the man came back and sat beside Jack. The man's English was slow and deliberate, lilting. "You have a new passport give to you in three days. You come here. You have copy of your of your traveler cheques, then also you may get new cheques from the bank. Bank of America. Here in Istanbul. Mr. Harry Bigelow is angry man, no?"

"I think his son died in Viet Nam." Jack says.

"Yes, is true. That is not..." He looks at Marie. "Excuse," she says. "That is not excuse. It is bad for him to be diplomat. For French Government, I say we are sad for this man do this to you. For next three days you must be very careful. No policemen."

"Why does your government care about me? How did you make this happen, I mean my passport and money?" Jack asked.

Marie said, "My father is the French Ambassador to Washington. He doesn't like Mr. Bigelow and was happy to call him. He is very good friends with that idiot's boss. But your Mr. Bigelow is a mean man. We have to go now and get you out of that hotel. Don't ask, I will show you why. Can he stay here?" she asked her friend.

"No. There is many problems for that. Papers of asylum must go to Paris. They must say his own government might hurt him. That is big problem. Is not possible. But, when I think Henri and François live in rented house, I think maybe there. They are both 'troupes de marine'. Very safe to be there." Marie jumped and came down with feet spread apart, arms in front with palms flat. "Ha!" she grunted. "Yes, Marie, karate," said the man. She hugged the receptionist and thanked her friend. The diplomat kissed her on the forehead, stood back and fingered the button near the top of his shirt. "Marie," he said. She looked down into her shirt, open to her bra, smiled and buttoned it up.

Marie led Jack up the four flights of narrow stairs to a door that led to the roof of the Hotel Gulhane. It was noon. The midday Mediterranean sun was shaded by tarps and blankets set on corner poles, like broom sticks or hoe handles and stretched tight by ropes tied to drain holes in the roof parapet. Fifteen or twenty of the kids from the lobby sat scattered about, small groups nestled around a tin pot on a stand above a Bunsen burner, boiling needles in water. On towels or pillow cases or shirts spread out beside the pots were thin, clear rubber hoses, spoons, vials and clear packets of powder. A girl leaned back on the brick wall at the building edge, a hose wrapped around her skinny arm just above the elbow while a boy, on his knees in front of her, slid a hypodermic needle into a small vein below the rubber hose, pushed the plunger all the way down and yanked the hose free. Her mouth was in an open childlike smile, eyes rolled up, looking at nothing, spit slipping down her chin. "OK?" Marie said to Jack. "Let's get you out of here."

Two days before Jack had arrived, a dozen Turkish policemen had arrested everyone in the hotel, including Gail Howland. They had done this once or twice before over the last few years. The amount of money gathered from the belongings of the arrested people provided sufficient funds to adequately compensate the hotel owner for lost business. The confiscated heroin sold handsomely, augmenting their meager budget. The kids arrested there would never lead a life anything similar to what their parents had planned, expected or wanted for their children. For all of them, for a long time, Turkish prison would be hell.

"Jack, you wear a motorcycle jacket, a black beret with a red star on it. You look just like Che Guevera and you're free and alive and not in Viet Nam. And, aside from all that, you're staying in a hotel full of heroin addicts. Even a better person than Mr. Bigelow might have a problem with that. Get your things, Jack. You can stay with Henri tonight. In three days we get your passport and money, then we go on an adventure, somewhere else. How does that sound?"

In Boston, Brenda poked her head into Special Agent Hancock's office. "You have a call from the State Department. Line one," she said. "Thanks," he said, pushing the lit button and picking up the phone.

"Tim, hi, this is Jason over at State. Remember you asked to be notified if anything came through DOS on a kid named Jack Duncan? Well we just got a communiqué from our consulate in Istanbul. Last night's daily log shows him asking for a new passport. The charge d'affairs denied his request. He states he thinks Duncan sold it to buy heroin. Do you want a copy of the communiqué?"

"Yes, please, as soon as possible. Are you saying that your consular person simply denied an American citizen a passport so he can never leave Turkey and has no legal document allowing him to be there? My God, Jason, he'll spend the rest of his life in a Turkish prison. As far as the heroin goes, our information would indicate that that is very, very unlikely. Does it say where he is staying? What hotel?"

"Yes, the Hotel Gulhane which is, according to Mr. Bigelow, a notorious heroin hang-out. Can you hang on a minute. I'm getting copied on an internal memo with this Duncan kid's name in it. Hang on... Oh, this isn't good. I think we have a diplomatic problem here. Tim, I'm going to have to call you back."

"Jason, I'm the FBI. You don't have to call me back. Just tell me what it is. Now. I don't have much time. I have to get through to my person in Istanbul before we lose this guy."

"Five minutes. I'll call you back." The line went dead.

"Brenda," Hancock said opening his door, "find the telephone number of the hotel Joe Cole is staying at in Oujda, Morocco. It's four-thirty here so it's five hours later or nine-thirty over there. He ought to be there. Get them on the phone and see if Cole is there. If you get him, hold him on the phone until I can talk to him."

When Hancock's phone buzzed again four minutes later, it was a Mr. George Turini who introduced himself as the Assistant Director of Middle Eastern Affairs at the State Department. "Agent Hancock, we have a bit of a problem here. You have asked for confidential information concerning events taking place in a foreign country. You also have, if I got this right, a person in Istanbul with whom you have an urgent need to communicate. Is this right?"

Hancock knew where this conversation was going. He knew this was precisely the reason Meritt didn't want himself or Hoover implicated. This was one of the things that might land him in a witness chair in a Federal trial. "Yes, Mr. Turini, that is correct."

"On issues such as these, Agent Hancock, we deal with the CIA. The FBI, as I understand, has no authority to conduct actions, investigations or surveillance anywhere outside the United States. If you could give me your contact at the CIA, I'd be happy to forward them the information."

"Mr. Turini, with all due respect, sir, this is an urgent domestic matter. We have reason to believe that Mr. Duncan has in his possession, possibly unbeknownst to him, documents which pose an immediate and grave threat to America's internal security. I repeat, internal security. We need to secure those documents. Now if you would like to confirm this with my direct and only contact at the CIA, feel free to put a call through to Admiral William Rayborn. I'm sure he'd be happy to chat with you."

There was no possibility that Mr. Turini could, would or wanted to call the Director of the CIA particularly after he had been bureaucratly nasty to an obviously well connected FBI agent. That was a call the Secretary of State would have to make and this did not seem to be an issue important enough to rise to that level. After a long pause he said, "The French Ambassador to Washington called my boss this morning demanding that a Mr. John Duncan be issued a replacement passport immediately and that that passport be delivered to the French Consulate in Istanbul. They would give it to Mr. Duncan, not us. He also made a few comments about the qualifications of our personnel. I am not at liberty to disclose that information."

"Why are the French involved?" Hancock asked.

"Because it seems that Mr. Duncan went into our consulate with the French Ambassador's daughter and unfortunately our charge d'affairs had him physically ejected from the building. She reported this to her father. That part, the ejection, did not appear in our consulate's communiqué of last night."

Brenda was waving at him from the door. "Thank you very much. You've been very helpful. Can I ask you a couple of quick questions?" "Go ahead," Turini answered. "When will this passport be delivered to the French Consulate?" "Three days. Friday noon, Istanbul time." Turini said.

"Thanks." Hancock said. "By the way, are our relations with France on domestic, or, I guess more like, civil rights issues still as bad as they have been?"

"Yes, they are. Worse actually. King's murder and the photos of the Washington and Newark riots really got them screaming. Christ, our police look like executioners. Their State Department has assisted in arranging asylum in Algeria for some of the more militant blacks. There are reasons for this that are too lengthy to go into, but if your Mr. Duncan is black or if the documents he has are pertinent to the issue of race, be very careful. Please do not get the French involved any more than they already are."

"I won't. He is not black and the documents do not pertain to race. Could you have someone forward me the communiqués, or at least the parts that you can share. Thanks again." He hung up. Having Duncan arrested, finding the list, and then arranging his release from prison was the cleanest option, but that was out. The French would know and they would scream. It was too risky. Sean O'Neal however, could probably get there within a day.

"Sean, how are you?"

"Fine."

"Any more on the communist attorney?"

"He's in Algiers."

"You know what your instructions are." That was an order.

"I do." That was an affirmation.

"Sean, listen. Do you remember that hippie party in Madbury, New Hampshire?"

"Yes."

"Do you remember the kid who lived there, Jack Duncan?"

"Yes."

"He's in Istanbul. He has on him or with him somewhere a really important list of names of people we believe are forming a revolutionary army to try to overthrow the government. It is the document we were looking for after the arrests in New Hampshire. We don't know what it looks like, but we're pretty sure that he has it. He is staying at the Hotel Gulhane. I want you to get on a plane out of Rabat tomorrow morning. Check into some other nearby hotel and find him. Search everything in his room. If you can't find it in his room, strip search him. But here's the thing. He's with a girl. A French girl. It is of the utmost importance that she not be made aware that you are doing anything. Do not let her see you. Do not get the French involved. If you have to physically search him, do it when he's alone and make it look like a mugging. Call me at the number I gave you, night or day, as soon as you have it."

"Or not?"

"Goodbye."

"No, Mademoiselle Marie says you cannot go out alone at night." Henri was firm. For two days, Marie had woken Sean up in the morning and stayed with him every minute of the day. They walked the waterfront watching the tug boats pull, push and steer the cargo ships into dock. Ships flying the flags of Liberia, Norway, China, Japan, Egypt, France, Canada, United States, Brazil. Istanbul was the nexus of land travel East to the Orient; through Iraq, Iran, Afghanistan, Pakistan, to India and Nepal and land travel to the west through the Balkans and Greece, Yugoslavia, Italy and into Europe. Across the Black Sea lay the Soviet Union. They watched the bartering in the Bazaar. Knives, jewelry, blankets, beads, burkhas and hookahs. Merchants worked their wares with passion; gesticulating, shouting, turning their backs in disgust at such a paltry offer but never giving up until a deal was done.

Deep beneath the city streets was a Turkish bath, hundreds of years old. Nothing Marie said about being alone with no identification in a place notorious for predators, replete with stories of bizzare sexual acts and certain to be a den for thieves swayed Jack in the least. He was going in. As he stood listening to her pleading, he saw a man he thought he recognized. Not surely, but familiar. A tall young man with copper skin and long, wavy black hair. He saw him over Marie's shoulder only for a moment, then he was gone down a narrow alley. "Are you listening to me, Jack?" "No, Marie, not really. I thought I saw a guy I recognized. I think he might have been at a party at my house in the States. I'm not sure." Jack said. "Is he a friend of yours?" she asked. "No, If it's the same guy, I think he is a narc. A federal narcotics agent."

"Jack, do you use drugs? Do you? Be honest."

"No. I don't eat them, smoke them, shoot them, buy them or sell them," he lied.

"I think we should go back to Henri and François'. You will be safe there. They are strong soldiers."

"Yes, I'm sure they are but they're at work now. So I'm going to go into a Turkish bath before I leave this country and I'm going in now. I'll be fine. There is nothing I've done bad. There is nothing anybody would want me for. If that guy is the same guy, he's not here for me. Marie, I didn't come all the way to Turkey to be intimidated by people from my own government."

"I think you are in danger here." She spoke softly.

"Maybe so, but I have seen enough bad things that people do to each other to know that the only way they succeed is if you're afraid of them. I am not going to let them do that to me. I am going down into this Turkish bath the same way men have been going in there for a thousand years. I'm going to come out clean and happy. Here, hold these for me." Jack gave her his wallet and the key to Henri and François' house.

He put his arm on her shoulder, stroked it up her thin neck to her ear and she looked at him with the fierce eyes of a French woman scorned. "I will watch from over there." she said pointing to a dark recess in the storefronts across the street. "What does this, what did you call him, this narc look like?"

"Tall, coffee colored skin, long black hair. Watch out, he's very handsome." Jack went through the door and down the steps into an ancient Turkish bath.

Everything was wet. Warm wet and white marble. The stair treads were cupped in the middle from a million feet descending carefully, heel first. There was no handrail. The marble wall on the down side of the staircase was worn with a cupped grove where hands had balanced bodies. A tall mustachioed man with a tall red fez sat on a short stool at the bottom of the stair. Jack held out a fistful of lira and the man took it all, reached behind him and handed Jack a checkered cotton cloth. Jack went into a room with dozens of wooden cubicles big enough to sit in and disrobe. He sat on a bench and stripped naked, putting his shoes and clothes on the shelf, wrapped the cloth around his waist, cinched it as tightly as he could and walked deep into the Byzantine Empire. A huge domed room with oculi, skylights that reached up to the cityscape above bringing light through the foggy steam into the subterranean cavern. The floors, walls and dome were gold, brown and blue with painted tile. Fat men, vast sweaty bellies and drooping man-tits sat around the perimeter on marble slabs, expressionless, silent, glistening sweat-wet waiting their turn. In the center of the round room three men, two belly down, one belly up lay stretched out on low marble tables while barefoot men in sarong-type cloths scrubbed their skin with rough, thick white mittens. The only sounds were the low grinding of the scrubber mitt and wet flesh slipping or slapping on stone when a fat man moved. When Jack came out of the domed room and into the shower his mind was light as air. His body tingled pink as though he'd just been born moments ago. His muscles had no muscle as he wobbled to his cubby. And his cubby had no order. His clothes were stuffed on the shelves, haphazard. Someone had been rifling through his things. Nothing had been taken, but then again, there was nothing to take. No wallet, no passport, no money, no keys. Everything was there except the paper he had in his shirt pocket with the addresses and phone numbers of the French Consulate and Henri and François' home. That was gone.

"He didn't see me but I saw him. Yes, he is very handsome, Jack, and he is looking for you. Why?"

"I don't know. I have no idea. I can't think of anything anyone would want me for, particularly an American cop. I haven't done anything. Aside from that Marie, nobody knows I'm here. I haven't told anybody. Not my school, not my friends, not my family."

"Mr. Harry Bigelow knows you are here. Mr. Harry Bigelow doesn't like you. The man could be one of his people trying to find drugs on you to get you put in jail." They were walking quickly along the cobblestones out of the center of the old town towards the consulates. "We are going back to my consulate now. You are going to stay there until Henri is off work. You will stay with him until your passport and money are here tomorrow." She was pulling him by the hand. "Those are not questions I said to you. Those are what you are going to do." Jack still tingled from the sauna scrubbing. Each time she swung her head back to issue another order, her long black braid swished against his forearm. When she strode, her hips swiveled swinging her ass slightly up on one side then the other. He didn't hurry to catch up. He let himself be tugged.

Marie went off to pack her things. Madam Chirac brought Jack coffee, cookies and the latest edition of Paris Match. He sat in the reception room, waiting, smiling occasionally at her, she smiling back. Henri was not there. It was his day off. Another guard, shorter and less affable, was standing in.

HIDDEN NAMES

Jack sat and waited while Sean, four blocks away, crept around back of Henri's rented house, waited until the din of a steel wheeled cart rumbling by masked any noise, then jimmied the window open and slid into the kitchen-living room area. He walked carefully, quietly across through the living room and up the stairs. He found the bedroom with Jack's things. He searched every pocket of all the clothes. He took every poem out of the folder, looking at each one, skimming the words, searching for any list of any sort. He searched the bed sheets, the pillow, the dresser. There was nothing there. Perhaps he missed something in the poetry folder. He took all the papers out and spread them across the bed. He shook the folder to make certain nothing was left in it. A small leather bound book, "The Prophet" fell out just as the front door downstairs, directly in front of the staircase, opened. He stood stock-still. There were two windows in the bedroom but neither was wide enough to fit through. Henri looked straight through the kitchen to the jimmied window and looked up the staircase to the opened door at the spare bedroom. Was it Jack? No, he had a key. Had whoever it was already left? Was he upstairs? He put his back against the staircase wall so he could see the hallway up above and step by step slowly, sideways climbed the stairs. He could feel someone there. At the top of the stair he leaped straight into the bedroom, crouched. Sean's boot heel caught him on the side of the head. He rolled away and up on his feet. As Sean tried to make it around the door, Henri caught him full in the chest with a straight right jab. Sean staggered, spun, kicked out in a sweep. Henri jumped back against the far wall, enough for Sean to make it around the corner, down the stairs and out the front door at a full run. Henri was behind him, running full bore but, at six-six, 230 lbs., he couldn't keep up. Sean, even with a bullet wound in his calf, was gone into a labyrinth of alleys.

"There was no list, Mr. Hancock. I searched through everything. Even his clothes when he was in a Turkish bathhouse. There was nothing. He has poetry, maybe thirty or forty of them. I read, or skimmed them all. No list of names, just poems."

"No, I don't know where he went. They have him stashed in the French embassy. I can't get very close. They have a big, and I mean big, French guard stationed right on the front steps. These embassies have secure entrances at the rear. You can't see anybody go in or out. You wanted me to keep the French out of it, right?" Sean didn't mention his altercation with Henri. "I've done some checking. It's not likely they'll fly out. It costs a lot and takes a few days to book a seat. They might take the train but it only goes two ways. Back to Europe or what they call the 'hippie trail', through Iran and Pakistan to New Delhi. They're either going to be on that or a boat. Two cargo ships leave tonight. One, a French freighter headed to Cairo and then to France, the other a Dutch boat going to Athens then to Israel and back to Holland. What do you want me to do?"

"Go to the train station. Given who he's traveling with, I think that's most probable. If they don't show up, so be it. Go back to Morocco. This Duncan kid will turn up somewhere soon enough. When he does, I want you there immediately and I want you to take every single piece of paper in his possession and get it back here. Call me tomorrow."

"I am not going back to Paris! I am on a six month adventure. That was what you said, Papa. I'm not going to come running home any time something happens!" The Ambassador smiled over the phone. Good girl. "We love you very much, mon cher. Stay safe."

The tides in the Mediterranean are small. It is not a big enough body of water for the moon to get a good grip on it. Not like the oceans. The surge of the Atlantic is strangled, used up as it funnels through the Straits of Gibraltar. By the time it has passed the boot of Italy, up the Aegean Sea to the Bosphorus at Istanbul, the changing sea just gently laps the seawall. Marie and Jack sat in the back seat of the diplomat's Mercedes, parked by the stone jetty at the dock listening to the ocean, waiting to board the freighter bound for Athens and Haifa, Israel. Francois stood by the hood of the car, his sidearm loaded. Jack had his new passport and his thousand dollars in new traveler's cheques. "So this is what my daddy said to me before I left Washington," Marie told him. `When you get past Europe, find a strong man to travel with. A man who can protect you from the things that other men might do, but make sure he's an honest man. Make sure you trust him, then trust him. Also, do not stay anywhere there are drugs. All of the power of my office cannot protect you from arrest for drugs.' "Then," Marie said, "my mother, who was born in China says, `Your father wants you to travel the world because that is how he found me. He came to China and we fell in love. I was his

215

first love. His only love. Do not, Marie, mistake desire for love. Help a man in his passion, let him help you in your passion, but before you bring him inside your body, be sure he is the only one who will become a part of you."

"Great," Jack said. "Do you always do what your parents say?" "Yes," she said, taking his hand and sliding it over her belly. "Usually."

Three other passengers were on board. A derelict drunk Englishman who said he was on his way to Crete to find his father who had never come home after World War II, Sven, a young Dane with a guitar and Ping, a raw boned Australian girl with a voice that carried half way across the Aegean Sea. The first night out, under the stars in a clear sky, the boat hull slapping the wave crests in metronome, she stood on the bow swigging a bottle of ouzo belting out: *"Big balls in cow town"*. Jack and Marie stood on the bridge with Wim Frank, the Dutch captain, talking about their lives, their hopes and the horrible situation the world had come to. The drunk Englishman down below sang, *"I have sailed upon a Yankee ship, Davy Crockett is her name, and Burgess is the captain of her, and they say she's a floating hell"* He sang it over and over again. He never got to the "leaving of Liverpool" part.

As they sailed through the pristine white Greek Islands—Kithnos, Serifos, Paros, Naxos—Jack sat with Marie against the gunwale on the bow.

"That man was looking for something in your papers. What do you think he wanted?" Marie asked.

"I don't know. Maybe he is from the *Atlantic Monthly* and they want to publish my poetry."

"Jack, don't be funny. What could he want?"

"Well, I've been thinking about that. The only thing it could be is a poem my brother gave me to mail to a girl in Istanbul. I forgot to mail it and she was arrested in a drug bust before I got there. Maybe they want that."

"Why didn't your brother mail it?"

"Because he's in jail, he's a draft resister. They don't let you mail stuff like that out of jail. He said it was some kind of love letter from a fellow inmate to his girlfriend."

"Can I see it?" she asked. Jack came back with all his poetry. "See if you can find it." he said. Marie read each poem. They were all handwritten in pencil on blank paper, some two sided. "The only thing we know is that the girl I was supposed to give it to was named Gail Howland." Marie read them all again. The ship rose and fell gently in the Aegean swells. Sometimes a slight salt spray blew over the bow. Sometimes terns or sea gulls squawked overhead. "I think this is it." she said after Jack got back from walking around the boat decks. "This doesn't seem like your words. It seems harder, less poetic. Is this it?" "Yes." Jack said. "You found it! But why would anyone possibly want that?"

Marie's face scowled as she read, her finger going along under each line. "What did you say the girl's name was? Gail Howland?" She clapped her hands. "Look here. Look right here. 'blow soft and clean or will a northern gale howl and...Gail Howland...gail howl and...Her name is in it. It's hidden in it. Why would he hide it? Are there other names in here?" Jack read. "I don't see any. Don't know. I think you'd have to know the names to find them. We never would have found 'Gail Howland' without knowing it."

"We?" Marie said, nudging him. She unbraided her hair, shook her head so it fell free nearly to her waist. She leaned over the bow rail smiling into the wind and salt. "Jack?" she said, motioning him beside her. "What if this poem is what they want. The guy who came to get it fought with Henri and got away. That means he is not a normal person. But he read all your papers and didn't take this either because it isn't what they want or, and I think this, he didn't recognize it. Then

Henri came in. That means he will be back. What do you think you should do?"

Sitting on the deck, Jack copied all his poetry into a new notebook, a gift from the captain. He told her he was going to mail the notebook home to his mother's house. If the guy came again, he'd just give him the whole file folder. Hopefully, he'd go away and not come back. "Give me the poem. I can figure it out. I know I can." She put the poem in her knapsack.

They steamed towards the harbor of Haifa, Israel. An hour out of port, Captain Wim rapped his knuckles on the side of a lifeboat. Jack and Marie, under the tarp, naked on their sleeping bags, were wrapped in each others' arms. "Up you get, lovebirds," he said in Dutch. The sun was rising over Mount Hermon sixty miles away on the Lebanon, Syrian border when they nosed to the docks.

"Tim, good to see you again." David Meritt was almost congenial. "I understand you're making some headway on our program. I briefed the Director on it this morning and I think it's safe to say that he is pleased. He wants some confirmation soon on progress on those three Panthers in Algeria but he thinks the person you've assigned to it sounds perfect for the job. No incentive to bolt. That's good. On the other front, we have some problems. I understand your Green Beret could not find the list we're looking for. That is very unfortunate. We are now certain Duncan has those documents." Meritt leaned forward. "In a Federal Prison there is a chaplain. He is no ordinary chaplain. He was at one time a Jesuit priest in the St. Peter and Paul church in Boston. His profligate ways got him banished and sent away by Archbishop Cushing personally. Why having sex with women gets a priest fired and sent to Catholic Siberia when having sex with little boys is wholly ignored is beyond me, but that's another matter. This priest wouldn't or couldn't stop. Well, it seems a few days ago this priest was involved in some particularly rough sex with the prison warden's wife and she died of asphyxiation. Right there in the chapel behind the altar. Since the prison is federal property, we were called in to investigate. This fellow wanted to cut a deal. Involuntary manslaughter, five years max, in exchange for information on a list of terrorists smuggled out of that prison. A call from Director Hoover and the Attorney General went for it. Here's what he had. He said he had eavesdropped on a conversation in the prison library. A Black Panther named Elroy Jenkins gave a poem to a draft dodger named Dwight Duncan. Duncan gave it to his kid brother, Jack, the day before this Jack flew out of the country. One of the guards saw the kid writing something on a piece of paper but they didn't find anything when they searched him on the way out. Well, of course they didn't. They couldn't tell one poem from another. The good Father, who never heard the poem, also said it was supposed to be mailed to a Gail Howland at a certain hotel in Istanbul. Neither she nor the hotel ever received it. We know that because she was arrested in a drug bust at the hotel two days before this Duncan kid got there. She's still in a Turkish prison and we're going to leave her there. Nice and safe and sound. The Consul General was kind enough to collect all her things for us and the poem was not one of them.

　　The Duncan kid never mailed it. He still has it. He probably doesn't know what it is. Neither prisoner will talk, of course, not Jenkins, not Duncan. Both of them are very smart. A de-frocked, sex addicted, murderer ex-priest said what? No judge would ever believe a thing he said. They know it. There's nothing we can do to them, for them or with them. We've searched all their things. It isn't there. So that brings us to this. Where the hell is this Duncan kid?"

"Maybe in Iran, Pakistan, India, maybe in Greece, Israel, Egypt. Maybe Yugoslavia or somewhere in Europe. We don't know. He got away from us. He's still with the French Ambassador's daughter as far as we know.

"Find him."

"How can I find him if I can't use the Agency, can't use Justice, can't use the State Department. I already went out on a limb daring a State guy to call Admiral Rayborn when Duncan turned up in Istanbul."

"Find him and get those lists. The Director is sure that that there will be a planned and orchestrated series of bombings all across the country starting within the year. He wants, more than anything else, to stop this now. We are trying everything we can to infiltrate these groups but so far they've seen us coming a mile away. We have nothing hard to go on but the poems that kid has stuffed somewhere in his knapsack. Find him and find him fast."

"Sir, many of these countries don't even require a visa to enter, just a stamp in the passport. If they issue a visa at the border, it takes two or three weeks, sometimes months for it to show up here. All I can do is hope his name turns up on some communiqué to CIA, DOJ, DOS or Interpol. We have some people, mostly lower level, in each of these organizations who will alert us if his name shows up. That's how we found him in Istanbul. None of them know why we want it. Sir, I'm doing the best I can what I have to work with. We can only hope he does something stupid. He already got in a fight with a colonel in the Turkish Air Force and lost his money and his passport. That's a good sign for us. But, sir, there's something I have to confide in you." Meritt stared at him. "Yes?"

"This Algeria thing makes me really nervous. I don't like ordering the execution of American citizens. Even if they are a danger to our country. Even if they are hiding out in communist countries. That's the work of the CIA, sir, and it is work that gets done with the specific approval of the President. We are way, way out there on this."

"None of those other agencies give a good goddamn about the domestic security of this country. That's our job. They won't help. And if we asked the President about this, he'd fire us all. Then we'd have to take him out as well."

"As well?" Hancock whispered. "What do you mean, 'as well'? As well as who?"

Meritt pushed his pudgy body up out of his chair. "Forget that. Find the kid and get rid of those terrorists. Period."

KIBBUTZ

"This is Sugar Abel, Sugar Abel... Come in International Operator...International, do you read me? This is Sugar Abel Sugar Abel...Come in International."

Yock was fifty or so. Twenty years ago he had come to Israel from the train yards of Chicago just after the end of World War II, a few years before it was Israel, when it was Palestine. The British, in their pith helmets and jodhpurs were still trying to control the affairs between angry Arabs and boatloads of immigrating Jewry; Arabs who had hoed this dirt and milked these goats, worked this rough plot for dozens of centuries and the Jews who had earned the right to a home, a safe home after similar centuries of nearly worldwide persecution and genocide. Palestine. Israel. The same small spot. The British lied to both of them. At some point before the United Nations granted the Jews their Sovereign State, the British left. They blockaded the Mediterranean waters off the coast, preventing boatloads of desperate Jewish refugees from landing on the shores. Boats sank, people died. The Brits walked away from their military outposts, still full of ammunition, carbines and machine guns. They handed the keys to the Arabs or to the Jews and sailed back to England

223

except for 38 British Officers who resigned their commissions immediately after independence was announced by Ben-Gurion, gathered together a Transjordanian army of volunteers from Libya and Yemen and Saudi Arabia and, along with 20,000 Egyptians, Iraqis and Syrians, attacked the Jews. Yock hated the British and blamed them for the bloodbath that followed. That was why there were no Brits living in the volunteers' bunk house at the kibbutz, just three Americans, three Danes, two Swedes and Marie. Israel still, in 1968, would not stamp a British passport. That's how Yock saw it and that's how he told it to Jack.

Kibbutz Sasa sits hard on the northern border with Lebanon, halfway between the Mediterranean Sea and the Golan Heights of Syria, twenty miles from either. Both Beruit and Damascus are about seventy miles away, a three day walk, seven minutes for an F-16. The volunteers' bunk house was the smallest of all the buildings. It was five concrete block rooms strung side by side, each with two beds, two bureaus, a steel front door and a high back window that looked out on a coiled razor wire fence. It was at the far back of the property where the land fell off to the south in a long desert valley towards the hills of Zafat and Nazareth. All the buildings, the commissary, dining hall, kitchen, radio and gun shack, adult housing and children housing were concrete block, some painted, others not. The kid's compound, where Marie worked, was painted with murals of children playing in playgrounds and animals. Everything was small inside. The doors were short, the windows low, the toilets about six inches off the floor and the tables so low an adult had to kneel at them. This is where kibbutz children lived. There in those rooms, together, not with their families. They all studied Hebrew, history, art and mathematics but also karate and marksmanship starting at ten years old. Every child was also taught to play an instrument, like a violin or a flute. The whole kibbutz was surrounded by waves of razor wire with one way out; a gate out by a guard shack on the border road. Everyone over sixteen carried a knife and a loaded pistol, always. No one had money. There was no use for it. Work translated directly into food, clothing and housing. A kibbutz is a commune. A communistic enclave in a capitalist society set hard on a hostile border.

In the week Jack had been at the kibbutz, he had never seen Yock without his cowboy hat. Sometimes he would push it back to wipe off sweat and Jack could see he was starting to bald and the skin on his high forehead was pink, unlike his face that was the color and texture of furrowed dirt. He wore cowboy boots, blue jeans, a denim shirt with sleeves rolled up above his bicep and an army issue pistol in a black leather snap shut holster. In the Six Day War, just a year before Jack arrived, he had been the Major in charge of the Israeli paratrooper division that dropped into the narrow cobblestone streets of Old Jerusalem.

Jack was in the radio house with Ted Hilliard, his friend from Deakins College. Ted had ended up on this kibbutz the same way Jack had headed for India; Professor Putz. Yock was in the radio house with them. It was a small block building with a thirty foot tall aerial on the roof, a steel door and no windows, only slits just big enough to stick the barrel of an Uzi through. Nothing was inside except a huge Ham radio and locked steel cabinets with the guns and ammunition. Yock touched the dial with one finger, just a wiggle enough to quiet the squeal and crackle.

"International, do you copy?"

"Kibbutz Sasa. Sugar Able Sugar Abel, this is International. I copy. Go ahead." The women operator's voice had no accent. Perfect English.

"Can you connect to," he read the place and numbers Jack had written..."USA, Briton Landing, New York, Deakins

College 528-567-6676." Yock looked at him. "To who?" Jack took the hand held microphone and pushed the button. "A Mr. Peter Putz," Jack said. "Peter what?" the operator said. "I will not! Sasa, what's the matter with you?" The connection went dead.

"Putz, Putz, don't you guys know anything? This is my Putz right here," he said pointing to the zipper on his pants. "How can anybody have a name like that? I mean anybody anywhere. Now she's really going to be a problem. Probably listen to everything, maybe even record it." He sat down and stared at them, shaking his head. "Okay, kids, give me another name, a good name this time, and I'll try again." "Aaron Earnstead" Jack said. "OK. She speaks German, French, Spanish and God knows what else. I hope Earnstead doesn't mean asshole in somebody's language." Yock got them through but not without a sinister warning about misuse of State controlled airwaves.

"Professor Earnstead, this is Jack Duncan. I'm in Israel. We couldn't get through to Peter..." Peter Putz, Jack's physics professor and advisor had arranged the program for him to study Dravidian at the university in southern India. "There seems to be a name problem with Peter." Earnstead laughed. "I can understand that. We thought you were going to study in India. Why are you in Israel?"

"I couldn't get my visa for India from the consulate in Istanbul. They said there were language riots and my studies might make some problems so they said no. I decided to take a cargo boat to Israel and see what turned up. What do you think I should do now?"

"I have a good friend there in Israel. Avraham Ben Yosef. Go find him. He can help you with your studies. He is a fine scholar. He wrote me a few days ago. He is on a small kibbutz in the north somewhere above the Sea of Galilee. He also said there was a Deakins student there. Ted Hilliard. You know him, don't you?"

Ted was standing over him now, hitting him on the shoulder and drawing his hand across his throat, like cut it off! Stop it!

"Mr.Earnstead, it looks like we have to get off the phone right now. There's some problem here. Thanks for your advice."

"You are welcome." He said. "Your college won't be here when you get back. The State revoked our accreditation. A Department of Health inspector tracking down a gonnahera outbreak stepped in a dog poop on the front steps and that was it for us. All the health stuff was a ruse. We're just too radical for this country. The faculty has all resigned. Make the most of your studies there. It might be all you ever get. Goodbye and good luck."

Tom turned to Yock. "Do you think she recorded that?"

"Yes, I'd say it's pretty likely she did. Why?"

"Ummm...I can't really say."

Yock moved directly in front of him. "You can't say? You can't say? No, you can't *not* say. Otherwise, I have no choice but to find out. We're very good at finding things out here. The best in the world. So, what is it? Out with it."

"OK." Tom cracked his knuckles, rubbed the back of his neck then turned around and wiped his mouth. "OK. My father is a Colonel in the United States Army. We don't get along at all. We never have. We hate each other. He's always wanted me to be just like him. He made me play football, lift weights, join the wrestling team. I didn't want to do any of that. I wanted to study English. He shut off my college money so I wouldn't have a student deferment anymore and got me drafted into the Army. I didn't want to. I don't want to be a soldier. I won't go to Viet Nam. So I left boot camp. I'm AWOL and I know he's trying to find me. I called my brother when I was in Cyprus and he said my father was calling everywhere in the world to track me down. He said it was all he talked about. Maybe it would make him happy to see me in a military prison or maybe he thinks he's so goddamn powerful he can fix it and get me killing people in some rice paddy where he thinks I ought to be."

"Young man," Yock said, "I don't like what your father or your country is doing in Viet Nam either. It's bad. It's bad like the British were bad. But two things you better think about: this country needs the United States, they support us and we support them. That makes our little problem here a political problem. But remember this; you've run from your army to a country where everyone your age is a soldier; every boy and every girl. If soldiers run away from this army, they get shot. No trial." He put his hand on his pistol. "Shot dead because we just couldn't trust them after that. It's dangerous here. Go back to your bunk house. For now, I'm only going to talk to one person, Avraham Ben Josef. Your Professor Earnstead is right. He's not at the Hebrew University anymore. He's here." Yock held the door open.

Ted's father was hunting him down. That made it hard. Yock had to decide if there was political danger to his kibbutz. Was Ted's fear of his father real, something that could come all the way to this kibbutz on the far northern border of Israel and Lebanon, all the way through the minions listening to taped conversations, through files the Mossad kept on foreigners, through all inquiries hundreds of government officials made to hundreds of State Departments? How thorough were these people and did Ted's father know he was in Israel? Did the Colonel ask Israeli Intelligence to help anyway, knowing he might have come here from Cyprus?

Ted might have been right to tell Yock about being AWOL but there was one thing Jack was sure of. Ted should not be messing around with a Sabra girl. Sabra. Israel's most treasured asset. A Jew born in the Promised Land. A Jew who spoke Hebrew as their mother tongue. Their future. They had only been a country for less than twenty years so there couldn't be many Sabra girls of child-bearing age in all of Israel and Ted, a goy like Jack, was rolling in the hay down in the cow barn with Aviva, their Aviva, their girl-child of Israel.

Ted said it was her idea. That while they were dancing she'd undone some buttons on her shirt and slid his hand inside against her breast and asked him to go with her to the barn. He said he didn't know what to do, that he knew he shouldn't do it, but what was he supposed to do? "What would you have done? Do you know how beautiful she is? Jesus Christ, she's the most beautiful girl I've ever seen." So he said OK and it happened. In the hay mound in the lamb's pen. "I think she was a virgin." he said. "There was blood in the hay." It had happened three weeks before on the night of the Purim celebration. The celebration of deliverance from extinction by the Persian Empire.

For the people here, Purim was a party that began in the early evening and didn't stop until it was time for the next day's chores. It was the one night when they all could laugh together, hug each other and tell jokes and drink. Most of them were from Chicago, some from New York. Twenty years ago they had come here. Most had worked in the grain yards and train yards with big machinery. Most had lost family in the holocaust. The new State had given them this outpost to protect the border and operate the machinery that turned the Hula Valley from a vast barren gulch into a fertile oasis. That was done.

On the afternoon of Purim, the names of all men and women of army age, between sixteen and twenty-two, were put in a hat, this time Yock's cowboy hat, and five were drawn to see who would stand guard around the kibbutz and five drawn to watch the children. If you got child-watch or guard duty one year, your name didn't go in the hat in the next year. The dining hall had been cleared out and tables put around the perimeter. Food on some, liquor on most. Double doors at the back of the hall led out to a dirt patio area where the older men and a few older women stood close to each other, looking out over Lebanon, drinking whiskey, smoking Turkish cigarettes, talking about the war. The war in '48, the war in '54, the war in '67 and the wars to come because they all knew more wars would come. Time between these wars was the time it takes to get ready for the next one; to have more children, to have more grandchildren, to feed them, to teach them to read, play music, to fight, to shoot, to fly the fighter jets. Tonight the old men wore their good linen shirts, untucked, and comfortable shoes. Tonight they took deep drags on their cigarettes and a long time blowing the smoke out, eyes closed, heads tipped back, smiling, lips slack. It was a full desert moon, a red moon rising over Jordan and if any one of those men had been alone, just all alone in this land of theirs, each exhalation would have been a howl, a high moan like a wolf on a bluff by its lair.

Inside, the others danced to Havanagila. One hundred linked together in a circle, kicking legs up at the Hava part, bowing at the Chemizmahad part, then paired off to the Tennessee Waltz, some waltzing with two arms out to the side, two to the waist, the younger couples holding all four elbows and hands tight in front between them, just rocking. They still had their green kakis on, their knives and pistols still on every belt. Arm wrestling had begun in the far corner. Israeli men, their army shirt sleeves neatly rolled up over their muscles had dragged a table out, set bottles of Jack Daniels at one end and two short candles, three feet apart at the other. Aviva was in charge. She lit the candles, checked the elbows for center, checked the free hands to make sure they were tucked in the back of their pants, not holding the chair, held her hand on top of the clenched fists moving them so they were square between both men, counted one, two three, GO! slamming her palm on the table. They pulled and pulled back and forth, always lower and lower to one side until flesh burned, the loser screamed and the winner jumped up, clapped his hands, took a swig of whiskey and Aviva called the next to try. Ted sat down at the table. Ted was big. Nordic big. As tall as the tallest guy there but wider. His shoulders hung like hams from his neck. He had taken his shirt off, slicked his hair back with beer and rubbed lime juice on his chest. He beat the first guy, the second and the third. The fourth was Yock. Yock had brought his own bottle to the table, an earthen jug with a thumb hold on it and all during the match he would take his free hand, sip the jug, wipe his mouth and adjust his cowboy hat. Most of the party had gathered to watch, yelling, drinking, slapping each other on the back. Ted had locked his shoulder. For Yock to win, he had to pull Ted's whole body over. He couldn't. Nobody won. At some point, Yock nodded to Ted, Ted nodded back and the dancing started again. By then it was deep into the night and Jack had to go bed. His job was not forgiven at Purim. This night Jack would only sleep for two hours and the Purim night would still be lit with laughter. It was after he went to bed that Ted and Aviva had gone to the barn.

Jack's work began at three-thirty every morning. He would find his way by moonlight or flashlight to the commissary by the dining hall, pack food for the day in a black leather iron-strapped box with a steel hasp and lock, load it in the back of a 1953 Jeep, whistle the German Shepherds awake from their sleep in the barn and drive out past coiled barbed wire pulled clear by the night sentry, swing open a set of chain link gates that closed the narrow border road at night and begin a slow drive, hunched forward over the steering wheel peering through the headlights at the dirt, searching for footprints and land mines.

His favorite food was baklava, sweet and crunchy, quarter-pound sticks wrapped in silver foil. Jack was only supposed to take one a day but usually took two or three. Soon enough the keeper of the commissary would find him out and he would have to offer some re-payment. Maybe a day's worth of mucking cow shit from the barn stalls. Maybe a week of kitchen duty. Not money. There wasn't any money on the kibbutz. He took a plastic jug of water, a tin of beans and flat bread, a thick skinned orange and Sasa apples, the same apples served at the embassies and hotels in Tel Aviv and Jerusalem, the pride of the kibbutz. Enough for breakfast and lunch. He filled a separate jug with water for the dogs, rinsed their ceramic bowls and filled a thin leather sack with dry dog food. The box had flares, blankets and a small steel radio that he never figured out how to work.

The Jeep had no keys. Flip a flat toggle switch up and push a thumb-sized button on the dash and the four cylinder Ford engine fired on the first turn. There were two seats; the driver's seat and one bolted on the front bumper. Set on a swivel in front of the bumper seat was the mount for a machine gun. Jack had no gun. No machine gun, no rifle, no pistol. He was not Jewish. He was goy. He was expendable. Yock had given him the choice of the Jeep or a horse; a great tall flat backed white Arabian stallion with a bright colored saddle blanket woven by the Druze, saddle, stirrup straps and girth hand tooled in Arizona and a rifle scabbard Yock said he stole from a British Officer's mount in Haifa while the officer was smoking hashish with an Arab gun dealer in the bazaar. Jack had always been afraid of horses. He chose the Jeep.

Desert dirt in the early morning, still damp before the dew has burned, can't be altered without trace. Any boot print caught in the low headlights, any dirt dug up or scuffed out to bury a coffee-can sized bomb can be seen from forty feet away. As long as his eyes fixed on the road and didn't wander to watch the free roaming goats dance on the morning hills or turn to see the black cloaked Arab men starting their morning fires beginning another day down in the Sayad Valley, just as long as every measure of his attention stayed tight to the dirt, it was unlikely Jack would be blown apart. The Jeep had a throttle knob on the dash. Jack could pull it out to a low idle and, in second gear, move slowly along without shifting or working the gas pedal. That way, all Jack had to do was steer and stare ahead. The dogs, Tof, a female and Yoffe a male, would lope along ahead of the Jeep, one on each side of the road, never in the road. Yock had spent a long time training these dogs. Their bark would signal a person anywhere within a quarter mile or so. Anyone, as Yock had put it, within rifle range. About six miles from Sasa down the dirt road towards the Mediterranean was a Border Patrol station. It was a concrete bunker with three rooms; one where the police sat, one where the kept their guns, ammunition, maps and supplies and a jail cell with bars as thick as a man's wrists. Jack would pull up to the front door to announce his findings; to tell them what he had seen, where and when. Sometimes someone, like him, probably not Jewish, probably a visitor to this land, someone from another kibbutz ten miles down the road west toward the sea, had finished their run of the road and he would see their prints in the dirt leading up from the road to the bunker. Whoever they were, they rode a horse and had only one dog. All the road, east to west, would now be checked clear. Bright yellow busses could take the children from all the small towns and kibbutzim to Quiriat Shimona without fear of the kids being blown to shreds before they got to school. This happened every morning before sunrise along the entire Lebanese border between Syria and the Mediterranean.

Jack drove about ten miles and hour and would check the odometer whenever he saw anything worth noting. That way, he could say, "One and a quarter miles out of Sasa, I saw three sets of footprints; two boots and one sneaker, crossing the road into Israel." The police would jump in their Jeeps and head off into the hills or down the road, always with someone in the bumper seat holding tight to the two handles of their machine gun. Many times in three months Jack reported boot prints. A half a dozen times he saw the dirt ruffled, a small speckled circle the size of a paint can shimmering in the headlight beam. He would stop, check the odometer, put the Jeep in four-wheel and drive up on the hill around the bomb. Once, Jack told them, the footprints went from Israel into Lebanon. They spit and swore and one slammed his fist on the oak desk. No Jew would walk into Lebanon. They had completely missed them. The Al-Fatah had been here, done something somewhere and slipped back to their camps in the hills far across the wide Sayed Valley.

After his early morning drive along the border road, Jack began the second part of his job. He drove about a half mile into the hills to let the cattle out of their corral so they could roam in the pastures of the hills above Lebanon. Tof and Yoffe ran the edges of the herd, keeping them in the high hills, away from the border road. Kibbutz Sasa had a hundred head of cattle, all Brahma or Brahma mixes and all taken from the Syrians within days after the Six Day War. Ten months ago, before the war, Kibbutz Sasa had no cattle. They were just farmers tending fruits and vegetables in the lush Hula Valley, a dry valley they made wet and fertile in the early 50's by diverting the waters of Lake Tiberius. In July of 1967, a month after the Six Day War, Yock and a dozen young men on horseback took Tof and Yoffe and rode east across the green valley and up the steep slopes of the Golan Heights. They stole every healthy cow they could find in every Arab village in a twenty mile radius. Three hundred head. They didn't sleep for two days. Some cows were lost in the steep descent from the high plateau back down into Israel, left with broken legs or necks for the dogs or vultures. They built a new barn for the milking cows at the Kibbutz and fenced in a corral out beyond the border station where the pastures in the valleys were deep and low, where there was more moisture, some grass.

Sometime late in the morning he awoke and heard the dog's distant barking. He had fallen asleep in the front seat of the Jeep. The sun was high and hot. He had slept for hours. The cattle were gone from the fields. None were there. Jack ran to the top of a rise and looked all directions. Behind him, south into Israel, west towards the sea, east towards Syria and then north down into Lebanon. He saw them there. All hundred head in the fields by the Lebanese town. Not in Israel. Jack ran across the field to the far edge of the road and stood right at the border. Sound travels better uphill than down. Sound waves going down bump into rocks and lumps and careen off up above the valley floor. He whistled his loudest pig-calling whistle, thumb and forefinger pinched in a circle pushed against taut lips curling back his tongue blowing shriek after shriek but dogs didn't hear him. They were running around the outside of the herd, trying to keep the cows packed tight.

Jack had never driven the Jeep more than ten or fifteen miles an hour. He drove it 50 mph all the way to the border station. The soldiers got Yock on the radio. Ten or fifteen minutes later, a Jeep with three boys, all younger than Jack, one out front in the shooters' seat holding tight to the machine gun, came fast down the road, pulled up by him and pointed the big gun down into Lebanon. Jack only knew one, the driver. He was David, Aviva's younger brother. He was tall and tussle haired with deep olive skin. They were all shouting in Hebrew. They all had 9 MM Uzi's out and were flailing their arms and guns around as Yock came over the ridge on his Arabian stallion riding hard down the hillside, drawing his Winchester 30-30 out of the scabbard. He fired two shots into the air. Both dogs bolted up the hill towards him and fell into formation, one on either side just behind the horse. Everyone stopped and watched as Yock, now not a hundred feet from the edge of town, swung his horse hard behind the herd and slowed to a trot while the dogs fanned out ahead, moving the cattle up the hill towards us. Yock kept his rifle set across the horse's back, pointed directly into the town. As the herd neared, the boys sprinted down the hill to help funnel the cows into file for the walk down the border road and back to the corral. A calf strayed out of the pack. As David ran to bring it back, the mother cow, a dirty white Brahma with twisted horns, lowered her head and charged out towards him. David stumbled back and back and back, hands pushing against thin air and heels slipping in the desert sand, back but not far enough back as she gored him straight through the stomach. David, not even sixteen, laid out on blankets flat out in the back of the Jeep with tee shirts tied tight around his belly, bled to death halfway to the hospital in Haifa.

The sun had set hours ago. The kibbutz was dark and quiet. Sleeping. Marie and Aviva sat in the dirt in the shadows outside a window to the commissary. Shoulder to shoulder. Aviva had been with her family all afternoon and evening. She was still crying for her brother. Sobbing. Smoking a cigarette. Gulping wine with Marie. Sobbing. The door to the commissary clanged shut and two men walked in, boots clicking on the concrete. They sat a table near the window and started talking in harsh tones in Hebrew. Aviva signaled quiet to Marie and cocked her head up to hear. It was Yock and Shlomo, the head of kibbutz security.

"Like you told me to, I called Major Eban and asked him to get in touch with the American Embassy. I called him two days ago. I told them there was an AWOL American soldier here, a deserter, and asked him what to do about it. He said keep him here. If the Americans agreed, he would send Interpol to pick him up here at the kibbutz. Israel couldn't arrest him for anything, he didn't break any Israeli laws and the Americans don't have any jurisdiction here, so Interpol would have to do it. They should be here tomorrow morning. How did you find out that this Ted Hilliard was having sex with Aviva?"

"Ari was in the cow barn a few nights ago. He saw them. Does her father know?" Yock asked. "No," Shlomo said. "Good. Let's keep it that way. What about Jack Duncan?"

"They can't really arrest him for anything. I just sent his name through with the Hilliard kid's name and asked them to take both of them. It's kind of sad really. But that's the way of youth. The Duncan kid has been a hard worker. He fell asleep. It was a hot out there. Anybody might have fallen asleep."

"No!" Yock's voice turned hard. "You wouldn't have. I wouldn't have. Even young David wouldn't have. None of us would have let our cows go back into Arab land. That is the problem with having goyim volunteers on our kibbutzim. They may work hard. They may be good kids, but they are not here to die for our country. Nobody should be here who isn't willing to die for Israel. The stakes are too high." Their boot heels clicked on the concrete as they left. The commissary door shut behind them.

Aviva slumped on Marie's shoulder, sobbing. Marie's arm was around her, her hand on her mouth to quiet her sounds. "What is it, Aviva? What did they say?" She told her, crying, tears streaming down her proud, golden Semite cheeks.

"Ted, wake up." Marie was leaning over him in the bunk house, urgently whispering, tapping his chest. It was midnight. Then over to Jack. "Jack, wake up," pushing his shoulder. They both woke and sat up in their bunks.

"You both have to leave the kibbutz, right now. Tonight. Interpol is coming for both of you in the morning. You will be arrested and sent back to America. Ted, they will arrest you tomorrow for being a deserter from your Army. Jack, they will take you with him. This is very bad. Very serious. Get up and pack. You must go now."

"Why? Why do we have to leave? What happened?" Jack asked.

"Because Ted, you should not have had sex with Aviva. She is Sabra. She is theirs, not yours. And you Jack. You have killed Aviva's brother. You should not have let their cows go to Arab land. These people are not happy. You have to go!"

"How do you know all this? " Ted asked.

"Aviva and I heard them talking in the commissary. This is what they said."

"Who?" Jack asked. "Yock and Shlomo," she said. "Oh, shit," Ted said. "Yock's the only one who knew about me. Where's Aviva?"

"You must not see her. Ted, why did you do that with her? Didn't you know what could happen?"

"It was her idea, Marie, not mine. I think it was her way of going AWOL without getting shot. You know what I mean?"

"You must go! You must go now. Both of you." Jack held her hands. "Marie, meet me in Marrakesh. Ten days." She kissed his cheek. "I'll be there," she said.

It took them twenty minutes to pick their way through the concertina wire at the low end of the kibbutz, behind the volunteers bunk house. The thighs of their pants and backs of their shirts were ripped and bloodstained.

"Let's not walk in the road, Ted, we should walk in the hills."

"What do you mean, 'walk in the hills?' We got thirty miles to walk in the pitch black carrying all our bullshit and you want me to walk in the goddamn hills."

"Well, actually I don't give a shit if you want to walk in the road and get your balls ripped off by a bomb full of nails. I"m walking in the hills cause you know what, they don't put landmines on hills. They put them in the road."

Late May in Israel and it's hot by eight in the morning. They had walked for seven hours, all along the ridges on the hills that rose up from the valley below, like pack goats. They saw a border road checker come from the east at about four in the morning on a horse with one dog. An hour later they saw a Jeep coming from the east, headlights on, going very fast towards Haifa. "That's my Jeep." Jack said. "Get down so they don't see us." They both lay flat in the high grasses. Yock was driving. Beside him in the front was a man in a suit. In the back was Joe Cole. Jack recognized his copper skin, his long black hair.

Outside of Acre, by that time exhausted, they went to the road and stuck out their thumbs. A fruit and vegetable truck bringing produce from the fertile Hula Valley to the seaport picked them up and took them all the way to the port in Haifa. They found a plywood kiosk down on the docks with a sign offering passage on cargo freighters. One was bound for Istanbul. Ted handed his passport to the young girl in the booth. She took it, looked at it and handed it back to Ted. Jack gave her his. She looked at it and also handed it back. She leaned forward and said very carefully, very quietly, "Someone who said they were Interpol was here with questions of both of you just ten minutes before. Leave from here very fast." She pointed up at the freighter. The captain, Captain Wim, the same Dutch captain who had brought Jack and Marie from Turkey to Israel three months ago, with whom they had laughed, drank and sang, stood on bridge. He jerked his thumb once towards the south and walked back into his cabin. It meant go!

Israel is a tiny country. The size of New Jersey. At its widest, from Gaza on the Mediterranean east to Sodom on the Dead Sea, it is 70 miles. From Lebanon to the southern tip is 240 miles. It's shaped like a knife, the north like a grip and the south like a dagger blade through the Negev desert to the port town of Eliat. The Israeli border at that tiny town where tankers bring oil and goods from the Far East is just a mile wide. When all the nations were debating who, what and where Israel was, the Jews demanded the Negev desert and that small spot on the on the Red Sea. They knew Egypt would never let goods bound to or from their new country through the Suez Canal. They needed a passage to the Orient without having to sail the Mediterranean, through Gibraltar and all the way around Africa to the Indian Ocean.

DOGS IN THE DESERT

"OK, Ted. How about we head south to Eliat and see if we can get on a cargo ship and get out of here that way." Jack said. "No busses, they might be watching those. Let's hitchhike and hope those guys don't stop to pick us up."

Hitchhiking in Israel was, in 1968, a matter of national security. Perhaps it was the law or maybe just a custom born of necessity that any hitchhiker was picked up by the first car to come. Most people in the country are soldiers in one way or another; soldier people who live on farms, on kibbutzim, in towns and cities, not on military bases and when there is calamity, when the Arab jets come and war rains down, everybody has to get to wherever they are supposed to be as fast as possible. It would take far too long to mobilize government vehicles to collect people and deliver them to all those places. Don't stick out your thumb, just point at the ground and that is precisely where the car stops to pick you up. Jack and Ted were 120 miles south in the Negev Bedouin town of Be'er Sheva by ten in the morning.

It was the first Tuesday of May and on the first Tuesday of every month Be'er Sheva exploded in a riot of color, noise and smell as the Bedouin came east from the Siani and west from Jordan and Syria to barter their goods. What, on a Monday, was a small nearly empty old town, was on a Tuesday, hundreds and hundreds of shouting, laughing, arguing nomads in hooded desert capes and hundreds of camels with bright woven saddle bags and spangled bridles and seemingly thousands of goats bleating and some roasting on spits over camel dung fires. Tents stretched out for miles in the undulating sand and the town was thick with spread-out carpets and goods for trade. Rope, knives, cheese, cloth. Be'er Sheva was the last desert stop on the Silk Road from Afghanistan to Alexandria. There was water under that sand and the wanderers had been stopping there since before recorded time. On Wednesday, it was all gone; empty, quiet and breezeless. On the first Wednesday of each month the sand stunk of goat shit.

From Be'er Sheva to Elait was another 120 miles of desert road. They waited for hours for a car to come but the first car that came, a Range Rover, took them all the way there. The only other traffic on the road was petroleum tanker trucks. Trucks full of fuel headed north to Tel Aviv, empty trucks headed south for more fuel. And trucks with goods from the East. There didn't seem to be any municipality in Elait; no government buildings or post offices, no library, no parks. There wasn't even a police station. It was like an outpost. Along the beach were people, houses, dirt roads and bars with western music and cold beer. At the far end of town there was a long wooden pier and a vast concrete parking for tanker trucks but there was no shack, no office, no building where anyone could ask about passage out. There was an occasional army truck with soldiers riding under canvas in the back. Halfway down the beach stood a guard tower with a Star of David nailed to the front. Six foot high rolls of razor wire spread from the base of the tower down the sand and out into the still warm waters of the Red Sea. On the other side of the guard tower, 10 feet away, was another guard tower, nailed to front of that tower was the four color flag of Jordan. Another spiral of razor wire rolled from its base down the beach into the still warm waters of the Red Sea. There was nobody in either tower. Just the flags standing guard. On the Jordanian side of the razor wire was port of Aqaba. Seemingly, except for the bars and cold beer, a mirror image of Eliat.

There she sat. A fat cargo ship, probably an oil tanker, about a half mile out. It looked as though she was dead center in the water between the two countries, too far out to read the name on the bow or see a flag fly on the stern. It could have come from anywhere and been there for either country.

"Swim?"

"Sure," Jack said, "Why not?"

"Because if we get there and they say 'sure' come on with us, our backpacks and passports and money are still all behind the bar counter. We'd have to swim all the way back to get it." Ted said.

"That's OK," Jack said. "If they say 'yes' we swim back and get somebody with a boat to take us back out. It probably takes a ship like that a long time to haul up an anchor and go somewhere."

They both stripped to their underpants and dove in.

The anchor chain was huge. Each link was two feet long, two inches thick. Jack started up first, scuttling along almost parallel to the water and then he began to rise on a slow catanary curve up and up and up until it was almost vertical and the ocean was a hundred feet below and his hands and feet were burning from the hot steel baked all day in the Mid-East sun. The hauser hole, where the chain went through the gunwale onto the deck was big enough to easily slide through. They looked aft on the ship. It was huge, as long as two football fields with the Soviet flag flying off the mizzen stay. "Russian." Jack said to Ted. "Russian," Ted said, "bad, but worth a try."

It is far easier to climb up than climb down. Things go well when you lead with your head and shoulders, pulling up and pushing with your feet and all things are in balance and solid underneath you. Like climbing a mountain face. Gravity is your friend. In reverse, you can't see anything. Your feet are your eyes and your hands just clutch. Going down, gravity is your enemy. At the slightest slip you're gone. Folks get off giant ships by getting on to some other smaller ship and going to shore. There wasn't one of those there for them and even if the people on board had said, 'Sure, for a few rubles we'll take you to Vladivostok with us. We won't turn you into the KGB or anything like that when we get there, you can just wander off into Siberia and find your way back to America'. Even if they said that, their clothes, money and passports were back in Israel on the beach in the bar with the Rolling Stones poster. They climbed one hundred and fifty feet of chain. One hundred feet above the water, through the hauser hole and onto the foredeck. There wasn't any way off the ship. They stood on the deck in their underpants. "Hello! Anybody here?" Jack yelled.

Far at the stern a man burst out of the cabin on the bridge and came running down the deck, one arm straight out in front of him holding a pistol, screaming in Russian. Ted and Jack were up on the gunwale and over the edge faster than minnows over a rock. They dove. Up higher than a ten story building they dove off head first. And then it was slow and it was weightless and went on and on and on. As Jack dove down he kept twisting his shoulders, arching his back and kicking his legs as high up as he could to keep his body straight down and hands thumb-locked together to split the water before his head split the surface. The speed of a free falling object is 33 feet per second squared. They hit the Red Sea at about 50 miles an hour and went down and down and it was then that Jack realized that he hadn't filled his lungs before he left the gunwale. When they came up gasping and flailing, the Russian was still screaming, still waving his pistol at them. But he didn't shoot. They swam like dolphins; under water, up for air, under water, up for air until, looking back, they couldn't see him anymore.

The Army soldiers in Elait didn't seem to care at all about what went on in town or what people were doing or not doing. They were there to protect Israel's vital shipping interests at this tiny touch of sand where, standing at the water's edge, you could see Jordan, Saudi Arabia and Egypt. The Red Sea forks at the southern tip of the Sinai Peninsula. A few ships go right, up the Gulf of Aqaba to these little ports of Israel and Jordan. Almost all go left up the Gulf of Suez, through the canal, across the Mediterranean to the ports of Europe. Most of the people in the town were either dockworkers or reprobates; people hiding out in broad daylight because there wasn't anybody to see them who cared at all, except perhaps soldiers watching soldiers.

She was young with dark skin, short cropped black hair and very tired, droopy, watery eyes. Ted was all over her.

"Ted, Ted, Ted, you got to stop talking to her. She said she's AWOL from the Israeli Air Force, just like you. Yock told us they shoot those people here and, you know what? The big goy white guy with his hands in her pants, they shoot him first. So let's get out of here, OK?"

"Five more minutes. I think I got it figured out. She's a junkie. Gimme five minutes."

A half an hour later Ted and Jack were walking due west across the sand dunes towards the Egyptian Siani looking for a deep wadi with a fig tree three miles out of town where a girl named Sherry lived in a green tent with her twelve dogs who were collectively named Captain America And All His Ships At Sea. It was a hundred and ten degrees, Jack had a belly full of beer and had left his hat in the bar. They were wandering across a blistering hot foreign desert in search of a heroin addict. A heroin addict who would miraculously cause whomever was chasing them to give it up. Leave them alone.

There was a fig tree and there was a big green tent and there was a horrific noise of barking dogs rushing up the dunes. Jack had had some difficulty a few years back with a German Shepard rushing down a farmer's long driveway late at night, snarling and tearing at his leg before the farmer drove his pick-up down the hill, got out and beat the dog into submission with a club he kept in the truck, probably for that very purpose. Jack had developed a serious phobia about unchained dogs. As Jack dumbly watched all twelve of the dogs dig and growl their way towards us up the dune, the pack lead by a big German Shepard, he lurched to run. Ted grabbed him. A whistle shrieked from down below and all twelve dogs stopped, stopped dead, turned around, ran down the hill and into the big green tent. Sherry waved, beckoning them to come on down.

"We have some money. We need a passport. And then we need some dope for the girl in town who told us about you."

"Who's that?" she asked. Sherry was in her early twenties. Tall, skinny, dark as a Bedouin with stringy dishwater blonde hair wearing a faded blue long sleeved men's dress shirt and the bottoms of a black bikini. She still had all her teeth. "Ruth," Ted said.

"Oh yeah, her. Pretty little Ruth. OK. I don't have a passport you could use but I know a guy who might not need his anymore. Give me forty bucks American and I'll give you some shit for Ruth and point you toward a guy you can talk to about it." Ted gave her two twenty dollar bills and she gave him a small cellophane bag thick with fine brown powder. She took them outside, pointed north and said, "About a quarter mile. Third tent. His name's Danny."

"The heroin in Eliat come from those places that have the cleanest uncut brown junk in the world. It don't get here by drug dealers because there isn't any market here and bringing it through Israel is suicide. It gets here from sailors looking for a little extra money in the port. Not like the stuff that comes overland to Turkey and gets cut with all manner of bullshit for sale to all the European junkies. This stuff comes straight out of Thailand on ships with rice, rubber and cloth. When you hear those shipments are coming in, you know the good stuff is coming with it. Don't take much to stay high here. Doesn't cost much either and nobody cares. Best place in the world for a shooter."

That's what Danny told them as he sat in his tent, boiling up his works in a pot on the floor. Danny didn't need his passport. He wasn't going anywhere. Even if he wanted to, it would not have been possible. He was so strung out on dope going anywhere was out of the question. He was tall and probably had been stout when he left home. His bones seemed thick. Now he weighed maybe a hundred and twenty pounds. His arms and thighs were like shoe leather from so many needles. His life was spent stoned in that wadi. He had three teeth left; two on the bottom, one up top. A little while after he tied off and shot up, he told his life story. He was Danny Higgins, a Canadian from Cobourg, Ontario, a small town 80 kilometers east of Toronto. He had two brothers and a sister. He was the oldest. He told about the schools he went to and that his father sold insurance and his mother's maiden name was Tingley and what she looked like or at least what she looked like when he left four years ago bound for Turkey,

Afghanistan and Malaysia. He answered every question asked, not looking at Ted or Jack, looking at the tent wall and talking in a dull monotone. They put a twenty on the table by his needles, took his passport and got up to go. He didn't care.

They went back to the bar in town with the Rolling Stones poster. Jack worked on his backpack. Inside the bottom was a reinforcing flap. He slit one side open and slid Ted's American passport inside, picked the threads out and cleaned up the edge. The bartender gave him a small tube of glue. He sealed the edge and repacked. Ted was Danny Higgins now. He even looked pretty much like Danny when Danny left home. Close enough anyway.

Sean O'Neal sat on the patio behind the bar underneath a palapa, the palm fronds rustling in a soft southerly breeze. He had rifled through every page of everything in Jack's knapsack while they had been out in the desert buying a passport from a junkie. He had finally found the poem. He found it because of Marie's scratchings and notes. He watched Ted and Jack through the window. They didn't see him. Sean had found a photograph in a little black book of poems written by a Lebanese poet. It was stuck in the book between a poem called 'Freedom' and a poem called 'Reason and Passion'. A picture of a beautiful girl leaning against an oak tree in purple and black stripped bell bottoms, a man's t-shirt cut off crooked high above her belly button, sandals, a string of flowers in her hair and a smile, head cocked to the side, eyebrows arched in silent invitation. It was Gwyneth, his sister. He held it in his hand; watching Jack stash the passport in the bottom of the knapsack, watching him pack his things, drink his beer.

"Who the fuck are......." was as far as Ted got before both his feet were belt high and the back of his head slammed

248

into the concrete floor, a foot away from Jack who lay sprawled face first in a spilled pitcher of beer.

"Don't," Sean barked at the bartender, who was wrestling with a sticky drawer behind the bar. "You pull a gun out of there and I'll kill you before you can point and shoot. Just get me a bucket of water. I want to talk to these guys."

Ted was gone. Sean had dispatched him with a curt, "I don't give a shit who you are, who you were or what you do. You don't know anything I need to know. Your buddy does. Interpol doesn't know what you look like. They got no picture, just a name and a description. They thought they were going to get you at the Kibbutz. Hit the road. Goodbye."

New passport in his shirt pocket, Ted shook Jack's hand. They hugged and Ted walked off to hitch hike north to Jaffa to catch a freighter bound for Europe.

"Where did you get this photograph?" Sean had picked Jack up, slammed him in a chair and told the bartender to bring two beers and a towel.

Jack stared at him. "Fuck You."

"I'm going to ask you one more time, real nice, and then I'm going to make you wish you never saw me. Where did you get this photograph?"

"I already wish I never saw you. What are you doing hanging out with my friends at my mother's house and then following me around the goddamn world. Who are you? What do you want? I'm not a drug dealer. I'm not a goddamn drug dealer, Mr. Narcotics Agent. That girl's a friend of mine. Leave her alone. She doesn't deal drugs either. Leave her out of this." Jack wiped his face and head and neck with the towel and took a long pull on his beer. He pointed at the blood on the stained towel, "Thanks a lot, shithead."

Two soldiers walked in the bar, their Uzis hanging loose at their sides. They looked at the Sean and Jack, looked at the bartender and said something in Hebrew. The bartender shook his head. They left.

"Who is Marie?" His voice was even. Flat. He unclipped a note from the back of Gwyneth's picture and handed it to Jack.

Teddy Gold, Cathy Wilkerson, William Ayers, Gail Howland, Terry Robbins, Mike Clonsky, Beradine Down (?), Diana Oughten, Jack Jacobs, Mark Ruddie (?) Steven Tappas (?) Jeffery Jones. (I don't know if these are their real names as they spell them but this is what they sound like when they are spoken.......The children in this little house all go to sleep at dark so I had hours and hours, days and days to crack this puzzle. It was fun.......and who is this girl? Is she your girlfriend?.................Marie

It took Jack a long time to piece it together. He read the note, looked at Sean, read the note, looked at Gwyneth's photograph, read the note, saw Gail Howland's name and realized that these were the names of the people in the poem he had smuggled out of his brother's prison. He could almost feel Marie's braids swishing against his bare body as he realized why she had gone into his backpack and put the names on Gwen's picture, not with the poem. Somebody wanted the poem, but nobody would connect Gwen's picture with that poem. Smart girl. Jack looked at Sean and said, "She is the daughter of the French Ambassador to the United States."

"He's with a girl. A French girl. It is of the utmost importance that she not be made aware that you are doing anything. Do not let her see you. Do not get the French involved."

Sean drank his beer, remembering Hancock's words. He ordered two more. The knot was getting too tight. He couldn't figure out how all this could play out. This Jack fellow may hang with hippies but he's got a backbone that won't snap. The French are all over this. What else do they know? If

I have done something that's going to cause an international problem, I'm never going to make it home alive. I can't just beat the information out of this guy. Gwyneth knows him. Doesn't just know him, he's her boyfriend. How can that be?

"What's your name?" Jack asked.

"Shut up, I'm thinking." Sean said.

"Good," Jack said, "That's good. Thinking is better than beating the shit out of people. Do you know this girl?" Jack said pointing to the photo.

"I said, shut up, I'm thinking."

Jack stood up, got another beer from the bartender and said, "I'm going to take a short walk so you can think and I don't have to watch you doing it. Don't worry, you got all my shit. I can't leave. I'll be back in five minutes." Five minutes later he came back.

"Where," Sean asked leaning over close to Jack, "did you get a picture of my sister?"

The sun perched on the on the western lip of the desert, seeming to roll slightly back and forth, to shimmy, to wiggle as though trying to find just the right spot, burning nearly vermillion as the whole orb, then the half disc, then just the faintest tip, like a hot match, burnt out into the vast brown sands of the Eastern Sahara. "Holy shit, did you see that?" Sean took a long toke off the dope pipe and handed it to Jack, leaning back against the stone jetty at the water's edge, staring off into the dimming nothingness. It had taken a hunk of hash the size of a big grape, but, by and by, piece by piece, toke by toke, they had told each other everything. When the sun had still been high in the sky, they realized that neither of them over the long haul had any other option. They were intertwined. Their government had for its own purposes taken these two disparate and independent strands of youth

251

and knotted them together. Were these purposes patriotic?
Were they demonic? They decided to leave that judgment to
the old white men elected by the people to do just that. Sort it
out. Right from wrong. The aging Belgian folksinger
bartender had been happy to give them the hashish and the
cheap clay pipe in exchange for Sean showing him how the
gun, now out of the sticky drawer, actually worked; where the
safety was, how the nine round magazine clip released out of
the handle, how you break it down, oil it and put it back
together and how you put soap on the drawer runners so they
won't stick the next time you need it. Sean also threw in the
bargain the agreement not to break his neck unless he talked
to anybody ever about what he had seen or heard. Sean and
Jack cooked up a plan while they finished the dope in the patio
behind the bar. Kidnapping the wife of an FBI agent struck
Jack as hairbrained; suicidal, with almost certain life-ending
consequences. Almost certain. Not completely certain. A
sliver of possibility it could succeed. That sliver of possibility
was the same sized sliver that either of them would live once
the FBI knew they both knew everything. As Sean and Jack
figured it out, it seemed like they had to do it.

Jack re-wrote the poem so the Weathermen wouldn't
get assassinated before they did anything illegal. Sean devised
a plan so the Panthers in Algeria wouldn't get murdered before
they committed any crimes. Maybe both groups had already
had committed crimes, but since Jack and Sean didn't know
anything about that, they decided they couldn't be the judge
and jury. It was up to people elected to make those decisions.

In the morning Jack found a 'World Almanac: 1960'
edition on a shelf behind the bar. He went down to the beach
and re-wrote the poem on a blank piece of paper. He gave it to
Sean who paper-clipped a note to it, 'I think this is what you
are looking for'. The Russian tanker was still at anchor out in
the Red Sea.

TONY IRONS

BRINGING IT ALL BACK HOME

there is no
weather where i am, deep down
underground in a bomb bunker
hunkered below my parent's home,
incubating my mother's nightmare.
never again will i care to sleep upstairs
in the mansion of my childhood
or hold my favorite bear,
a round brown
teddy, rose and velvet eyes,
silk shirt.
the spell of china's finest,
the damning spell cast on western greed
as round and blinking, days on end
eyes and hours tick on and on.

can our land be bright again?
will sun from the east
bring clean light or will a northern
wind howl and
hurry true men
from their ancestral homes?

i am subterranean,
sick at heart for my land now lost to greed
i sing loud, my songs
fill more than space, they
pierce the soul.

i circle plastic icons
of contemporary culture

in a round ring about me and
ignite them singing
jimmy d! jimmy d! as my voice tells a
tale or two to a deaf nation.

we hope the god
ulysses grant us power;
washing ton after ton of guilt away.
but i climb out now
into the fray
like the beanstalk man, now
mad and soon
to find my path, to
clear new roads ahead.

i need sun to see it right
i'm off to spain for boots
of spanish leather.
and then to france
to stroke the sculpted bronze of maceo
jeffersons joans of ark and jesus
and then back here
to fight, to free my home of fear.

SUBVERSIVE VERSES

The freighter out of Haifa was a stinking, belching Liberian scow. The steel decks were awash in some rancid fluid like year old fish oil or melted blubber. The crew seemed to have mastered the art of walking without legs flying about like a funny man in a vaudeville skit, but for the others; Jack, Sean and six Spanish Jews returning from their once in a lifetime pilgrimage to the Holy Land, walking was not possible without using both hands to hold onto the gunwale rail. Whatever paint had been applied had long since peeled off and washed out to sea giving way to a thick, bubbling scale of rust. She was a fat old aunt moments away from her funeral. Her hold below was packed from stem to stern, from keel to deck with crates of apples and lemons and an army of happy rats gnawing away at the fresh produce bound for the first port of call on the Mediterranean coast of Spain then off to Barcelona bistros, bars and four star restaraunts. Sasa apples. The finest apples in the world. Hula Valley lemons, plump and tart but not bitter. The Jews had been to Jerusalem, to the sacred site of ancient Judaism, the Wailing Wall, the second temple of Soloman where they had stood before the great stones and, mumbling things that reached their mind from the deepest places of their heart and soul, slid little handwritten notes, secret notes, on folded paper into the cracks between the stones just as Jews had done before them for thousands of years. Now, on their way home, these merchants huddled together in an alcove under the ship's bridge rising only to grasp their way to the gunwale, lean over and barf up what little gefelefish was left in their stomachs.

For the benefit of his two young American voyagers, Ragnald of Oksfjord, the captain, a soaring Norwegian with skin like sun dried sea-kelp, stood on the bridge and, in heroic tenor clear and lurid as a fog horn, hallowed Dylan's, *'Zee Hour Zat Zee Ship Comes In'*

Three days at sea, two days of trains and ferries, Jack and Sean reached Marrakesh, Morocco nine days after Jack had been booted from the kibbutz. Marie arrived the next afternoon. Young people of the sixties did not have to make elaborate plans as to where in a city they would meet. It was unwritten but universally understood that the meeting place would always be the International Youth Hostel. That is where Marie was, sitting in a ratty, overstuffed chair in front of an abandoned fireplace reading an old copy of Le Monde. She threw her arms around Jack and looked straight over his shoulder into the eyes of Sean O'Neal. Their eyes locked. Her mouth opened. The human eyes do nothing more than admit light, refract it into shape and color and send the data to the brain where one's conscious knowledge in the past and in the present melds with the synaptical spectrum of the subconscious creating an image that is drawn in the physical sense and painted thick or thin with emotion in the spiritual sense; thick or thin with fear or hate or sympathy or love. Instant energy, laser fast, zapped between them. Bold, bright magenta. Desire.

After explaining everything to her father and making specific plans over the phone with the French Embassy, Marie and Sean, aka Jacques Botier, caught the early train from Marrakesh through Tangier through Oujda, both with French passports, three hundred miles across the northern fertile plain into the train station in Algiers. Marie was veiled, both of them wore cloaks. Sean's was tied at the waist with ten wraps of thumb-sized rope and a tassel hanging down. Ten wraps, thirty-two inches each was a four inch wide band thirty feet long, easily enough to tie up three men. Inside his cloak was a six inch double-bladed horn-handled goat-skinning Berber knife he had bought in Marrakesh. He had sharpened it on a smooth flat stone he had found in the walkway outside his hotel. Fifty times each side, spitting on the stone every ten strokes. Remembering how Popcorn hated the sound. They walked together, side by side, shoulders touching, not talking. They walked through the throng of the central city until the main boulevard forked three ways: the right branch to the French section, the center branch to the government quarter and the left branch up into the labyrinth of winding narrow cobbled streets of the Casbah. Marie's father had told his daughter to present herself to the Ambassador in the French Embassy, no one else. No one else! She was to wait there until a man named Jean arrived from France. He would be carrying a black diplomatic passport. Make him show it to you. And then come immediately home. Immediately. Do you understand? Yes, Papa, I understand. I love you.

It was a black night. The moon and stars were lost in space somewhere above the storm clouds that stretched across the Mediterranean. Get the hardest first. The rest is downhill. Sean found the darkest, most remote corner of the barricades that separated the debauchery of the international port from the abstinent, puritanical Muslim city and shed his Berber garb, hiding it in a trash can. In blue jeans, black tee shirt and black watch cap with his rope and knife he made his way past warehouses and machine shops towards the harbor and the bars. The blackness of the night gave way to and eerie yellow illumination at the water's edge where stevedores loaded and unloaded cargo freighters around the clock. The dockworkers were not Algerian. They were Bulgarian, German, Russian or French. When their shift ended, they went to the bars and whorehouses and when they could take no more drink, no more flesh, they went to sleep in barracks made of corrugated tin. The basketball player was here somewhere. He came every night at about this time. There were four bars. Sean found him in the third bar standing at the counter knocking back a whiskey with a beer chaser. Sean picked a tall French girl sitting in the back with a coterie of whores waiting for work. He paid her 500 dinar to coax the big man outside and around the back of the bar to the whorehouse shack. She was good. Within a few minutes she had his hands inside her blouse and her hand inside his pants. Out back at the door to the whorehouse, under the dim red light, she motioned for him to wait a moment. She held up her hand in a stop signal, pointed to her eyes then put her head on her hands, tipped to the side. The universal sign for a head on a pillow. She was going to see if there was an open bed.

When the door closed behind her, Sean hit him across the back of the head with a 4X4 piece of dock blocking and all seven feet of him crumpled into a heap in the dirt. He tied his hands together, tied his feet together, tied them both to each other, stuffed a rag in his mouth, tied it around his head and dragged the man into the dark. Ten minutes later, at exactly ten o'clock, the limousine from the French Embassy met them at the barricade where Sean had entered. Sean and the driver stuffed the big man, now conscious, in the back seat and the car pulled away. Sean put on his Berber garb and walked off in the dark, up the hill to the Casbah carrying a liter jug of goat blood the driver had given him.

The others went in a similar way. The German boy had left before first light and the candy salesman clapped his hands in happiness. 500 dinar had bought all the sweets and rented the cart for an hour. The trussed playwright rode in the storage bin under the candy shelf through the narrow cobblestone alleys, riding a deafening din all way to the foot of the hill. The little man with a head like an eggplant made no fuss about it at all. Sean had poked him in the chest outside the café then broke a stout wooden railing with one blow of his bare hand. Mr. Moussa-Faki, Elroy's lawyer, let himself be tied up, gagged and stuffed in the trunk of the limousine. Sean dribbled goat blood on the floors of each house. In the big man's house, he busted furniture, smeared blood on the walls and left his bone-handled knife on the floor.

When all three were in the basement of the embassy, Sean tied a hood fashioned from a bed sheet on each head, splashed some goat blood on their neck as though their throats had been slit and, from twenty feet away, took a Polaroid picture of each one separately. He went upstairs to wash up and find Marie.

"The man who brought you here is a United States Special Forces Green Beret. He was sent here by your government to kill you. He has chosen not to. He made that decision by himself, voluntarily. He has made it clear that if he can come into Algeria, capture all three of you and bring you here to this basement, the next assassin can come here and kill all three of you just as easily as he could have. If your government believes you are still alive, there will be a next assassin. And he might just do what he is told to do. This soldier has chosen instead to deliver you into the custody of the French Government. You will be moved to an undisclosed location and kept under house arrest until such time as it is safe for you to be returned to your country. Your government, as well as the Algerian government, will be advised that you are dead. All three of you. You were murdered by an unknown assailant and your weighted bodies were dumped in the sea. You will moved tonight to the docks where you will be put in wooden crates with air holes and shipped by freighter to another country. The trip will be approximately ten hours at sea. Good luck."

The man with the black passport, Jean, was tall, tanned, well built, in his seventies with close cropped white hair and a hard stare. The same man who met Joe Cole on the veranda in Tangier. The same ex-CIA agent now working for Marie's father. It had not been hard for the Ambassador to convince the man that not only was he the right person to do this, but it was the right thing to do.

The three Black Panthers were still bound and gagged. They were hooded and bound, sitting on the concrete floor in the basement of the Embassy. They could hear the wooden crates being slid across the floor and the tick, tick purring of a diesel truck waiting outside the door. Part of the CIA man's charge had been to make sure that the Ambassador's daughter was safely conveyed back to Paris. While he was talking, Marie and Sean had left the Embassy. Holding hands they had sprinted five blocks to the station and taken the last train back to Morocco.

"Mr. Hancock, the three men in Algeria are at the bottom of a thousand feet of water. Nobody will ever find them. I mailed an air express package to you from Rabat that has all the paperwork Jack Duncan had on him including the list of names you were looking for. I've flagged that piece of paper. I included Polaroid photos of the each of the three Panthers before they were bagged up and dumped. I'm going to take some R&R over here and I'll be stateside in couple of weeks. I'll call you when I get there. And, Mr. Hancock, when I get there I want to see my sister. We did what you wanted done. I want it over."

"You've done a great job, Sean. I'll expect a call in two weeks."

Five days after talking to Agent Hancock, Jack, Gwyneth, Sean and Marie walked together out of the Washington, D.C. office of the French Ambassador to the United States. Marie stayed with her father. The other three took a bus back to Boston. The Ambassador had asked them to tell him everything. Everything. They had. Almost. Sean downgraded the murder of "a mafia hit man" to assault but Gwyneth had been forthright in describing what the man had done to her. After they left, M. Chevenaeu sat in quiet reflection for a half an hour pondering how it was that a nation could treat its children that way and realizing that any nation could and many did, particularly when they were suffering daily domestic and international trauma. Even France might do that.

"Annette, would you please place a call to Dean Rusk." It was not unusual for an Ambassador to call the State Department. It was unusual for the call to be placed directly to the Secretary of State. Later that afternoon Dean Rusk was telling the Ambassador what the likely upshot would be. "Jacques, I will advise the President but I am quite sure that in an election year this is not an avenue he would wish to pursue. I think he will say that this is a matter best looked into early in the next administration. Are all of the young people safe? Good. I'll get back to you. And Jacques, thank you for helping them."

The President, LBJ, did not say such thing as 'it's best to pursue this later.' He said, in his Texas drawl, "Why would I want that fucking pervert Hoover humping my leg in public. That's just shit crazy, Dean, and you ought to know that."

"Yes Sir, I do know that. I told the Ambassador I would bring it to your attention."

"Yeah, well you tell that little Frenchman to sniff up somebody else's skirt, OK?"

"Agent Hancock, do you know something that I don't know and the Director doesn't know. He would like an answer to that question. Director Hoover is standing right here beside me in my office and he is not happy!" Meritt's voice was going up into the soprano range. "Do you?"

"About what, sir?"

"About this supposed list of subversives. About this poem that you say was smuggled out of the penitentiary and retrieved by your operative in Israel. Do you know anything about this that you haven't told us? If you do, you had better start talking right now."

"I do not know anything about that list that I haven't told you. I received it Air Express mail two days ago. The operative retrieved it from the person, a Mr. John Duncan, who we believed had it in his possession all along. He did have it and he must have received it from his brother the day before he left the United States. I immediately sent it to our encryption lab. What is the problem, sir?"

"The problem, Hancock, is that the lab ran that poem six times and came up with the same list of names every time. Do you know what those names are?"

"No, sir, I don't." The Special Agent fidgeted with papers on his desk.

"OK, I'll tell you. In order: *Teddy Roosevelt, Eisenhower, Wilson, Harry Truman, Fillmore, Pierce, Taylor, Ulysses Grant, Washington, Madison.* You recognize any of them? Does that sound like a list of subversives to you? You've been played, Hancock. Somebody knows about our little Program. You've been had. You've been duped; played for a patsy. Director Hoover wants to see you here Friday, 0900. You clear on that?"

"Yes sir." He really didn't want to go back to Lincoln, Nebraska he thought as he hung up the phone.

"Have somebody talk to that Vannie Druggan fellow. Tell him Hancock is going to squeal on him about being an informant. Tell him whatever he wants to do is fine with us," Hoover said to David Meritt as he left his office. "I'm out of town on Friday."

"There is nobody going to do anything about this unless we do it ourselves, just like we talked about in Israel. Marie's father said no go. Some bigwig said sorry, can't help. Our time is running out. Hancock expects me back in a week or so. If we're going to do it, we gotta do it now. Soon. We have to do it before Hancock expects me back. He might have something planned for me. If these guys find out what we did in Algeria, we're all dead. Bang. Dead. All of us. All three of us. We all know everything that happened. We all know what they did and what they are doing. They wouldn't hesitate a second. They don't seem to give a shit if people live or die. Jack, you in?"

"Yeah, I'm in. But we have to be really careful with what we do. Somehow we have to have a plan where we don't actually 'kidnap' anybody. We want to make sure that nothing bad happens to this guy's wife and kid. They didn't do anything. I guess what I mean by that is no Vannie Druggan, no mobsters or all that shit you talked about on the beach. None of those guys trying to turn the tables on the FBI. Nobody but us."

"OK," Sean said, "I did talk to one of the boys last night. Just to find stuff out. They know these things. They need to know these things. It might be important to them someday.

263

Here's what it is. She's an alcoholic. Big time. He also said she volunteers as a children's librarian at the Somerville Elementary School every day from 9 to 12. He said they'd seen her a couple of times buy a bottle of vodka at Mt. Auburn Liquors at noon on her way home from the library. Noon. Jesus Christ. Nothing else, just a bottle of Smirnoff Vodka. Her daughter comes home on a school bus from the Arlington Elementary School at three-fifteen every day. Daddy is usually home by six. That's all. Pretty simple."

Last night Jack's brother Dwight, two weeks out of jail, had spent the evening with them going over all of the events that had transpired. He told them where the poem came from. Who had given it to him. Sean sat quiet, listening to him, piecing it together. Dwight wrote letters for them. One was addressed to Senator Frank Church, Chairman of the Senate Intelligence Committee, cc'd to no one. Concise, powerful, constructed with proper legal language. The signature line was for Special Agent Timothy Hancock, FBI. The other was much longer, written in layman's language with statements and allegations that would be red meat to any investigative reporter. It was addressed to Executive Editors, New York Times, Washington Post, Boston Globe and copied to Mr. Ramsey Clark, U.S. Attorney General and J. Edgar Hoover. It contained no names and had no signature line. After he drafted the letters, Sean asked Dwight to do him a favor. A big favor. Something that was very important to him. He told Dwight that there was no way that he could go into a Federal Pen without risking his life, but if Dwight could do this for him he would be truly grateful. Please tell Elroy that his brother wants to say something to him. I was in Nam with his brother. He's was my friend, but I think he's dead now. Tell him he wanted to say that the Viet Cong might be brothers in your eyes, Elroy, but they are actually ruthless killers. Murderers. What you're doing with those Black Panthers, Elroy, is wrong;

killing innocent folks. Elroy, you're no different than the Cong. Please Dwight, if you could tell him that it would make some sense out of all this madness. Dwight said he would think about it.

Jack, Sean and Gwyneth were in a coffee shop on Tremont Street looking out on the Boston Common. Dwight had left that morning for a board meeting of the War Resisters League in Philadelphia. On the cafe table were the letters Dwight had drafted. That day's copy of the Globe lay open to Metro Section; *Community Events.* Gwyneth started making little clucking sounds. Her lips pouted out and her tongue was clicking on the roof of her mouth. Clucking. She stood up, pulled her hair into a pony tail on top of her head and knotted it. She buttoned up the top button on her shirt, pursed her lips into a severe little downturned crescent, put her first finger on her lips and went, "Shhhh...Shhhhhh!...Do I look like a librarian? Read this." she said tapping the newspaper. "

Open House For Children At Boston Library

Roald Dahl loves nothing more than reading "James and the Giant Peach" to spellbound children. He will be at the Boston Public Library Wednesday afternoon as part of a kick-off celebration of children and children's literature

Volunteers are welcome to assist.
Call Nancy Demond at 617-997-0033.

"Get her to volunteer. Perfect. This is perfect. No kidnapping. It gives us all day tomorrow to get ready. But we can't let her drive her own car. She could leave at any time and ruin everything," Jack said. "I think we need Bill Bear. He's the 'wheelman' from New Hampshire. You met him when you busted my house. He can get us anywhere anytime and he

265

won't ask questions. If anybody runs plates, they won't find him. He borrows license plates." They were all bunked in the youth hostel on Tremont St. a block out of the Combat Zone. "I'm definitely going to have to lie to him. 'Hey Bill Bear, how'd you like to help me kidnap the wife and daughter of an FBI agent?' Not cool. How about, 'How'd you like to drive an hour and a half to give a woman and her daughter a lift to a library five miles away?' Not cool. How about, 'My buddy got this woman knocked up and she needs an abortion, can you help me?' He'd go for that."

"Yeah, I remember him. Cool guy. Very together. Should have been Special Forces."

"No," Jack said. "Should not have been Special Forces. Hippies don't shoot people."

By ten o'clock that night, they had a plan. "As long as Marie's father calls while I'm sitting there, it should work. Otherwise we're all dead." Jack said.

The Salvation Army had racks and racks of clothes that must have been donated by retiring librarians or school secretaries. Gwyneth, in tight brown tweeds and sturdy brown shoes looked as though she would not tolerate even the slightest transgression of any rule. Not even the thought of it. Her lipstick was scarlet. Eyebrows penciled brown. Black rimmed glasses with clear lenses perched on her nose. Bill Bear's first impression was that her moral stricture would be as rigid as a rod. Mission style. But as they drove along, he began to feel a strange underlying aura. Perhaps, he mused, with the top knot down and the tweeds in a heap on the floor, she might have some seriously deviant ideas of good clean fun. Mother Mercury lumbered into the driveway at 348 Arlington St. in Watertown at three-thirty in the afternoon. On the driver's side door were stick-on letters that said, 'Public Library' with a round seal under it with a picture of a baseball player on it. It was the only round sign Bill Bear could find. A

Boston Red Sox sticker. He assured them all that if Mrs. Hancock had packed in a few vodkas, she'd never know the difference. At a hardware store he'd bought a small, magnetic, battery operated yellow flashing light which he had stuck on the roof and turned on. The roof of this 1958 Monterey Phaeton behemoth was over seven feet long. The light looked like a pimple.

Bill Bear and Sean got out and stood beside the car trying to look like library maintenance personnel. Gwyneth knocked on the front door. She had called Mrs. Hancock an hour earlier and Susan, she said please call me Susan, had been delighted to help. Becky would get to meet Roald Dahl. It sounded like a wonderful event. Gwyneth had told her that there was absolutely no parking anywhere near the event so the Library was sending out cars to pick up all the wonderful volunteers. That was very thoughtful of them, Susan Hancock had said.

"Hi," Gewneth said when the front door opened, "I'm Eunice Snead from the Boston Library. We spoke earlier." Mrs. Hancock's eyes, a little bit rheumy, a little bit watery widened perceptibly when she saw Bill Bear, 250 pounds with a full beard and wild hair. With the flashing yellow caution light behind him, he looked like he was adorned with a massive flickering hairy halo. He was grinning and pointing at the 'Public Library' sign on the door of the car. Sean stood by the back bumper, almost at attention.

"Yes," she put her arm around Becky's shoulder, "yes, I think we're ready to go. Let's see. I left a message with my husband, dinner is thawing. Um, you said we'd be back by six, right?"

Eunice Snead nodded emphatically. "We certainly will have you home by six. The first thing we need to do, which we do with all volunteers, is get a picture of you so you can be recognized in our monthly newsletter." Sean walked over and the four of them, Sean O'Neal, Susan Hancock, Becky Hancock and Gwyneth O'Neal stood on the lawn in front of Agent Timothy Hancock's house. Bill Bear told them to all say 'Susie Creamcheese' and snapped a couple of Polaroid pictures. "OK, We're off the see the wizard," Bill Bear said holding the back door open for the three girls.

Mother Mercury lurched and pulled but kept on rolling down Mt. Auburn, onto Memorial Drive, along the Charles River and over the Longfellow Bridge. As she lumbered down Cambridge Street past Beacon Hill, she began a terrible jerking. "Goodness Gracious!" exclaimed Bill Bear as he purposely jammed his foot on and off the gas petal causing the old car to simulate her death throes. "Heavens to Mergatroid!" he shouted.

The girls in the back seat were bouncing around all over each other and Betsy was wailing. Bill Bear jammed the brakes, stomped on the gas, jammed the brakes on, put her in neutral, turned the key off and coasted into a store parking lot at the corner of Bowdoin and Cambridge, three blocks from the federal building, eight blocks from the library. "Hell's Bells," he said, "I think the old goat might have given up the ghost."

A young man in a clean, button down white shirt and a linen jacket with a shock of black hair falling over his eye and cheek, knocked on the window. "You guys all right?" he asked.

"Oh, yes" said Bill Bear getting out of the car, "I think we can walk from here." he said slipping the Polaroid picture into Jack's hand. "We'll be just fine. Thanks for asking." Jack Duncan put the picture in his pocket, walked behind the convenience store and sprinted off to the Federal Building, just two minutes away.

At ten minutes of four, Jack handed the secretary at the front desk of the FBI offices the Polaroid picture and told her it was extremely urgent that he talk to Mr. Hancock right now about his wife and daughter. The secretary recognized them in the photograph and went directly into Hancock's office. They both came back out into the hallway, Hancock ordering the secretary to call his home and call the Boston Public Library and get Agent Conrad in his office right now. "You," he barked at Jack, "Get in here."

"Where is my wife and where is my daughter?"

"I don't know, sir, I wasn't with them."

"Where did you get this picture?"

"A hippie gave it to me." Jack said pulling the letters out of the inside pocket of the jacket and laying them, with the envelopes, on Hancock's desk. His hands were shaking.

"Do you know Sean O'Neal?"

"Yes, sir, I do."

"Who are you?"

Jack laid out a copy of the poem. "I'm the guy who had this poem and I'm the guy Sean O'Neal would have killed to get it. My name is Jack Duncan. If you don't sign the letter to Senator Church within fifteen minutes, the other letter will be mailed to the newspapers."

Brenda, his secretary, opened the door and told him that there was no answer at his home, his wife was not at the Public Library and there was no one named Eunice Snead who worked there. That's the person, Brenda told him, his wife had mentioned when she left a message a few hours ago about going to the Public Library. Agent Conrad, she said, was on his way to the office from a meeting in Saugus. Hancock waved her out and read the first letter.

Dear Senator Church,

I am a Special Agent of the Federal Bureau of Investigation. I am director of the Drug and Racketeering Division of the Boston office.

For the past year I have been an active participant in a secret program directed by the headquarters office in Washington, D.C. The program was designed and is being executed with the specific purpose of disrupting the activities of various civil rights and dissident groups. This program has wiretapped, incarcerated, coerced confessions and assassinated American citizens with no legislative, executive or judicial authorization.

If I, and two citizens I personally have coerced into illegal activities, are granted immunity from prosecution at the local, state and federal levels, I am, and they are, willing to give full and complete testimony to your committee, in closed session, regarding our knowledge of these activities. I only know what I have been told to do and what I have personally done. I suspect there is a great deal more to this program. I submit this for your consideration because I believe the dignity and integrity of our country is at stake.

Sincerely,
Timothy E. Hancock

At four o'clock exactly, Brenda opened the door again and said there was an urgent call for him. He said he was busy and she said the caller knew he was busy and who he was with and what it concerned. Brenda pointed at Jack. Hancock told Jack to leave the office and sit in the waiting room. When Jack had left, she told her boss it was the French Ambassador to the United States and that he wanted to talk about Sean O'Neal and a few assassinations in Algeria. "Put him through." Hancock mumbled, staring at the photograph of his wife and daughter bracketed by Sean and Gwyneth. Staring at the letter.

When Jack came back into the office, Hancock was not the boyish man he had been. He was slumped. He was holding the letter to be sent to the newspapers. The letter that described everything the Agent had done in infinite detail. The letter that described the involvement of the French Government in their efforts to prevent the American

270

Government from assassinating her own citizens on foreign soil. It described how a senior State Department official had denied a young citizen the right to have legal documentation in a dangerous country, in effect sentencing him to prison for the rest of his life. It described how young people had been coerced into undercover service for the FBI and forced to commit illegal actions, including murder. The letter described parts of J. Edgar Hoover's COINTEL Program perfectly.

"Nobody kidnapped your family, sir. They went willingly. I'm sure they're fine. Your daughter might meet a famous author." Jack then touched the photograph and touched the letter to the Senator. He said, "Sean said to tell you one thing. He said to tell you, 'Your country will be proud of you.'

Special Agent Timothy Hancock signed the letter, handed it to Jack and turned his back, looking out his window at the Boston skyline.

Jack dropped the letter in the Post Box on the street. A Boston cop was telling Bill Bear to move that hunk of junk from in front of the Federal Building and was starting to make all the moves that cops make just before they arrest somebody when Susan Hancock sweetly told the nice policeman who she was. She thanked Bill Bear, Sean and Gwyneth for making it possible for Betsy to meet Roald Dahl even if it was just for a minute. Jack told her that she should go up and see her husband. He's not doing very well, he told her. "Oh, dear," she said, taking a last swig on the ginger ale that Bill Bear had spiked for her. Mother Mercury lurched into traffic as Susan and Betsy Hancock went in the front door.

Gwyneth was at home with her mother and father telling them how fascinating her college experience had been. How much she learned every day. Sean and Jack were on their way to the Olde Dublin Pub when Vannie Druggan stopped them on the corner by the pub. Vannie gave Jack a ten dollar bill and told him to beat it, go drink his beer. Charlie Markham, the hit man, was across the street, within sight, out of earshot. His hand was in his jacket pocket, his eyes locked on Sean.

"No! I'm not doing it. Vannie, I'm not killing anybody. Not now, not anytime. I'm done with that. As matter of fact, I'm done working with you altogether. I'm looking for a new life so just let me go. Let me out of all of it."

"Sean, Sean, Sean," Druggan said putting his hand on Sean's shoulder, "you don't want your mother and father hearing things about Gwyneth and the priest from Saint Peter and Paul's, do you? You wouldn't want that spread all over town, would you? It may kill them. Might break their hearts." Druggan gave him that slight glimpse of the secret. Just a corner of the card. "Aside from that, this bastard Hancock tried to ruin your life and your sister's life. He deserves it."

"You're a bigger prick than I thought. The answer is no."

"Charlie won't take a cop down. He's scared to do it. You do this, you work with Charlie on this tomorrow morning," Druggan said nodding his head towards Markham across the street, "and you walk free forever. Your sister walks free. Her good name walks free. It goes like this, Seannie. She didn't seduce that priest and get him excommunicated from Southie. She didn't do that. He raped her and nobody needs to know anything about it. Ever. And that scumbag Benito Romo. She was never there with him. Never happened. That's what Don Anquillo will say. And you Seannie, you didn't snap his neck. Why would you do that? You never even heard of the sonofabitch. You were with me, drinking a pint right here. That's what the old barkeep would say. Four, five, six other people would swear you were there with me." Druggan backed up a step and put both hands on Sean's shoulders. "This is a promise from me. This is my word. You can't get better than that, Sean." He shook his head slowly. "That FBI guy? What does he care about you? He's a cop."

On Wednesday morning at 6:15, as he did every Wednesday morning at that time, Agent Timothy Hancock, still in his pajamas, was carrying the trash from the garage to the curb for the weekly pickup. His wife and daughter were still sound asleep. Charlie Markham and Sean O'Neal pulled into the driveway in a late model Chevrolet, blocking his path. Charlie got out and asked him how to get to the Mt. Auburn Cemetery. Sean got out of the passenger side and came up behind Markham. Special Agent Hancock never showed up for work that day. He never showed up at J. Edgar Hoover's office on Friday morning.

Agent Conrad knocked on the door around noon. No answer. Silence. He walked around the house to the patio where the apple trees blossomed. No answer at the back door. There were no lights, no sounds. In the garage he found Charlie Markham kneeling on the floor. His arms and legs were tied behind him and lashed to the leg of the workbench. He had a ghoulish grin on his face, eyes bugged out. The rope and duct tape around his head and neck were bound so tight he could only manage a squeak of air through his nose. On his chest was pinned the letter to the newspapers and a note that said, "Mr. Hoover and Mr. Druggan,—The Ship Came In—Your Days Are Numbered."

What Timothy Hancock liked most of all about the villa in France was sitting on the veranda with his friend Jean, the CIA man. They sat and watched Becky ride the wine wagon. Marie had affixed a saddle to the top cask, tying the girth straps to the side boards and ropes up from the headboard so Becky could pretend she was the driver. Sean led the horse from where the trucks off-loaded the empty casks down the dirt path to the wine cellar in the bottom of the barn where they would be filled with Virginie Deneuve's fine, fruity Rose de Provence. J. Edgar Hoover was dead before Senator Frank Church's gavel pounded down and Timothy Hancock raised his right hand, swearing to tell the truth, the whole truth and nothing but the truth, so help him God. Vannie Druggan had disappeared into thin air.

Acknowledgements

Jim Stockard and Sally Young at the Loeb Fellowship gave me the time and space to study writing with Anne Bernays at the Neiman Foundation. I am very grateful they allowed me to move from being an architect to being a writer.

My brother Peter, author of many books on constitutional law, gave me incredible encouragement, proclaiming this book to be the very best of this genre he had ever read. He remains adamant that this opinion is not at all influenced by the fact that the book is dedicated to him. It is so dedicated because he gave years of his life in a federal penitentiary so that we all might be a bit more free.

Scotty, Susan and everyone in the Todos Santos writers group have been wonderful. My closest friend, Bob Mangold, is the inspiration for more than one character. He has spent his life laughing, loving and doing things for others that are often dangerous or difficult, but always meaningful.

I have spoken with many soldiers who fought in Viet Nam. Without wanting any credit, they have shared their painful experiences. Thank you all for what you did and what you said, particularly you, Mike.

Two of my sons, Moses and Zackary poured over early manuscripts and gave me wise advice and insight into my writing and their understanding of the social upheaval of the 1960's. Most of all, I reach out and squeeze the strong, warm hand of my wife, Lee, and she squeezes back.

About the Author

Tony Irons was born at a Manhattan Project reservation in Richland, WA where plutonium was enriched for use in the H-Bomb. When he was ten, his father died. His mother, a poet, moved the family of seven children east to Exeter, NH. During the heart of the Vietnam War, he served three years as a Consciencous Objector working with soldiers addicted to heroin. He dropped out of college after nine months and became a carpenter, a contractor and taught himself architecture. He became one of the last self-taught architects in the country, becoming licensed in California in 1994. Mayor Willie Brown appointed him City Architect of San Francisco. In 2000, Tony was awarded a Loeb Fellowship in the Graduate School of Design at Harvard University.

At Harvard, Tony studied creative writing with Anne Bernays through the Neiman Foundation. He and his wife Lee lived in a small apartment just off Harvard Square. It was there that Tony wrote many of his short stories about his experiences in Mississippi and Alabama during the Civil Rights Movement. He and Lee live in NH.

Tony's second novel, *Sacred Ground*, set in the Blue Ridge Mountains, will be published in Summer of 2013.

CPSIA information can be obtained at www.ICGtesting.com
Printed in the USA
BVOW072334301112

306971BV00001B/3/P